Horse Dreamer

A Novel
by

Daniel W. Homstad

AmErica House
Baltimore

First printing

ISBN: 1-58851-042-5
PUBLISHED BY AMERICA HOUSE BOOK PUBLISHERS
www.publishamerica.com
Baltimore

Printed in the United States of America

In memory of my brother Chris

Acknowledgements

February 29, 2000 Apple Valley, Minnesota

I would like to thank the following people: Jerry Anderson, a Civil War reenactor with the First Minnesota Regiment, for insight into daily army life from that period; Professor Carol Chomsky, University of Minnesota Law School, for information about, and insight into, the trials of the Dakota captives; Trudell Guerue, Esq., for insight into life as a person of mixed heritage; Carolynn Schommer, Shakopee Mdewakanton Sioux Community, for help with the Dakota language translations; Chris and Melody Westerman, and Floyd Red Crow Westerman, for their encouragement of this book; members of the Minneapolis Writers' Workshop, for their honest critiques; the research staff at the Minnesota Historical Society; my parents, who taught me the value of a good book; and my wife, Heidi, for her love, enthusiasm, patience and gentle criticisms.

A word on language used in this book

The Dakota-U.S. Conflict of 1862, and its aftermath, remain emotional subjects in Minnesota to this day. Nowhere is this more evident than in the language used to describe the people and events of the conflict. At the time of the conflict, the terms "Sioux" and "Indian" were used, most often by whites, to describe those Native Americans in the Dakota Nation. The terms "half-breed," "mixed-breed," and "breed" were used, most often by whites, to describe people who came from both white and Native American heritage. The terms "Sioux Uprising" and "Sioux War" were used, again most often by whites, to describe the conflict itself. While most of these terms are rightly understood today as politically incorrect (at best) and racist (at worst), they are used in this novel because, simply, people used them back then.

Contents

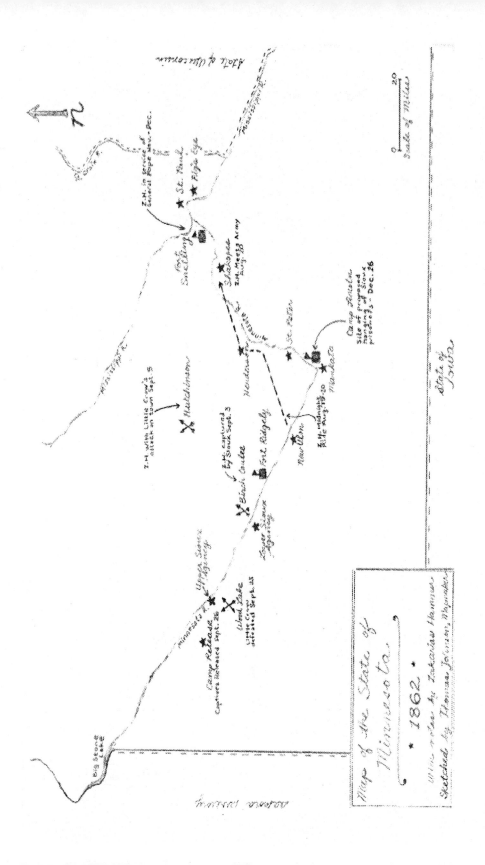

Map of the State of Minnesota

* 1862 *

With notes by Zacharias Horner

Sketched by Thomas Johnson, Mapmaker

BOOK I:

Half-Breed

A very nice and pretty bird of all colors came and sang beside our Dakota village. A voice said, 'Listen not to him; pay no heed to his song; look not at his colors.' He went away.

He came again with finer colors and sweeter songs, and he continued to do so until we heard him, and he led us away to die. The bird is the big knives — the white man; his songs are his fair words and lying promises; his colors are his paints, the beads and goods he gives us for our land.

Woe to us, for the day we hear the big knives' words, we go to our graves.

— Anonymous

1. Overture (I)

SPARKS SWARMED in the night sky like a million congregating fireflies. Superheated to a brilliant orange glow, they whipped pell-mell into each other until they massed, frenzied, above the roaring bonfire before careening into the heavens. Only the pale phosphorescence of the stars overhead eventually dimmed the trail of glowing embers as they migrated into the infinite space above the sprawling prairie.

From a distance the fire appeared insignificant, nothing more than a tree or bush that had been ignited by lightning. Close up the fire would have given pause to wary wolves and coyotes as they stalked the night, steely-eyed and sullen; however, the incandescence of the flames spread outward only a few yards, merely a pinprick of light on the darkened canvass of grass.

But the men gathered around the fire were anything but insignificant. The flickering light framed the hardened, weathered faces of the region's greatest Dakota chieftains, resolute men who were guiding their people out of the past and into an uncertain future. They sat cross-legged in a circle, facing each other across the flames, smoking their pipes, murmuring among themselves, and nodding their heads when standing orators raised agreeable points above the crackling, popping, and hissing of the blaze.

Little Crow spoke first. "I am the greatest of all the chiefs. You have chosen me as your spokesman in our dealings with others. You are wise to seek my advice."

He paused, allowing the weight of his authority to sink in. He carried himself as a gentleman, the warm orange glow of the fire complementing soft and dignified features. Splendidly dressed, he wore a headdress of eagle feathers and weasel tails, and bore a bright blue painted circle around one eye.

"This is the *bdo te*—the land where we settled on earth and became human beings," he said in his deep, authoritative voice. "But now things have changed with the arrival of the *wasicun*, the whites who have flooded the land like a tide of roaring waters. They say the land belongs to the Great White Father in Washington. They call us the *Sioux*—the word of the Chippewa, our enemies, for `snake'—and

17

treat us as such in our dealings with them." He paused, puffing at his pipe. "We are the *Dakota*—the allies—and we are a part of this land. And we have reached a crossroads in our existence."

The men around the fire nodded silently, solemnly, as Little Crow introduced the topic that led to this great and historic gathering.

"I will direct our people in the proper direction," Little Crow said. "But let every man among us speak his mind before I direct that course."

The first man spoke after only a brief silence.

"I want to kill all the whites now," said a chief named Shakopee, venom in his voice. "I want to drive the Americans from the land."

A murmuring of assent rose from some of the men. Shakopee stood in front of them like the powerful chief he was, tense, coiled like a rattlesnake about to strike. The firelight raged in his piercing eyes. Little Crow would listen closely to his words.

"We used to live on our own, camping by the rivers in winter and migrating to the prairies in summer to hunt the buffalo," Shakopee continued. "But as the whites have come, crowding us, we have sold our lands near the rivers and moved permanently to the prairie. It is hard on the prairie. We have been forced to give up the hunt and learn farming. Our hands are raw from wrestling the plow—but when the crops fail, we must rely on the white government agents to provide us with food." He paused and clenched his fists. "But they are not honest with us. Our people must pay the traders more for pork and sugar than the whites pay at their settlements. Then the traders put up signs saying they will sell nothing to the Dakota on credit. They say if the Dakota are hungry they can eat grass!"

He puffed up his chest and defiance flashed in his eyes. "All the whites will die, and Shakopee with them, before he will eat grass!"

Some of the men shouted in support of Shakopee. Others shouted against him. Little Crow raised his hands to quell the din. Before he spoke again his face twitched thoughtfully as he struggled to find the right words.

"We should not speak of war with the whites," he said. "The Dakota are brave but not foolish. There are many Americans and few Dakota. There are as many whites as there are leaves on trees. Count on your fingers all day long and the whites—protected by the long knives, the blue-coated soldiers—will still be coming."

Once again agreement rose from some of the men. Wabasha spoke in agreement with Little Crow.

"We have no cannons and little ammunition to fight the long knives, who will come just as sure as I breathe," he said. "Little Crow is right. To speak of war with the whites is to speak of our own destruction."

"But all the white soldiers are to the south fighting the other white soldiers," Shakopee retorted severely. "They fight amongst themselves as we speak. But there will come a time when the Great White Father Lincoln stops it. And then the land will be full of whites and the Dakota will have lost their chance."

He shook his fist at Little Crow and Wabasha. "The Dakota will never have a better chance! The policies of the *wasicun* have left us starving! They have blood on their hands! Now it is time to get our own hands bloody!"

"Those are the words of a child!" Little Crow snapped. "Shakopee knows very well that blood cannot wash off blood!"

Shakopee strode around the fire and faced Little Crow. He stuck his nose only inches from Little Crow's.

"The young braves want to kill, too," Shakopee growled through clenched teeth. "Has Little Crow not heard their voices, raised in battle cries? They want to kill!" Fury seared his face. "If the chiefs stand in the way, they will be the first to die!"

Little Crow stood unflinchingly. "Dakota chiefs do not fear to die," he whispered hoarsely. "They do what is best for their people and not what will please children and fools! What Shakopee proposes is madness!"

Shakopee spun and shouted to the men in the circle. "Little Crow is afraid of the white man! Little Crow is a coward!"

In one swift motion Little Crow snatched off Shakopee's headdress and flung it to the ground. Shakopee shrank away as Little Crow shook his fist at the men around him.

"Little Crow is not a coward!" he shouted. "And he is not a fool!" He calmed himself and spoke quietly, resolutely. "Braves, you are like little children; you know not what you are doing."

19

The men sat in rapt attention as he continued; his tone and inflection punctuated by urgency.

"You are full of the white man's devil-water. You are like dogs in the Hot Moon when they run mad and snap at their own shadows. We are only little herds of buffalo left scattered; the great herds that once covered the prairies are no more. See. . . ! The white men are like locusts when they fly so thick that the whole sky is like a snowstorm. You may kill five-ten; yes, as many as the leaves in the forest. Their brothers will not miss them. But kill five-ten; and ten times ten, and times ten again will come to kill you."

The men sat silently. Little Crow's words hung thicker than the smoke in the air.

"Yes, the whites fight amongst themselves away off," he continued quietly. "But do you hear the thunder of their big guns? No, it would take you two moons to run down south to where they are fighting, and all the way your path would be among white soldiers as thick as the tamaracks in the swamps of the Chippewa. Yes, they fight amongst themselves, but if you strike at them they will turn and devour you and your women and little children like wolves."

He paused dramatically. He clutched them all in his grip now.

"You are fools. You cannot see the face of your chief; your eyes are full of gun smoke. You cannot hear his voice; your ears are full of roaring waters. Braves, you are like little children. You will die like the rabbits when the wolves hunt them in the Hard Moon."

Little Crow stopped. All eyes locked on his face—soft features chiseled into stone by his excitement. But then, as they watched with amazement, his features at once relaxed again. The lightning that flashed only a moment before now faded, and he peered at them with only love and concern. His body relaxed as if he'd shrugged off a boulder. How his mind worked the men could only guess, but to a man they realized they were witnessing a transformation, some inexplicable metamorphosis within the great chief.

Perhaps Little Crow remembered how it used to be. How they had lived at the confluence of two of the region's greatest rivers—the one the *wasicun* called the Mississippi, flowing south on its winding path to the Gulf of Mexico, and the other they called the Minnesota, dissecting the western prairie that marked the eastern edge of the Great

Plains. How they had always been on the move between these two rivers—in the winter, living in permanent elm-bark lodges on the banks of the Mississippi, the men hunting deer and the women gathering maple sugar, and in summer, traveling west to hunt the great buffalo herds on the prairie by the Big Stone Lake. How it had been a hard life, but also simple and satisfying. Their only enemies had been the Chippewa in the north. Game and fish were plentiful. The Dakota had lived off the land, as they had always done.

But the *wasicun* came, the white men who would alter everything forever. The first ones came up the rivers in canoes by themselves, lonely bearded men who came for the adventure and settled with the Dakota and married their daughters and fought the Chippewa side-by-side with them. Some came later with the Word to convert them and ensure their only way to salvation. Others came against their will, men shunned by society or men fleeing the law, rejecting all others as they sought anonymity in their isolation.

Then came the explorers in great longboats and barges. They claimed the land in the name of a King or a Queen or some Other Authority. They claimed to "discover" the land and announced their intent to "civilize" it. *But you cannot discover what already exists*, said the Dakota. *You cannot own something that is alive. The gods and spirits are alive in the land, in each rock and river, in the deer and buffalo, in sticks and trees.* Nonsense, was the reply. Here's a piece of paper to say we have claimed it. And you'd better agree, if you know what's good for you—our armies fight now in far-off places to preserve our rule there, but one day the Army will arrive to establish our rule here.

Finally an army did come—hordes of blue-coated soldiers brought to the frontier on the backs of fire-breathing dragons, massive steamships churning north in the mud of the Mississippi. The Stars and Stripes flew from the ramparts of a massive fort right at the *bdo-te*, dominating the bluffs above the rivers. The land around the fort became barren; the forests cut to appease the appetite of the behemoth on the hill, the villages of the Dakota pushed away.

The white politicians came with treaties, pieces of paper written only in English demanding that the Dakota sell their land. Hundreds of thousands of settlers would arrive in the territory, which would soon be a state. They cajoled and begged and reminded the Dakota that the old hunting grounds were thinning out and that beaver and muskrat were now scarce. Selling the land of the *bdo-te* could be the only sensible course. The Great Father in Washington would pay millions of dollars for the land. Their paradise waited for them out on the western prairie of the territory—a reservation of land ten miles wide on either side of the Minnesota River just south of the Big Stone Lake. They could hunt in the old ways, even go west to the remaining buffalo herds. With annuities from the sale, the Dakota could live comfortably for generations to come.

And so the Dakota moved, but with each new treaty it was the same old thing. Usually nothing came for months—no flour, no blankets, no meat, and no money. Nothing. *It is out of our hands*, the government agents said. *The politicians in Washington are to blame.* Finally, when the shipments arrived, they were inferior; beads, ribbons, and silk handkerchiefs cannot feed starving children. What little meat arrived was already spoiled. There wasn't much money. The traders already claimed most of it as compensation for the credit they had given out of inflated prices.

In desperation, near starvation, the Dakota chiefs had mourned.

In the end, perhaps Little Crow realized the truth in something his friend Wabasha once said to him:

There is one more thing the government can do. It can gather us all out on the prairie and surround us with soldiers and shoot us down.

Perhaps, despite his own certainty of the calamity that would surely befall them, Little Crow would not let his people go down without a fight.

"Little Crow is not a coward," he finally said, peering at Shakopee. Tears flooded his eyes. "He is not a coward!" He clenched his fists.

"We will fight! Little Crow will die with you!"

2. Neither Fish Nor Fowl

"NO DIRTY Indian's gonna get the best of me," the tall boy growled menacingly as he advanced steadily with fists in front of him, his three cronies fanning out to encircle their prey. Zak looked nervously around him for any route of escape, but he was surrounded by the four boys prowling around him like a pack of wolves. He searched frantically for any allies, anyone who could help him. But he was new to the school, his father just having moved them to the reservation. All he saw in front of him were the faces of the white boys, the sons of the white traders, and they all wore the same frightening expressions—faces twisted with rage, eyes flashing with hate.

Zak spoke pleadingly to the tall boy. "Look, Asa, if this is about yesterday, I sure didn't mean. . . "

The tall boy cut him off quickly. "You're damn right it's about yesterday," he said curtly. "You showed me up in front of all my friends. In front of the *girls*. When my old man found about it he tanned my hide. Said no son of his is gonna get humiliated by no redskin. So the way I got it figured, you caused me twice the pain." He grinned wickedly. "But now you're gonna get yours."

With a sickening feeling in the pit of his stomach, Zak realized there was no way out of it. Nothing—no amount of begging, pleading, or talking—would stop what was about to happen. He was trapped. He would have to fight them. And all over a stupid incident with a horse.

He'd been on his way home from school, having stayed late because it was his turn to clean the blackboards. As he walked home, he heard a commotion down one of the side streets. Curious, he walked there to see what was happening. He came to a corral behind a house. Many of the students were gathered around the corral, watching something that was happening inside. They were yelling and screaming, laughing and pointing.

He'd looked into the corral and recognized a white boy named Asa Dawkins trying to mount a horse. He'd heard Asa talking that day in school about it. Asa's father had an unbroken colt, and someone dared Asa to ride it. He'd boasted he could ride any horse, broken or not.

He was having trouble with this colt, though. The colt accepted a bridle in its mouth and a saddle on his back, but Asa could not get in the saddle for its first ride. Every time he tried to mount the horse it spooked, throwing him and bolting for the other side of the corral. The watching children laughed at Asa, teasing him about his earlier bragging. His face red, Asa began whipping the colt with his riding crop.

After a few blows, Zak couldn't watch any longer. He climbed the fence and dropped into the corral. He grabbed the crop from Asa and pushed him away.

"Quit hitting him," he said. "It's not his fault. You're doing it all wrong."

Asa appeared taken aback by Zak's bold move, but when the children began teasing him he quickly recovered.

"Oh, yeah?" he sneered. "Whatta you know about it, ya *dumb Indian*?" He emphasized the last two words, drawing them out mockingly.

Zak hadn't answered him. He turned away, threw the riding crop over the corral fence, and walked slowly toward the colt.

"Easy, boy," he said soothingly. The colt turned wary eyes to him. "Easy, boy," Zak said again. "I'm not gonna hurt you. There, there, that's a good boy." He crept even slower now, nearing the frightened horse. He put his hand out to touch him. Once he thought the colt would bolt, but it didn't. Zak patted his flank and continued to talk soothingly to it.

He knew what to do now. He'd seen Joe LaCroix break in a colt just like this one before.

"You need to practice putting weight into the stirrup so he gets used to your weight," Zak said to Asa. "You gotta do it a few times." And he did just that, holding the left rein and the cheek piece of the halter with his left hand while stepping up and down several times in the left stirrup. The horse looked back skeptically at Zak while he did this, but he did not move away. "Good boy," said Zak.

"Then you gotta stand in the stirrup a few times," Zak said to Asa, "and test your weight again." After doing this several times, Zak stepped out of the stirrup. "Now he's ready to have me get up there, but not too quickly. You gotta pat him on the rump as you get up and then lean over the other side and pat him there, too. See? He's getting used to me moving around up here." He looked at Asa, who stood there frowning, arms crossed.

"You were dragging your leg over him as you were getting up," Zak continued. "That spooked him." Carefully he avoided touching the horse as he swung his right leg up and over him. Finally he placed his right foot in the stirrup and slowly sat in the saddle.

The colt's eyes rolled back and his ears pricked up, but he didn't move. Zak nudged him a little with his knees and the colt began to walk slowly around the corral. Soon he responded to the reins, turning slow circles as Zak guided him right and left.

After a few minutes Zak dismounted and walked the horse over to Asa, and handed him the reins. "He's ready to ride," he said.

The watching children clapped, and soon they cheered Zak as he climbed out of the corral and walked home. But he'd known it wasn't over. He'd just shown Asa up, humiliated him in front of the children. He knew Asa would have to try settling the score with him.

And now it was happening.

Zak fought back as best he could, swinging wildly and kicking out with his feet. He felt several of his blows land and heard the cries of their recipients. He fought very well for over a minute, but in the end there were too many of them. He felt punches and kicks landing all over his body—his face, the back of his head, his back, his legs. Blood filled his mouth, coppery and salty, and his head rang from the blows. He realized he was overmatched, so he went down as much out of self-preservation as from the pain, curling into a protective fetal position, shielding his privates with one hand and his face with the other. His attackers finally stopped only because they exhausted themselves.

Zak lay still for a few minutes, recovering his strength. No one helped him. Slowly he got to his feet and stumbled home. He knew he'd been bloodied and bruised, but at least he was still walking. On his way there he took stock of himself—a bloody nose and a fat lip, and one eye was swollen shut, but that was about it. He felt his side—good, no broken ribs.

25

He held his head up. He'd taken the best they had and survived.

"A `half-breed' are you?" the schoolmaster had bellowed at him on his first day at the reservation school. "Well, that's too bad."

Zakarias Hammer was his Christian name, but most people he met didn't care. When you're half white and half Indian, you're neither fish nor fowl. He'd been told he was some sort of "breed." He'd been told he was a "mixed-breed," the product of a mix-up, as if his father's Norwegian blood and his mother's Dakota blood were incompatible like oil and water. He'd also been told he was a "half-breed," basically only half a human, as if his Indian blood irreparably tainted his pedigree-quality white stock. Someone once said people "pigeonholed" him. He wasn't exactly sure what that meant, but if it meant what it sounded like—cramming a beautiful free bird down into a dark hole where it didn't fit—then he had a good idea.

Zak had faced the scowling schoolmaster, an enormously fat man wedged tightly between his chair and desk, chunky hands folded above a protruding belly. His beady brown eyes peered at him between the folds of bloated pink cheeks and the brim of a flat-topped straw sailor's hat. He wheezed as he breathed, and he frowned with distaste as if he was in the company of a leper.

"How old are you?" he demanded.

"Sixteen, sir."

"Sixteen, hunh? Bet you can't even read English."

I can read, Zak thought. He and his mother had learned to read together. But he didn't say it.

"Well, it wouldn't make any difference if you could," said the schoolmaster severely. "You just remember you're no smarter and no better than any of the white children in this school. Even the dumbest one, the poorest one, is better than a half-breed like you and always will be."

Zak felt the eyes of the other students searing holes in the back of his dusty blue overalls. Two half-breed girls sat in the back of the room, but they didn't rise to his defense, their eyes downcast.

His ears burned, as they always did when embarrassment overcame him. He shuffled his feet, looking down at the ends of his ragged leather boots. He clutched at the collar of his cotton shirt, which suddenly scratched at his neck like soggy wool. Although it was late spring and cool outside, the room felt suffocatingly hot.

"Well," the schoolmaster said, his mouth twisting upward in a fake smile, "We'll work especially hard on you." He snorted. "All that is Indian in the man should be dead. Kill the savage and spare the soul."

Zak winced. He suddenly felt about an inch tall. He didn't *feel* like a "savage." He didn't think he *looked* like a "savage." Savages were like the desert island natives he'd read about in *Robinson Crusoe*—ugly, threatening, naked cannibals that boiled people alive before eating them! True, he'd inherited some qualities from his mother that made him look different than any of the white children—black hair framing a long, thin, face that looked like it had a deep permanent suntan. Brown eyes above a small nose. High cheekbones and a crooked smile that revealed straight teeth. But he still wanted to cry out to the schoolmaster that he was really only half Indian, that he was also half white!

The walls of the one-room schoolhouse had seemed like they were closing in on him. He started to clear his throat to speak, but before he could the schoolmaster unfolded his flabby arms, leaned forward in his groaning chair, and stabbed a thick index finger toward Zak's chest.

"Inside every Indian is a white man wanting to get out," he said.

Zak always wondered what made people say such things. It had been that way his whole life. "They just don't know anything about you," his mother said once. "They are afraid of what they don't know."

He never wondered what his father thought about him, though. He knew he was only an asset in his father's enterprise for profit.

Born Brandt Olaf Hammarskjold, his father fled Norway as an angry seventeen-year-old in 1840, having been cut out of his father's will as the family's only adopted boy. He made the eight-week sail to America aboard a two-masted brig, emptying refuse pails from steerage overboard to pay his fare. He arrived in New York twenty pounds lighter with a case of the scurvy and with a new name, shortening his last name to "Hammer" not only so Americans could pronounce it but also as one last blow to his dead stepfather. He arrived in Minnesota territory four years later after a failing as a farmer and being shunned

27

for refusing to join the church in a Norwegian settlement near Lake Koshkonong in southern Wisconsin territory. "They had faith and charity," he said about the settlement. "As long as it was for themselves."

Zak often heard him speak of his arrival in Minnesota territory. "I steamed up to Fort Snelling on the *Argo* in 1844," his father would say in his thick Norwegian accent. He did not pronounce his "H's," his "T's" sounded like "D's" and his "G's" like "K's," so it sounded like he "steamt up to Ford Snellink on da *Arko*." "Lucky I did then, 'cause it sank a couple years later at Reed's Landing. Twenty people on board. Anyway, I barely got one foot in the fort when Sibley comes up to me and gives me a gallon of whiskey and tells me to get an Indian wife." He would puff his pipe, relishing the knowing nods of his listeners. Most of them had received the same introduction to trading from Henry Hastings Sibley, the territorial director of the American Fur Company.

"Sibley says to me, 'I don't know you from Adam, but if you work for me you do it my way.'" He would imitate Sibley's deep, authoritative voice, often drawing laughter from his audience. "And my way is keep tribes happy. Happy Indians hunt and spear. We get fur, we are happy. Get to Little Crow's and marry yourself squaw. I did it, so will you.'"

He would take another puff of his pipe, knock out the burnt coals on his boot, and stuff it in his front pocket. He would smile, his sharp, tobacco-stained teeth showing through his blonde beard, his blue eyes sparkling, and he would cram his muskrat-pelt hat further down on his head.

"So I just fixed on one that wasn't too fat or too thin. She's Wounded Hand's daughter, you know, one of the farmer Sioux. I took the whiskey Sibley gave me and five more gallons, ten blankets, a gun, and a pony. I put them outside the old man's lodge and knocked on the door. Three days later he brought her and said I keep her long as I want."

He would pause and nod toward Zak. "Good for business to have Indian wife and child."

Zak's mother, born *Tanagidanwin,* or Hummingbird, was only sixteen when her father gave her away. Her mother often told her the story of how she'd gone into labor alone in the woods, as all the women did in their village, and, at that critical point when the labor could go either way, how a pretty hummingbird visited her as she lay writhing in pain in the grass. The bird had spoken to her and calmed her and helped her through the most difficult part of the labor.

Hummingbird looked like the tiny, fluttering bird she was named after. A small thing of beauty, her deep-brown eyes exuded kindness and understanding. Her lush black hair graced her gently curved back all the way to her diminutive waist. Her round face framed her sparkling eyes, as she would fondly describe her childhood at Little Crow's village at the *bdo-te.*

"It was a hard but happy life," she would say. "Some left by—I'm not sure of the white man's word—suicide, yes, suicide. Especially women who were treated badly by men. But my father, Wounded Hand—*Nape Taopi*—he was kind to mother. We lived poor but we loved each other. I was the middle child. Whirlwind—*Tateiyumni*—your uncle, he is a little older than me. Circling Hawk—*Cetan Okinyan*—a cousin living with us, he is your age. My whole family lived there, with my uncles like my father, my cousins like brothers and sisters."

Later, when Zak visited the village, he thought of it as kind of run-down and shabby compared to the white New England-style buildings that were springing up in St. Paul. You could see a couple dozen permanent elm-bark houses that housed four or five families each and some teepees. Next to the lodges were large wooden racks used for drying meat. Gaunt, flea-ridden dogs shuffled aimlessly throughout the village, wandering dull-eyed around the camp, scrounging for food and generally shunning the affections of anyone but their masters. Women worked the corn fields that surrounded the village. Moored in front of the village at the river bottom were several dug-out canoes. Behind the village, perched on the rolling green bluffs overlooking the river, lay the cemetery of burial scaffolds, the bodies of loved ones of the past perched high enough on their forked-post pedestals to avoid scavenging wolves.

Wounded Hand prepared a great feast for the wedding of his daughter and Brandt Hammer. "I honor you as my son and welcome you to the family circle as one of us," Wounded Hand said to Brandt at the wedding feast. Wounded Hand gave a wedding feast as large as anyone had ever seen. A *shaman,* or Dakota holy man, performed the ceremony, making a long speech extolling the virtues of a productive man and fertile woman. The feast lasted an entire day, and featured shooting and riding contests. Wounded Hand gave away two horses, which brought much acclaim from the villagers. To give was much better than to receive and brought status.

All of his new Dakota relatives welcomed Brandt except Whirlwind, who refused to either shake his hand or smoke a pipe with him.

"I am here only to show respect for my sister," he said. "It does not mean I support the marriage. Dakota should be with Dakota. White men do these marriages only to help themselves." The family thought badly of Whirlwind's comments, but the family was not there two days later when Brandt took his bride to Fort Snelling for a civil marriage ceremony, with none of her relatives present, so they could have a "proper marriage."

3. *A Spirit on the Trail*

AWESOME IN its dimensions, the prairie sprawled flatly across western Minnesota like the floor of the heavens. In all directions lay a wondrous expanse, with only an occasional tree to interrupt a meditative twenty-mile gaze. Tall enough to hide buffalo, the bluestem grass heaved in the ceaseless prairie winds, sighing with a wistful loneliness that beckoned to all who ventured upon the rolling sea. To those who found the emptiness liberating, the prairie offered anonymity, renewal, and hope.

But the Indian reservations, to which Zak and his family had moved in the spring of 1862, blighted the surrounding paradise like cancer on the skin. The government agencies on the reservations—the Upper Sioux and Lower Sioux—were nothing more than bleak outposts, two tiny towns made up of a few residences, a couple of doctors, a couple of mission schools, and the numerous stores of the white traders who sold goods to the Dakota spending their annuity proceeds. The Dakota that chose to learn farming lived in or near the towns and bought their supplies at the traders' stores at greatly inflated prices. The Dakota that chose to remain faithful to the traditions of hunting and gathering—those in the villages of Little Crow, Shakopee, Medicine Bottle, and Red Middle Voice—lived on the periphery of the reservation, well away from the towns. Poverty and restlessness reigned.

Zak and his family lived in a log cabin within shouting distance of the Lower Agency. Brandt Hammer worked in one of the stores that supplied farming equipment. He sent Zak to the school devoted mainly to the children of the traders, refusing to place him among the "Sioux heathens" at the mission school devoted mainly to the full-blood and mixed-blood children of the reservation. He likewise refused to accommodate Hummingbird's Dakota family or heritage, permitting no visits to the household from her kin—in fact, allowing virtually no contact—and permitting no "heathen influence" in the house itself. He countenanced no Dakota prayers, rituals, or customs.

Not long after moving to the reservation, though, Zak spied two familiar-looking Dakota riding toward him on horseback. As they neared him, he recognized them as his uncle, Whirlwind, and his cousin, Circling Hawk. He hadn't seen them since the move west.

Circling Hawk, dressed in white man's pants, white shirt, and hat, looked much older than Zak did, even though only a year separated them. His oval face framed delicate features—gentle brown eyes, small round nose, ready smile. His straight black hair fell only to his shoulders, much shorter than other boys his age.

Whirlwind looked as hard as Circling Hawk did soft. His waist-length black hair whipped wildly in the wind. His square jaw was set perpetually in a steely resolve, and life and passion raged in his black eyes. Ever the traditionalist, he wore leather leggings, a porcupine-quill vest, and iron bands that ringed his sinewy, tough arms. He painted his face in gaudy greens, reds, and yellows. He always carried a rifle and he always scowled. Zak felt that small shudder of fear that always rippled through him when he saw his uncle.

"Greetings, cousin," Circling Hawk said to him, smiling. "I am pleased so to see you. How are you?"

"You speak English!" Zak exclaimed, taken aback.

"Very goodly, I am pleased to say," Circling Hawk said. "I have been to the school at the Mission. They teach me to read and write, first in Dakota, then in English. I can write my name and can read books."

Whirlwind snorted derisively. He spoke in Dakota.

Circling Hawk cast his eyes downward and then looked embarrassingly at Zak. "Whirlwind I am afraid does not approve of me learning the white man's ways. He says those that school and learn farming are wanting to be like the white man and he is ashamed."

Whirlwind spoke again.

"Whirlwind says that those who learn farming and give up the hunt are favored in every way, getting new houses and more of the money from the Great Father. The government agent and the traders cheat all the others. Whirlwind says he will not be a part of it. He will not join the 'pantaloon band,' those that cut their hair and wear pants like the whites."

An uncomfortable silence settled over them. Finally Zak found his voice again in the face of Whirlwind's stern gaze.

"Where do you live?" he asked.

"I live near the mission with my father and mother, in Little Crow's village," Circling Hawk answered. "Whirlwind lives at Shakopee's village to the north."

Zak contemplated this. He found it curious that, despite these differences, Circling Hawk and Whirlwind appeared headed in the same direction.

"What are you doing now?" he asked.

"We are going down to the Agency," Circling Hawk said. "The Dakota gather there because those in Shakopee's and Red Middle Voices's villages are hungry. Little Crow is already there, though. He does not want to see fighting. He wants to council for peace."

Ever more curious, Zak asked to go with them.

"Why, that's fine and dandy," Circling Hawk said. "You may ride my horse with me."

Several dozen Dakota men on horseback surrounded the Agency building. Facing the Dakota, a company of blue-uniformed soldiers from nearby Fort Ridgely kept a nervous vigil. Several of the white traders stood with guns at the ready. Zak's stomach turned when he saw his father. When his father spotted him on the back of Circling Hawk's horse, his face clouded over and he scowled.

Nobody uttered a word, in English or Dakota. All eyes gazed upon Little Crow, who suddenly stood in his saddle to speak. A missionary stepped forward to translate.

"Little Crow says the Dakota are hungry. The Great Father promised money and food, but there has been little of either. The food and supplies in the storehouse belong to the Dakota; but the money they have been promised has not arrived yet and so they cannot pay. It is unfair for the traders to deny credit suddenly and leave the Dakota with little or nothing."

The men around the storehouse stood silently, sullenly.

"Little Crow says he is for peace but he is afraid of losing control of the younger braves. When men are hungry, when their children are hungry, they help themselves."

A trader stepped forward.

"Myrick," Whirlwind snorted with contempt and spat. Other Dakota turned suspicious eyes upon the trader.

33

"No money, no food, no exceptions," Myrick shouted. "The Sioux'll pay their debts, too, before these doors are opened. If the Dakota are hungry, they can eat grass!"

Myrick's words surged like lightning through the Dakota men. Whirlwind, his face twisted with rage, raised a clenched fist in the air and shouted.

A stricken look paralyzed the interpreter's face. He drained of all color.

Myrick demanded he translate, but the interpreter's mouth didn't move.

"Translate it, damn you!" shouted Myrick.

In a timid voice the interpreter squeaked, "He says he will shoot the dogs who deny him credit."

The soldiers shifted their rifles. Two of them cocked their muskets. The throng of Dakota men surged forward menacingly. But Little Crow rode forward, raising both hands in the air frantically.

"Dakota men, stop!" he shouted. "Conflict here will only end in defeat! The agents have promised the annuity will arrive soon. Go home now like men and we will have a council to discuss this further!"

Grudgingly, after a few minutes of indecision, the Dakota dispersed. But to a man they shot murderous glances at the soldiers and traders. Whirlwind smiled at Myrick as he passed, but it was a deadly smile, one that promised only retribution.

Circling Hawk gave Zak a ride back to his cabin.

"Pleased to see you again," he said. "I would like to enjoy with my cousin again. We can be friends."

"I'd like that," said Zak.

Zak's mixed-blood friends at school, Mirna and Minnie LaCroix, were twins who had been raised solely by their father, Joe, the son of a French trader and Dakota woman. Over the years Mirna and Minnie had suffered prejudice in the same ways as Zak, but their father dearly loved them. The twins were fast friends and now impervious to the teasing. In them Zak found two sympathetic ears and some strength in his heritage. They teased him about being such a quiet boy, but they seemed to like him.

Zak took every opportunity he could to be with his two friends. He visited often at their little farmstead, only a half-mile from his house. It was in one of these visits that Zak had realized his lifelong dream to learn to ride a horse. His father showed no interest in teaching him how to ride. But when Mirna and Minnie told their father that Zak had never done it, he huffed and puffed, dumbfounded.

"A boy's got to know how to ride a horse!" he exclaimed. "Why, we're goin' outside right now and learn you how to ride my paint!"

The paint was an aged stallion that had seen better days, but Zak didn't care. He'd never seen an ugly horse. When Joe LaCroix helped him up into the saddle, it seemed to come naturally. He balanced without holding the reins, and when Joe showed him how to ride—knees bent, head up and looking over the ears, back and shoulders straight but not stiff—Zak took the paint forward first at a walk, tentatively, then more surely. As he learned the interaction between his hands and legs—hands to position the horse's head and neck, and legs to urge forward movement—Zak increased the walk slowly to a lazy trot. The paint, as moody and cynical as any old horse, seemed to sense Zak's joy and responded eagerly, and soon they were in sync as one.

"Why, the boy's a natural," Joe LaCroix said elatedly, slapping his thigh with his hat. Mirna and Minnie giggled delightedly.

To Zak, it seemed as if he had never been so happy, so *alive.* Things may be rough at home, he thought, but he had three new friends. Four, if you counted the paint. He thought things might not be so bad after all.

But in June of that year something dreadful happened that changed the course of his life, and consequently, those of many others as well.

The corn in the field outside their cabin stood almost as tall as Zak already, despite the better part of the summer looming ahead. The blackbirds massed to fight for their share of the bounty, and they raided the corn in swirling, frenzied clouds. Exasperated, Zak and Hummingbird cut four six-inch trees and cleared a small patch in the center of the field, sinking the four posts into the reddish-black soil in the shape of a square. They fit four thick branches into the crooks at the top of the posts, forming the sides of the square. On top of these they lay several branches to form the platform of the tower, tying everything down with rawhide. Atop the platform Hummingbird built a crude sun shade out of willow boughs, bending them into a dome shape and tying them down, placing a blanket over the top. For two solid weeks she sat in her tower, waving her arms and screaming shrilly, a possessed scarecrow banishing the blackbirds that dared to invade her territory.

The terrible thing happened almost unbelievably quickly on the last day of the month. Hummingbird scrambled up the platform just after the sun rose in a sultry dawn. As the humidity rose thickly from the sweating land, towering storm clouds exploded upwards, dominating the late morning sky with sinister-looking blues and blacks. Just after noon the storm broke with a cannonade of rolling thunder and wild lightning that danced across the sky. The maelstrom howled and battered the prairie for only a tension-filled half-hour before fleeing to the east, but in that short time it wrought havoc upon its helpless victims. Apple-sized hail battered the corn stalks into useless pulp. Straight-line winds snapped helpless trees in half, whipping them into gnarled hulks and rolling them over the land like tumbleweeds. Zak and his father huddled in the cabin, which shook as if a giant pounded on the roof with both fists. As soon as the wind died and the first ray of sunshine burst through the window, Zak's father bolted for the cornfield and Hummingbird.

When he did not return immediately, Zak left the cabin. But he met his father at the edge of the field, face ashen; a lifeless Hummingbird draped over his shoulder.

"Lightning got her," his father said. His face showed no emotion, only strain at the burden he carried.

Zak felt like he'd been clobbered in the jaw. He stood, paralyzed, staring at the body of his mother. He tried to speak, but all that came out was a dry, sickly wheeze.

"She never knew what hit her," his father said dully. "She didn't suffer."

The rest of the day became only a blurred memory for Zak. In an almost catatonic state, he managed somehow to mount his father's horse and ride to Shakopee's village to find Whirlwind and Circling Hawk.

He did not cry. He couldn't think. He might as well have been dead himself.

Whirlwind and Circling Hawk returned with Zak to the cabin. When Whirlwind strode through the doorway Zak's father sat seated at the table, simply staring at the bed where Hummingbird lay. His face contained no grief, only a blank look of uncertainty. He cradled a half-empty bottle of whiskey between his hands.

He did not acknowledge Zak and Circling Hawk when they entered. He barely raised his eyes as Whirlwind moved purposefully around the cabin, grabbing a blanket off a shelf with one hand and a chair with the other. Whirlwind moved next to the bed, paused a moment to look at his sister, and then covered her up to her chin with the blanket. He set the chair close to her head and sat facing her, his back to the rest of them, folding his arms across his chest.

After a couple of minutes he spoke over his shoulder.

"Whirlwind says he is going to sit there until the sun goes down," Circling Hawk translated. "He says he will sit and wait in cases she revives."

"In case she revives?" Zak asked incredulously. "She can't. . ." he began, but Whirlwind raised his hand, cutting him off.

"It is customary for the Dakota to postpone the burial until the family has waited, like Whirlwind will do," Circling Hawk said. "It is only when hope for life has truly vanished that mourning may begin."

Zak looked out of the corner of his eye for his father's reaction, but there was none. He sat on the floor to maintain his part of the vigil. Soon he dozed, numb and exhausted.

At twilight Whirlwind, still seated beside Hummingbird, finally stood. Circling Hawk nudged Zak, who had dozed throughout the afternoon.

"Whirlwind says the vigil is over," Circling Hawk said. "Gather up some of your mother's personal things and put them in a pack. We will take them with us when we go."

Whirlwind murmured while standing over Hummingbird. He stretched out his arms, and still speaking, raised his head, his eyes fixed on a place in space far beyond the roof of the cabin. Then, silently, he picked her up in his arms.

Turning to face everyone, he spoke. "It is time for Hummingbird to return to her people." His face showed no emotion, only steely determination. He started for the door.

Zak's father, shaken from his dazed state by the sudden activity, stood unsteadily. He cleared his throat.

"She ought to have a Christian burial," he slurred weakly. Circling Hawk did not translate. "She. . ." he began again, but he did not finish. Something in Whirlwind's eyes, something definite and deadly, made him sit back down at the table and return into his shell.

Zak did not let his father see him cry. After he had pored over the cabin for a few of his mother's favorite things, grabbing her awl kit and sewing kit, his eyes blurred with building tears, he left the cabin without speaking. Only out on the prairie, after they tied his mother to a travois behind Whirlwind's horse and set out, did he sob quietly, his shoulders shaking as he rode on the back of Circling Hawk's horse. They did not look at him as he wept.

Zak saw the huge bonfires of Shakopee's village well before they arrived. What looked at first like a distant prairie fire evolved gradually into a burgeoning sphere of incandescent orange light. Zak distinguished the silhouettes of teepees set in a great circle around two huge swirling fires in the center. Giant sparks leapt from the fires, racing skyward in blazing arcs. Zak felt as if he were entering another world.

When they penetrated the village circle the activity ceased. The sudden silence was eerie and overwhelming. The flickering light from the fires enveloped them, reflecting off the bleached white hides that comprised the teepees. Zak now recognized the faces of many of his relatives, some of whom he hadn't seen in years. His grandfather, Wounded Hand, greeted them solemnly with a raised hand. His face was expressionless, but Zak thought that the great wrinkles on his face were more pronounced than ever. His flowing ghostly-white hair swirled in the hot wind emanating from the fires. A tall woman greeted Whirlwind and then turned and smiled at Zak when Whirlwind gestured toward him. Goodness, thought Zak. That's Whirlwind's wife, Dying Rice Moon. How long had it been since he'd seen his aunt?

Many other people looked vaguely familiar to Zak, but they seemed as if they were from the distant past, or even another life. But there was no division among the Dakota that night in Shakopee's village, no distinguishing between farmer Indians and traditional Indians. All stood ready to receive Hummingbird, one of their own, back into the village.

Wounded Hand closed his eyes as the group passed with his daughter. They parted their way through the people as Whirlwind worked his horse and travois toward a teepee. Some reached out to touch Hummingbird as she passed. Others stood silently still. Somewhere in the back of the crowd a dolorous wailing began, and others soon joined. When Whirlwind dismounted at the teepee the village women were joined in their cry, a collective soul-wrenching howl that rose with each new voice. Whirlwind untied his sister from the travois and gently carried her into the teepee.

"The teepee's set up specially for Hummingbird," Circling Hawk explained. "She will remain there while we mourn her death."

Whirlwind came out and pointed across the village circle. "We will sleep tonight in my teepee," he said. "Come now and we will eat something."

Zak sensed, rather than saw, his entry into the smoky, lighted teepee after being outside in the dark. He heard bubbling and smelled the smell of boiling meat. He felt the warmth of the cooking fire and then his eyes adjusted. He saw Dying Rice Moon hunched over the fire to the left as he entered, stirring the cooking pot. She smiled at Zak when he entered the teepee behind Whirlwind. Then, keeping her eyes down, she said a couple of quiet words to her husband, who grunted in response.

Zak, merely wanting to stay out of the way in this unfamiliar territory, sat to the left of the fire behind his aunt. Whirlwind and Circling Hawk looked at each other in confusion and then some merriment. Dying Rice Moon, seeing their faces, turned and looked at Zak. She raised her eyes almost imperceptibly, smiled, and gave a low chuckle. She turned to her husband and said a couple of quiet words.

39

Whirlwind began to laugh and Circling Hawk, seeing this, began to laugh, too. Zak's face flushed and he felt his ears turning red. What now? he thought.

Circling Hawk translated as Whirlwind spoke. "You are sitting on the wrong side of the teepee. Men always sit on the right, women on the left." Zak's face felt hot and he started to speak, but before he could, Whirlwind cut him off with a brief wave of his hand.

"It is all right," he said, smiling again. "You are used to the ways of the whites. The whites are always mixed-up and confusing. Besides, I can never tell the difference between the men and women among them because they all dress the same, clothing yourselves from head to foot in white shirts, pantaloons, and hats." He chuckled again.

"We are a traditional people and we cherish our ways," Whirlwind said. "Our ways our as old as we are as a people and are the reason for our existence." Zak nodded, but he did not completely understand. This must have shown in his face because Whirlwind continued.

"Look," he said, standing near the center of the teepee. "This teepee is in the shape of a circle. The circle is the sacred hoop. The power of the Great Mystery works in circles: the sky is round, the earth is round. Wind, in its greatest power, whirls in circles. Birds make nests in circles. The sun rises and sets in a circle, and the seasons form a great circle in their changing and always come back to where they were."

He stepped outside the teepee. "Come out here," he called. Circling Hawk and Zak followed. "This camp is in the shape of a circle," he continued, passing his arm dramatically over the panorama of the village. "You see," he said, turning to them, "The families in each teepee are part of the circle. But they are not just a part of the village; they are also a part of the past. All of our ancestors are still with us, if only in spirit. This is all part of the greatest circle, the eternal cycle of our people."

Zak nodded.

"Good," said Whirlwind. "You, too, are part of the circle, even if you have lived as a *wasicun*. Your mother lives through you, and you are welcome here, for as long as you live."

The sun rose red and ominous the next morning. When Zak left the teepee much of the village already stirred with activity. Whirlwind returned dour and empty-handed from a hunt. After another meal of boiled venison—the last in the teepee—Wounded Hand announced that mourning for Hummingbird would begin. Dying Rice Moon immediately left the teepee and soon Zak could hear wailing over by the teepee in which his mother lay.

Whirlwind motioned for Zak and Circling Hawk to follow him into the death teepee. Inside, Hummingbird lay like a statue on buffalo robes. She wore her favorite quilled dress. Her hair had been neatly brushed and her arms folded across her chest. She wore moccasins with beaded soles. Her face had been painted to reflect her status in the community.

Tears welled in Zak's eyes. She looks the same, so beautiful, he thought, and peaceful. Maybe she is finally at peace. He placed his hand upon her forehead, hard and cool to the touch. To himself he said a little prayer for her.

"It is proper to show our respect and our grief by giving of ourselves," Wounded Hand said, "as Hummingbird gave of herself in life. As we give thanks and atonement each year through the ceremony of life at the Sun Dance, so do we give of ourselves in the ceremony of death." And they gave of themselves—men slashing their arms, women butchering their hair—methods of grieving in the Dakota tradition. Horrified, half-sickened by what he saw, Zak summoned all of his strength to remain quiet out of respect for the tradition.

The next day Dying Rice Moon wrapped Hummingbird in a buffalo robe. They painted her face with the marks necessary for her journey. Circling Hawk explained that Hummingbird's spirit would leave her body to travel the Spirit Trail, and in order to make it, she had to pass an old woman that would examine her for the marks before allowing her to move on. If she did not see the marks the old woman would push Hummingbird's ghost from the trail, and it would fall to the earth to wander forever.

Whirlwind took Hummingbird and placed her on a travois. Dying Rice Moon pulled the travois out beyond the village and into the prairie. Zak, Circling Hawk, Whirlwind, and Wounded Hand followed. A suffocating humidity rose thickly from the prairie grass. The silent, solemn column cut laboriously through it and over the gently rolling hills to the burial ground.   One lone scraggly pine offered meager, fleeting shade as the procession brought Hummingbird to her waiting burial scaffold.   Suddenly a cooling wind rose from the west, and everyone looked toward it and smiled.

"It is *Tate,* the wind," Circling Hawk said. "*Tate* will move your mother's spirit more easily along the Spirit Trail."

Whirlwind worked quickly and with certainty.   Seemingly unhindered by the self-mutilation he'd performed in mourning, he deftly lifted Hummingbird from those offering her below and placed her gently on the scaffold. He took Hummingbird's sewing kit and awl case from Zak and placed them with her inside her buffalo hide. Then he drew from his pouch four thick rawhide ropes, wrapping each one tightly around the body and scaffold, tying them tightly to enclose the hide and avoid exposure to the rain and endless prairie wind. When he was done he jumped from the scaffold and walked away without looking back. The others followed, Zak last of all.

Zak's father did not appear at the village during the mourning period.

Circling Hawk and Whirlwind wanted Zak to stay with them.

"You are nephew and cousin," Whirlwind said, "but you are also a friend. You may be white in your upbringing but you have the soul of a Dakota. You should stay with Dakota."

The decision tore Zak in two directions. These people were dignified and treated him well. Most of his family lived here. But at the same time he was not ready to adopt this way of life, their religions. All the Dakota prayers to the Great Mystery and the various spirits? What did that get them? What good did it do? Their suffering was as bad, if not worse, than anyone's. No, he was not ready for this.

So Circling Hawk took Zak back to his cabin.   When they arrived, Zak, surprised, saw that his father's horse stood in front of the cabin, saddle packed and cinched. Zak dismounted. Just then his father came out of the cabin with another bag slung over his shoulder. He gaped at Zak with his own surprise.

Neither spoke, the silence between them saying volumes. Circling Hawk shifted uncomfortably on the back of his horse and said good-bye.

Finally Brandt Hammer cleared his throat and spoke. "Well, let's get a move on. We're moving over to St. Peter. It's no use to stay around here no more. There'll be work there at a foundry. Get to packing. I've started on your things, but you're here now and you can do it."

When Zak entered the cabin he saw with dismay that none of his things were packed. He lied, he thought. *He lied.* He was fixing on leaving me. My father was going to just leave me. Five more minutes and he'd have been gone.

It was hard to believe, but not that hard. Zak thought about the offer that Whirlwind and Circling Hawk had made him. He began to wonder if he'd made the wrong decision.

4. Sun Dance

ST. PETER, a frontier town of about two thousand people, lay on the western edge of the Big Woods, a sprawling forest of cottonwoods and oaks surrounding the Minnesota River. The St. Peter Company dominated the town, exporting grain and lumber north to the burgeoning twin cities of Minneapolis and St. Paul. In just five years since its birth the town boasted a flour mill, a foundry, a brewery, a jail, a forty-room hotel, and assorted tanneries and markets. Just to the north of the town was a site called Traverse des Sioux, where the Dakota had signed one of the treaties selling their land to the U.S. government.

The St. Peter Company put Zak and his father up in a log cabin on the northern edge of town. Twelve hours a day his father worked in the company foundry, manufacturing stoves and other appliances. The sand to construct the molding for the stoves was procured right in St. Peter on the banks of the Minnesota River.

"No better grade of sand can be found in all the western country," Mr. Essler, the foundry manager, said when showing Zak and his father around.

If the death of Hummingbird could have served as a catalyst for better father-son relations, it unfortunately didn't happen. When his father was home he hardly spoke to Zak, often grunting in response to things he said, sometimes not acknowledging him at all. He ate what food Zak prepared without thanks and would leave again, heading to the town's only tavern. When he was home he continually drank whiskey, often passing out head-down on the table.

They never spoke of Hummingbird. Zak wanted to, and mentioned her one day, but his father dismissed the topic with a wave of his hand. *I'm so lonely,* Zak thought. *I don't have anyone to talk to. I miss my mother.* He looked at his face in the mirror. It was a sad face, with dark lines under defeated eyes, his mouth set in a frown that he feared was becoming permanent. It looked like the face of a ghost.

And then one day, toward the end of their first month in St. Peter, Zak met a friend he'd never forget. Toward sundown on a pleasantly cool day Whirlwind and Circling Hawk arrived at their cabin on horseback. Whirlwind led a third horse by the reins, a handsome

45

painted colt. Whirlwind dismounted, tied his horse to the rail outside the cabin, and handed the reins of the colt to Zak.

It was the most beautiful horse Zak had ever seen. He walked around and around the majestic animal. He figured it was about fifteen hands high at the shoulders, equal in height to him. He stroked the colt's golden-chestnut base coat, the brilliant white splashes on his back, flanks, shoulders, and chest. A thick black mane flowed dramatically down the colt's strong, thick neck. When he came around to face him, Zak saw a bushy black forelock atop the horse's gently sloping head. A black star sat right between his eyes. Long black eyelashes accented the friendliest-looking eyes Zak had ever seen. Looking into the horse's large dark eyes, Zak felt like he'd known this colt for years.

Zak looked at Whirlwind in amazement. What was he doing? Was he giving the colt to him? As if in answer to his wordless questions, Whirlwind nodded to Circling Hawk and pointed to the horse, speaking in Dakota.

"Whirlwind says the colt is for you," Circling Hawk translated. "He is a fine horse. Whirlwind won him in a shooting contest four moons ago. He says he knows how hard Hummingbird's death was for you. He saw your ghost face and saw how sad you were. He says you should have horse as a friend."

Zak heard a noise behind him. His father stood on the porch, his mouth half-open as if about to speak. Zak's heart sank. His father would never let him have the horse.

But something defiant in Whirlwind's blazing eyes stopped Brandt Hammer in mid-thought. Twice he opened his mouth again, but twice he shut it again. Finally, with a little shrug of the shoulders, he turned and went back into the cabin.

Stunned and enraptured, Zak couldn't believe what was happening. He didn't speak for a long time.

"Does he have a name?" he finally asked Whirlwind. He held his breath, hoping the answer was *no*. He'd always wanted to name a horse.

Whirlwind frowned at Zak, as if he didn't understand the question. He spoke.

"Horse is not like son or daughter," Circling Hawk translated. "Whirlwind did not name the horse. Just call him 'Horse.'"

Zak let out his breath in a gush of relief.

"The horse is a friend to the Dakota," Whirlwind continued. "But it has not always been that way. Dogs and people did all the work, pulling the teepees and packs on travois and on backs. When the horse come, the Dakota did not know what it was. Taller and thinner than buffalo, with a head not furry like the buffalo's. They looked like big dogs. The Dakota were scared at first, but the big dogs offered no harm. When finally a brave warrior got on the back of the first big dog, it only resisted a little. From then on the Dakota rode the horses! What a gift from *Wakan Tanka*!"

Whirlwind paused, stroking the colt's neck. "Dakota love their dogs, but this animal is bigger and better than any dog. This is *Sunka Wakan*—'holy dog.' Many Dakota believe the horse to be their spirit helpers, and they call themselves 'horse dreamers.'"

Whirlwind turned and mounted his own horse. "I give you this horse to be your spirit helper. You are Horse Dreamer now. You remember your Dakota family when you ride him."

Zak stood transfixed, enthralled by Whirlwind's words.

"When the moon of the ripening chokecherries comes I will dance for you in the Sun Dance," Whirlwind continued. "I will pierce my skin with hooks attached to rawhide and will hang on the cottonwood tree, praying for the Great Mystery to help you. When you ride your horse you think of the Sun Dance—in the golden of the horse you will see the sun I will stare at; in the white patches you see will the clouds that will provide some relief from the sun; and in the black tail and mane you will see the earth, to which we all belong and on which I will dance. The Sun Dance is the key to salvation for the Dakota, and I will dance for yours."

With that, Whirlwind and Circling Hawk wheeled their horses around and galloped away. Zak stood, still unbelieving, looking at the colt in wonder.

"Thank you," he whispered. "Thank you for this gift." He walked around the colt once more, patting its flanks and scratching between its eyes.

"The Sun Dance," he said. When he looked closely he *could* imagine what Whirlwind had talked about—the sun, the clouds, the earth.

"I will call you Sun Dance," Zak finally said. The colt turned its head and looked at Zak as if he understood him.

"I will call you Sun Dance," Zak said again, to hear the name out loud again. "Or, 'Sunny,' for short. You will be my friend forever."

That night his father left. With no warning another thunderstorm rolled belligerently over them, the land shuddering from thunder and wincing from the pelting rain. Hail clattered off the cabin's roof. But despite the din, Zak slept, dreaming of his new friend. Between these distractions his father stole away, and Zak heard nothing. When the sun cast its first rays through the cabin's windows, he realized he was alone. There was no note, no explanation.

He'd been abandoned.

Zak waited almost a week before he decided that his father wasn't coming back. During the first two days he thought perhaps he had just gone to the nearby towns of Mankato or Henderson on errands for the foundry and merely neglected to tell him. He frequently looked both ways down the road for a sign of his return, half expecting to see the familiar buckboard at any time, but all he saw was the mailman and a couple of the brewery's wagons hauling barrels of beer north to St. Paul. On the third day he mounted Sunny and rode into the foundry to see if his father had indeed been sent on business, but Mr. Essler told him that not only had his father not been sent out on business, but that he hadn't been to work at all. Zak hung his head and left.

On his way home a sudden rush of inspiration and dread surged through him, and he rode to Dr. Mayo's office. Maybe his father had taken ill or had been injured and was under the doctor's care in the tiny hospital behind his office. After all, the doctor didn't know who he was and maybe had not been able to get word to him.

But his father was not there, either, and Zak rode home. During those first days he went about his normal chores as if nothing had happened, gathering driftwood down at the riverbank and tending his small garden behind the cabin. At times he liked being all alone. He felt grown up and independent on the quiet little farm.

He managed a few meals of corn and potatoes from the garden and some lumpy bread he made by mixing flour and water and baking the dough in front of the fireplace, but he had come up empty hunting and the lack of meat was dissatisfying. He had no money to buy any from the butcher in town. On the third day he got off a fairly clean shot at a doe down at the river bottom, but the ball sailed over the deer's shoulder and tore a chunk out of the tree behind it. Before he could re-load—he'd never been as fast as his father at this—the doe bounded away, its white tail flicking up and down as it ran. On the fourth day he did shoot a rabbit that strayed near the garden and he made a pretty good stew of it, but the animal was small and provided only a couple of meals.

After four days Zak began to feel lonely. Father wasn't much company, he thought, but at least he was company. He tried whistling to add a little noise while he worked, but his notes sounded hollow and airy. He tried singing a few songs he'd heard in church at the Agency, but he couldn't remember most of the words and he was thoroughly disappointed with his off-key singing. He talked to Sunny and rode him two or three times daily, a bit of consolation. But all the while he looked for his father to return. His spirits leapt with each sound of approaching hoofbeats, only to sink lower each time as they passed. His head jerked up with every sound. He thought he heard the door bang open and slam shut, and he jumped to his feet to shout, "Father?" only to have eerie quiet answer him. Sheepishly he realized it was only the wind pounding against the side of the cabin.

At the end of the week, visitors called upon him. When he heard Sunny nicker to signal their approach, he put down the breeches he was sewing and went to the doorway. Riding up the lane was Mr. Essler, the manager of the foundry, and someone else. Zak squinted to see who it was. His heart sank.

Judge Flandrau.

Zak knew all about the town's most distinguished citizen. After reigning as the agent at the Lower Agency, Judge Flandrau moved to St. Peter to help form the company for which Zak's father had worked. He worked as a highly respected lawyer and judge. At six-foot-three, he towered over almost everybody in town. His full beard and ample belly were marks of distinguishment. As he rode up behind Essler, tall and erect in the saddle, Zak could see why people in town did what he told them to.

Essler nodded at Zak as they came up, but he didn't say anything. He looked uncomfortable, shifting twice in the saddle before trying to speak. When he began, he stammered a couple of unintelligible things before the judge raised his hand, stopping him.

"Hello, young man," the judge said, simply enough. Essler appeared relieved he didn't have to speak. "May we come into your house?" the judge asked.

"Ah, sure," Zak said. "You can tie your horses on the rail there."

"Very well."

Inside, Judge Flandrau sat directly at the table and motioned for Zak to do the same. Essler remained standing, hat in hand, looking around the inside of the cabin. When he saw Zak's mending on the bed, he looked knowingly at the judge.

"Young man," Flandrau began, "James here tells me that your pa's gone. That you've been here all alone for some time now. Is that true?"

Zak sat silently. He'd always known, deep down in his heart, that this would come. But he wanted to stall it.

"Ah, I'm not sure," he said.

"I see," said Flandrau. "But James here tells me that your pa hasn't been in to work in quite some time. And I don't see him hereabouts." He stared at Zak for what seemed like a full minute, but then his features softened.

"Look," he said. "I'm sure you are confused, wondering what has happened. But James was concerned enough to come to me about your situation. And I'm concerned now. I can understand if you don't want to say anything about your father."

"It's not that. It's just. . . "

"Yes, son?"

"It's just—I don't know if he's gone. He probably is," Zak said bitterly. He still couldn't believe he'd been completely abandoned, thrown away like garbage. He stood, walked over to the doorway and looked out, slamming his hand against the doorjamb.

"He's probably gone," he said again. "He never liked me. How could he do that to me?" He looked at the judge imploringly. "I never did anything to him."

"Of course not."

"I know why you're here," Zak said. "You think that because he's gone, I can't take care of myself. You think I'm too young."

"We think you're too young to have this much happen to you so soon," Flandrau said. "I know about your ma's death—remember, I used to be the agent over there. And I know enough about your pa to know about you and him."

Zak sat down again at the table. "You do?"

"Yes. I heard how he treated you and your ma." Flandrau spread his hands in front of him. "Your pa had some good traits, but he had his demons. Many of them lived inside the bottle. But others, too. They kept him from getting close to you, seeing you as a person. Do you see what I mean?"

Zak nodded. He sat quietly again.

"What do you want?" he finally asked. "I'm not going to live at The Poor Farm." That was the town's house of charity, where destitute and mentally ill people lived. Zak had heard of it, particularly of a man named Napoleon Busby, who had tried to burn down the town's brewery because he thought it was the "house of the devil." Zak shuddered.

"No," Flandrau said. "We want you to come live in town. At the boarding house. It's a nice place to live and Mrs. Hinkel will cook and do laundry for you. You can have your own room."

"But I don't have any money!" Zak sputtered.

Flandrau waved that off. "Don't worry about that. It's on the company. Your father worked for us. We take care of our own. You can earn your keep with Mrs. Hinkel by helping her with chores around there, and you can come by the foundry and help James clean."

"I don't know," Zak said.

"Really, Mr. Hammer, it's the only way," Essler said earnestly. "It's the only way."

Zak considered this. "What about Sunny?" he asked.

"Sunny?" Flandrau responded.

"My horse."

51

"Oh, that's easy. You can put him up in the company stable. Full board. You take care of him, and you can take him out at any time."

"Why are you doing this?" Zak asked. It seemed almost too good to be true. He felt like he didn't deserve it. "I have relatives back on the reservation I could live with."

"No," Flandrau said.

"A boy living among wolves will grow up as a wolf," Essler said. The judge shot Essler a disapproving look.

"That's not just it, Zak," he said, still glaring at Essler. "You need to be in a town, with a firm roof over your head, and a school that's not just for the mixed children. Don't worry about the cabin here," he said, looking around. "We'll get you a fair price for it and put the money in a trust for you ."

Zak didn't say anything, but Flandrau must have taken that as assent.

"Good," said the judge. He rose from the table. "It's settled then. You're doing the right thing. I'll send some men out here tomorrow to help you move your things."

Zak couldn't sleep that night. Questions raced through his mind. What if his father came back? What would he say about the sale of the cabin? What would it be like at the boarding house? What would it be like at the school? Were there any other children like him? After a couple of hours of tossing and turning, he got up, slipped on his boots, and walked out to the stable.

The moon bathed the stable in a pale light. Zak opened the door and went inside. Some light filtered in and he saw Sunny standing in the corner of his stall. Sunny blew out his nose and gave a knowing nicker. He must have heard me coming, Zak thought. He ducked under the rail and entered the stall.

Sunny snuffed again and Zak patted his flank and stroked his mane. Sunny nuzzled the side of his head. The horse's scent filled these close quarters—musky, with just a touch of hay. That's the best smell in the world, Zak thought.

My trusted friend. My mother may have passed on, and my father may have abandoned me, but I still have Sunny.

"We're moving to town," he said softly. "We're gonna live at the boarding house." Sunny looked at him silently. His brown eyes looked completely black in the faint light. "You're going to live in a nice big stable—a lot bigger than this crummy little one. And you'll have lots of company there."

Sunny bobbed his head. He really seems to understand me, Zak thought.

"I'll come and see you every day, and I'll feed you, and take you out, and brush you down. It'll be just like now. It'll be great."

It'll be great, he said again to himself. But he wasn't really sure. They could move him into town and keep him from going to the poor farm, but it would still just be the horse and him. He didn't have another friend or relative within a day's ride.

He signed deeply, wondering, uncertain.

Mrs. Gretchen Hinkel, a short, round, middle-aged German immigrant, beamed at Zak when Judge Flandrau introduced them, and she declared, in her peculiar backwards way, that "it would be like here having another grandchild." Her dead husband, a Bavarian named Otto, had opened the land to farming near the German enclave of New Ulm, just a day's ride to the west. Just five years before a heart attacked felled him and Mrs. Hinkel sold their homestead and moved back up the valley to St. Peter, "frontier close enough for anyone."

She introduced Zak to her current tenants as her "guest of honor." The tenants took turns greeting him. Jim Johnson, a tall man with an angular face and sparkling blue eyes, pumped his arm furiously and said he was paddling a canoe up the Minnesota River to "see the frontier before it's gone." Zak declined his offer to accompany him. Prentiss Pike, a squat bald man with narrow brown eyes, shook his hand morosely and said he was here from St. Paul to negotiate a contract with the brewery and that he was not happy being in "this backwater town."

The other tenants were Mr. and Mrs. Foreman, who said, "Oh, call us Herbie and Gertie." They were on their honeymoon, traveling by steamboat up the Minnesota River to "see Indians."

"Are you an Indian? Are you?" Gertie Foreman asked him hopefully, eyeing him up and down.

Mrs. Hinkel treated Zak like a guest of honor. She sent Louisa, her cleaning help, to tidy Zak's room first thing in the morning, and she often baked delicious cookies for him. She allowed him to make his transition gradually, not probing him with too many questions and keeping quiet when Zak left unannounced to visit Sunny at the Company stable. She left him little notes in his room, which welcomed him and indicated she looked forward to knowing him.

Zak did some chores around the hotel. He emptied and cleaned chamber pots from the rooms, chopped wood, and painted. On Saturdays he worked for a few hours at the foundry, cleaning and painting. He began to attend school. He was the oldest boy in school; others his age were working or farming with their fathers, and the older ones were all in the Union Army, fighting down south in the war between the states. Zak wondered a couple of times what it would be like to be in the Army. He wondered if he would have the courage to fight in battle, or if he would run away like a coward. I guess I'll never know, he thought.

Zak thought he'd seen a couple of other boys his age around town, but they weren't in school. The one boy, the taller one, wore a dirty brown derby cocked haughtily to one side. They didn't seem to work anywhere, and when Zak asked Mrs. Hinkel about them she huffed scornfully.

"That's Dougal Black and Jimmy Cronk. Hooligans they are. Do nothing but cause trouble. Quit school they did and cause trouble in town. Away from them you stay."

But something drew him near those boys, something he couldn't recognize and surely couldn't resist. Maybe the teasing from the white children at school got to him. Maybe the absence of his friends Mirna and Minnie got to him. Maybe the painful knowledge that he had been discarded like yesterday's newspaper by an unloving father served as the final straw. Maybe he just wanted friends, *any* friends, even outcasts. Whatever it was, it was natural enough that Zak felt no real surprise when finally encountering Dougal Black.

He'd skipped school and ventured down to the river flats when, consumed in his thoughts, a shout of "Hey!" shook him out of his cocoon.

He wheeled and faced the boy with the brown derby.

"Hey!" Dougal shouted again. "Who the hell are you and what are you doing here?"

A couple of inches taller than Zak, he adjusted his dirty hat haughtily. Bushy black hair poked out from beneath the rim of the hat, some falling over his dark brown eyes. His sharp, thin nose twitched above a twisted sneer that seemed to shift his entire face to the left. He wore a dirty long-sleeved white shirt beneath brown suspenders, which held up heavily-patched brown pants. He wore heavy brown boots.

"I said who are you?" he demanded again.

"I'm Zak."

"Zak, smack." Dougal giggled at his own joke, his high nasally voice shifting into a series of gurgling sounds. He sounds like a sick crow, Zak thought.

"Zak, smack," Dougal taunted again. "Do you know who I am?"

"Yeah, I know."

Dougal pondered this a moment. "Well, what are you doing here?"

"Nothing. Just standing here."

"Just standing there?" Dougal repeated. He looked suspiciously at Zak. "What do you mean, just standing there? Nobody just stands somewhere."

"I am."

Dougal peered at him with his beady eyes a moment and walked closer to Zak. "Well, go stand somewheres else. This here's my riverbank."

Zak looked at Dougal Black. His senses told him Dougal was dangerous, a bully. But he thought he could give him a good fight if he had to.

"Your riverbank?" Zak looked around. "I don't see any signs with your name on it."

Dougal Black, temporarily speechless, recovered quickly. "Don't need no signs. I'm a-tellin' you it's so."

"I got as much right to be here as you do."

Dougal tensed. He moved toward Zak, but then stopped. Maybe it was something he noticed, maybe the way Zak didn't back down but took a solid defensive posture, that stopped him.

After a minute he squinted at Zak. He seemed to give a new appraisal of him. "Say, I know you. You're that Injun living up at the hotel."

"Maybe I am."

"What's an Injun doin' livin' up in a hotel? Think you're better than everyone else? I seen that flea-bit horse of yours, too."

"He's not flea-bit," Zak retorted. He saw now he may have to fight this Dougal Black after all. He moved closer to Dougal. Their stare-down seemed to last an eternity, but neither pushed it any farther.

"How come you're not in school?" Zak finally asked.

"School's for fools." Dougal bent down to pick up a rock, turned, and skipped it twice on the river. "That's what my pappy says."

"Pappy? I've never seen you with no pappy."

"Well, I got one." Dougal sneered, suddenly defensive. "Just cause you ain't seen him don't mean I don't got one. He's just busy all the time, too busy to come into town."

"What does your pappy do?"

"None a your business. I said he's busy all the time. What about yours? I seen you with some old man once but I ain't seen him around for a far piece."

Zak didn't answer right away. He bent over, picked up a rock himself, and skipped over the river's surface. "He's gone," he finally said.

"Gone? Gone where?"

"I don't know."

"What do you mean, you don't know? Your pappy's gone and you don' know where?"

"Nope."

Dougal stood silently for a moment, calculating. "Is he dead?"

"No, he ain't dead. He just left."

"What'd you do to make him leave?"

Zak spun to face Dougal. "Nothin'. I didn't do nothin'. He just up an left one day. Ain't seen him since."

Dougal looked at Zak. Then he turned and nodded toward a thick grove of cottonwoods just up the riverbank. "Want to see my place?"

"Your place? You mean your house?"

"Naw," Dougal said, grinning. "My *place*."

Curious, Zak agreed. They walked together up to the grove of cottonwoods, Zak looking all the time to see what Dougal was talking about. But he couldn't; the trees were too thick. But right when they got to the edge of the grove Dougal pushed through some thick bushes and disappeared. Zak hesitated, but an arm came out and waved him in. Zak stepped through the bushes. They were so thick he could not see on either side of him. When he stepped through, they were in a tiny clearing, a clearing that had been chopped out of the underbrush. Set in the middle of the clearing was a tiny shack, four walls of planks nailed to a frame and a flat roof. A stovepipe stuck out of the roof.

The shack nestled against the riverbank. Zak looked behind him. He could not see the river through the thick bushes; in fact he couldn't see anything on the other side. He looked up. The tall cottonwoods all but blocked out the sunlight. It seemed apparent nobody could see the shack from the outside, probably even in winter when the leaves had fallen, and it seemed clear nobody could see it from the bluff above.

Dougal stood with his arms folded, looking proud of himself. "What d'ya think?"

"It's sure neat," Zak said. "How did you find it?"

"Find?" Dougal asked incredulously. "I didn't find it. I built it. Couple of years ago. No one else knows it's here." A shadow seemed to pass over Dougal's face. "You better not tell anyone about it."

"I won't," Zak said. Dougal squinted at him. "I said I won't," he said again. Dougal stopped squinting but still didn't seem entirely sure.

He sure is suspicious, Zak thought.

Dougal disappeared through the creaky shack door. Zak entered behind him. In the darkness his eyes lost focus, although he distinguished a single kerosene lamp burning in the corner. He saw the shape of another boy sitting behind the lamp, but his eyes had not adjusted enough to recognize him.

The shape spoke. "Who's that? Who said he could come in?"

"Shut up, Cronk," Dougal said. "This is my place, and what I say goes." Zak's eyes grew accustomed to the dim light. Seated in the corner was the other boy Zak had seen with Dougal.

"Is that that Injun kid we've been seein'?" Cronk asked.

"Yeah. Zak Smack."

"Zak Smack." Cronk giggled wildly, as if it were the funniest thing he'd ever heard. "Zak Smack. Zak Smack." He quit giggling, stood, and walked over to Zak. Shorter than Zak, he appeared even short for his age. His skinny face sported freckles and large buck teeth that stuck out in all directions. He wore a dirty white shirt with brown pants and suspenders. Like Dougal, he wore heavy brown boots. Like Dougal, he wore a derby, cocked to one side. Dougal Black's little flunky.

"Are you a real Injun?" he asked.

"I'm only half Indian," Zak answered.

"An Injun is an Injun," Cronk said. He turned to Dougal. "Where'd you find him?"

"Down at the river bottom," Dougal said.

"What were you doin' there?" Cronk asked Zak.

"Nothin'."

"He was just standin' there," Dougal said.

"Doin' what?"

"Just standin' there, he says."

"Just standin' there? Doin' nothin?"

"You deaf?" Dougal asked. "You sound like a parrot. Whyn't you shut your face?"

Hurt, Cronk retreated to his corner seat. Zak looked around the shack. There were no windows. The shack only offered a table and three chairs, a small pot-bellied iron stove with a pipe leading up and out through the roof, some fishing poles haphazardly thrown into one corner, and a shelf with assorted bottles on it. The kerosene lantern on the table in the corner cast a sickly yellow light upon the inside.

"What do you guys do here?" Zak asked.

"Nothin'," Dougal answered. He and Cronk glanced at each other and giggled.

"Yeah, nothin'," Cronk said.

"What?" Zak asked, perplexed.

Cronk looked at Dougal, who nodded. Cronk turned in his chair and brought down a bottle from the shelf. He pulled off the cork and handed it to Dougal, who handed it to Zak.

"Here," he said.

"What is it?" Zak asked.

"Just drink it."

"Yeah, just drink it," Cronk said.

"What is it?" Zak asked again. He put his nose to the mouth of the bottle.

"Don't smell it, drink it!" cried Dougal. "What are you yella?"

"Yeah, he's yella!" cried Cronk.

Zak felt his ears burning. He was glad it was fairly dark because they probably couldn't see his red face. He put the bottle hesitatingly to his lips and tilted his head back. Warm liquid trickled down his throat. He swallowed and immediately coughed. His throat burned and his eyes watered. He coughed again, resisting the urge to gag. Dougal and Cronk laughed uproariously.

"Whiskey," Zak croaked when he'd recovered. He knew the taste of whiskey, having sampled his father's bottles once when he was away. He wiped his mouth and shuddered, took a deep breath and handed the bottle back to Dougal.

"It's whiskey all right," Dougal said.

"It's whiskey, all right," Cronk said.

Dougal took a gulp from the bottle, looking at Zak the whole time, shook his head vigorously from side to side, and swallowed without flinching. He smiled. "That's what we do here," he said.

"Among other things," Cronk said. He pulled a corncob pipe from his pants pocket and lit it. The smell of tobacco filled the small place.

"We do what we want down here," Dougal said. "Nobody bothering us, tellin' us to do chores or go to school. It's like a club, and I'm president."

"I'm vice-president," Cronk chimed in self-importantly.

"What do your folks say about all this?" Zak asked them.

"Mine don't know," Cronk said. "They don't care none about me anyway. Just 'clean the barn,' or 'fetch some water, and go to bed,' is all I get. They think I'm going to school." He laughed.

"Didn't anyone from the school tell 'em?"

"Yeah, they came out one time and my pappy skinned me something fierce, but they ain't been out agin' so's I'm in the clear for

59

now. I just leave ever' morning like I'm going to school and come home every night and they don't know nothin' different."

Dougal didn't answer Zak's question, so he asked it again.

"My pappy don't care none either," Dougal said.

Cronk giggled. "Why, your pappy's gone!" he exclaimed. Dougal shot a severe look at Cronk.

"You shut your face!" he yelled.

"But it's true! He's in jail!"

Dougal punched Cronk in the shoulder. "Ow!" cried Cronk. "What'd ya do that for?"

"Keep your big mouth shut," Dougal said. "I told you never to tell anyone that."

"Sorry. Geez," Cronk said. His eyes had watered and he was rubbing his shoulder.

"Your pappy in jail?" Zak asked Dougal. "What for?"

"None a your business," he said angrily. "I'm going out ta get some more wood for the fire." He stormed past Zak and out.

Zak and Cronk were silent. Finally Zak asked, "What's his pappy in jail for?"

"Killed a man, that's why," Cronk said.

"Killed a man! Gosh almighty!"

"Yep. Killed him deader than a doornail. They was a fight at the tavern in town. His pappy and another man got into it over who knows what and they got to tusslin'. He says the other man pulled a knife and got it into his pappy but his pappy got it back and stuck it into the guy like a fatted calf. Stabbed him five times. But when the sheriff came, the witnesses, who were the dead guy's friends, said it was the other way, that his pappy pulled the knife. Took a manslaughter deal for ten years in the state prison to avoid double that for a full-up murder rap."

After a few minutes Zak asked, "How come the sheriff doesn't come get you guys and bring you up to school?"

"We're both over sixteen. You can quit if you want when you're sixteen. How old are you?"

"Same."

"Why do you go? Everyone's dumb there."

"Some of them are," Zak said.

"They're all dumb. Have some more whiskey."

60

5. Into the Abyss

WHAT IS the matter with you? Zak would ask himself. Are you going bad? You can't be. Anyway, there's no way you're as bad as Dougal and Cronk. They smoke and drink, for goodness sake. They're only sixteen.

Listen to yourself, the other side of his mind would say. *You're the one cutting school and spending time with two hooligan drop-outs that like to smoke and drink. You've* been drinking whiskey and cutting class. *You're* only sixteen years old, doing the same things they are. Don't think somehow you're better than they are.

Maybe, he would respond back. But they're like me. Their fathers all abandoned them, in different ways. At least they understand what I've been through. They have shared the same experiences and have asked a thousand questions, with no answers. At least with them I'm not just a dumb Indian. I've been accepted by somebody, finally.

That's no excuse, the other side would retort. You know what is happening. Sure, you've been accepted, but at what price? This will cause you nothing but trouble. You are making the wrong choices.

If Zak harbored any doubts about this, a chilling and foretelling incident should have banished them.

"Hey, you're cheating!" Dougal screamed at Cronk one afternoon while they played poker.

"Am not!" Cronk retorted. "You're just sore you're losing again!"

"You're cheating! That's an extra ace!"

"Will you two shut up?" Zak cried. "You're hurting my head."

"Cheater!" Dougal screamed again. Suddenly he pulled out a revolver from his waistband and stuck it in Cronk's face.

Cronk froze. The color drained from his face. He stared, cross-eyed, at the barrel between his eyes.

Nobody spoke. Nobody moved. Finally Zak broke the tension. "Dougal, put that away!" he snapped. "What's the matter with you?"

"Nobody messes with me," Dougal said through clenched teeth.

Cronk's face, a sickly gray, dripped with sweat. He began to blubber.

"Dougal, it's only cards," Zak said pleadingly. "Even if he did cheat, this isn't worth it."

Dougal peered sideways him. He swung the pistol around and pointed the barrel at his chest. Zak felt his stomach drop.

"Nobody tells me what to do in my place," he said. "I let you in here in the first place. You don't tell me what to do."

"All right," Zak whispered. He barely croaked the words out his constricted throat.

"I could shoot both of you," Dougal said. His gave his crooked smile. His eyes glossed over, as if he really considered the idea to be attractive and feasible.

"But I won't." He stuck the gun back into his waistband.

Cronk slumped in his chair, wiping his forehead. Zak breathed again.

"All right, Jimmy, new game!" Dougal cried, reaching over and cuffing Cronk affectionately on the shoulder as if nothing had happened. He began to deal the cards. Still petrified, Zak and Cronk could only look at each other in disbelief.

"What's the matter, Jimmy, you're not still scared, are you?" Dougal taunted him.

Dougal and Cronk acted differently the next night, as if they sheltered a secret between them without including Zak.

"What's going on?" Zak finally asked.

"It's a surprise," Dougal said.

"Yeah, a surprise," Cronk mimicked.

"What kind of surprise?"

"You'll see," Dougal said. "But first, some whiskey."

"I'll give you a hint," Cronk said. "Where do you think we get all this whiskey?"

"Shut up, Billy," Dougal said.

"And the tobacco?"

"I said shut up, Billy!"

"Where do you get all the whiskey and tobacco?" Zak thought for a moment. "Cronk's pappy?"

Cronk giggled. "Not even close."

"Billy!"

"All right, don't get sore," Cronk whined to Dougal. "I was only givin' him a hint."

"I told him it's a surprise. Now don't ruin' it. He'll find out soon enough."

"I don't like surprises," Zak said. He thought about his father leaving unannounced in the middle of the night. No sir, I sure don't like surprises.

"Well, yore gonna like this one," said Dougal. They drank for a while.

Dougal finally said, "All right. Let's go."

"What're we doing?" Zak asked. He felt strange. The whiskey made him warm all over. His head tingled pleasantly. He liked the way he felt.

"Shut up," said Dougal. "Get up. Grab that iron bar over there." He pointed to the corner.

Zak stood and almost fell, dizzy. He put his hand on the table to steady to himself before he shuffled clumsily over to the corner to retrieve the bar.

"Look, he's drunk," cried Cronk. "A drunk Indian!"

"A drunk Indian," said Dougal. "That's like sayin' a black nigger!"

Cronk giggled.

"Shut up, Billy," Zak said, slurring his words. "You're short."

"Yeah, but you're drunk. Drunk Zak."

"Zak smack," said Dougal.

"Zak smack!" chimed in Cronk.

Now Zak even found this funny. He began to laugh. Bolstered, Cronk repeated "Zak, smack" over and over. They began to laugh uncontrollably, rolling on the dirt floor, tears coming out of their eyes.

The night was pitch black. Stumbling, crawling, scrambling to the top of the riverbank, they saw silhouettes of buildings ahead of them, dark, barely distinguishable. Only a few lanterns glowed from behind window shades. No movement. The town was theirs.

They crept through the streets, Dougal leading. Zak whispered once, but Dougal cut him off with a motion, a savage finger across his throat. They were behind the mercantile. Dougal grabbed the iron bar from Zak and tried to force the door open, but it didn't work. Dougal yanked the derby from Cronk's head. He stuck his fist in it, placed its crown against the windowpane in the door and quickly, expertly punched into it. Shattered glass tinkled to the floor. Dougal reached in and unlocked the door.

Inside, Dougal handed Zak a match and ordered him to light it. In the faint orange glow, Cronk was behind the counter, one hand in the sourball jar and one hand in the jerky jar. The clanking of bottles came from the storeroom. Dougal emerged with four whiskey bottles, two in each hand. When the match died, Zak lit another one. Cronk, pockets stuffed with contraband, had a bottle in one hand and a pack of tobacco in the other. Dougal and Cronk giggled.

They were like kings. Kings of thieves.

Zak woke in his bed with a start. The sun shone through the open window. He remembered he came in the same way he left, using the trellis and the roof so no one downstairs could see him. He lay back down on his bed, head throbbing. His mouth seemed full of cotton, his tongue like leather. He dozed the rest of the morning.

A sharp rapping on his door startled him awake. Sheriff Gibson Patch filled the doorway with his six-foot-two frame. He looked like a giant. He chewed tobacco slowly, methodically, asking permission to spit in Zak's chamber pot.

Zak denied he was anywhere near the mercantile during last night, saying he was in bed the whole time. Ask anyone downstairs, he said. No one saw me leave after dinner.

Shame overwhelmed him as he lied.

The sheriff nodded slowly, chewing, contemplative. He hitched his thumbs in his belt and nodded some more. He looked at Zak, hard, and said he didn't like break-ins in his town. He didn't know who would have done it, but whoever it was, they'd better watch out. Old man Olson carries a pistol under that overcoat of his and he's sick to death of the break-ins. Says he and his three brothers are gonna shoot whoever they catch.

Zak nodded dutifully, agreeing that would be justified.

"You better not have told him nothin'," Dougal said when he found out the sheriff had been to see Zak.

"I didn't say anything," Zak said.

"I'll kill you if you do," Dougal said.

A week later they broke into the mercantile again, but this time it all went horribly wrong. Dougal managed to pry the lock off the door and they were inside with as little effort as the last time. Once again Dougal pilched whiskey while Cronk stuffed his pockets full of assorted goodies. Zak acted as a lookout, and saw nobody outside. What he did not see was who was inside.

"Hold it right there!" a voice commanded in the darkness. They heard the *click* as the hammer was cocked on a gun. "You better not move if you want to walk out of here!"

They heard the scraping of a match being struck against the wall and suddenly the pale yellow radiance of a kerosene lantern illuminated the room. When they looked in that direction they saw Olson, the mercantile owner, pointing a pistol at them.

"I knowed it was you troublemakers," Olson crowed triumphantly. "I knowed it all along, but I couldn't prove it. Now I can. All right, face me and keep your hands where'n I can see them. Let's just get along now and I'll be turning you over to the sheriff standin' up instead of lyin' down."

Dougal snickered.

"Oh, this is funny?" Olson demanded. "Yeah, it's funny, ain't it? Breaking into a man's business, his livelihood. Well, it ain't funny." He pointed the pistol at Dougal. "I got a notion to put one in your leg right now. Self-defense, I'd say. Nobody would say nothin' different. My word against yours. I could do it. I got the power."

Dougal snickered again. "You ain't got no power," he said. "You'd never use that on no other person. You're just an old man bluffin'. You ain't got it in you."

"Oh yeah?" demanded Olson. "Regular smart guy, huh? I got it in me. You make a move and I'll do it, I swear."

"No, you won't." Dougal smiled wickedly at Olson.

"I will!" But now Olson looked from one to the other of them. He seemed unsure.

"You won't." And with that, Dougal grabbed a jar from the counter and flung it into the opposite corner, where it smashed loudly. Olson, momentarily distracted, glanced in that direction. Dougal pulled his pistol instantaneously. To Zak, what happened next seemed to take place slowly, as if they were all in water with sluggish motions. It would be etched in his mind for the rest of his life.

A flash from Dougal's barrel temporarily blinded him. The blast pierced his ears, and after a instant of deafness he was left with a loud ringing. Out of the corner of his eye he saw Olson go down and heard the thump as he hit the floor. He heard shattering glass as the kerosene lamp shattered. Olson writhed on the floor in pain.

"I told him he didn't have the power," Dougal said. Then he turned and walked out of the store. Cronk followed him.

Zak rushed to Olson, curled in a fetal position, holding his leg. Blood soaked the trousers beneath his hand. He moaned in pain, his words indecipherable. He looked up at Zak with shock-filled eyes.

Torn, Zak faced a moment of complete indecision. He knew he should stay and help the man. The wound needed dressing and probably a tourniquet. He should run and get help.

But terror petrified him. He couldn't think straight. His legs felt like buckling.

Without the backing of any reason, without any forethought, the decision emerged in his muddied mind. Deep in his brain, perhaps in the part that provides the instinct, he knew he was wrong. Maybe his heart attempted to overrule his mind. He had an inkling that his future, his life, depended on this decision. But through some defect in his mind, his personality, his *soul*, he couldn't control himself. He felt like someone else was deciding for him.

Before he knew it he undid his belt buckle and removed his belt. He tossed it down to Olson.

"Put that around your leg above and pull it as tight as you can," he said. "Maybe you can save it."

And he turned and fled.

Sheriff Gibson Patch came for him two hours later. Zak, dozing on his bed, opened the door expectantly.

"Hello, Sheriff," he said. He turned around and sat on his bed.

The sheriff walked in with his deputy, Bernie Smith. The sheriff's face drooped with sadness. He rubbed his temples and chewed his tobacco slowly. He exhaled tiredly and sat in a chair across from Zak. He sat quietly from a minute, staring at his shoes.

"I know, you told me so," Zak said.

Patch looked up. "I'm not goin' to say anything like that. What's done is done."

He paused. Mrs. Hinkel now stood in the doorway.

"I just spoke to Olson," Patch said.

"So he's alive?" Zak asked. He breathed heavily with relief as the sheriff nodded.

"He's lost some blood, but he's gonna make it."

"What's happened?" Mrs. Hinkel asked.

"We can't talk about it now, Gretchen," Patch said. "You'll know soon enough. You go on back downstairs now."

She did not move, her worried face struggling to keep composure.

"Go on, now," Patch said gently.

She cast a worried glance at Zak but left the room.

The sheriff turned back to him. "I think I have a pretty good idea of what happened from what Olson says. But I don't know everything." He looked hard at Zak. "A guy's gotta protect himself. A guy who was there but didn't do all the bad things would make it easier on himself if he said exactly what happened. Easier legally and conscience-wise. See?"

Zak nodded silently.

"So how about it?" Patch asked.

Conflicting emotions boiled in Zak. On one hand he felt the sheriff was right, but on one hand he remembered the threats Dougal had made. Judging from Dougal's recent actions, he seemed perfectly capable of carrying through on them.

"I can't," Zak said.

Patch shook his head. "You can," he said sternly. "Don't you worry none about Dougal," he said, as if reading Zak's mind. "He's not gonna do anything to you. I'll see to that."

"I just can't right now." Zak ached with misery.

The sheriff's face fell again. "All right. But you think about it. A man's gotta look out for himself." He stood. "Come along now."

"Am I being arrested?"

Patch nodded. "I'm sorry. Until I find out exactly what happened and who did what. I know you were there. That's probable cause to take you in."

Zak nodded. Tears welled in his eyes. "What about Sunny?"

"Your horse? He can stay where he is. I'll have Bernie feed him and take him out." Smith peered sideways at the sheriff, obviously annoyed at being volunteered to do something.

The sheriff's features softened as he looked at Zak. "I knew your pa, son. I know what you've been through. I know about being with people who you think will take you as you are, even if they are rotten apples. There'll be a trial, but I'd put in a good word for you. But you gotta help me some."

He paused. "Remember this. Man looks into the abyss. He sees there's nothing there. At that moment he finds his character, and that allows him to go on. Do you understand?"

"I think so," Zak said, although not completely sure.

The deputy moved toward Zak, drawing a short length of rope from a pouch in his fist. "Give me your wrists," he said.

Zak offered them forward. But the sheriff shook his head sharply at the deputy. The deputy shrugged and put the rope away.

Zak stood. He looked around his room, at his bed, at the nightstand. This had been his home for the last few weeks and now he was going to jail, and who knew where after that. Would he go to the state prison? Do they have a prison for boys his age, or would he be locked up with bad guys older than him?

"Can I see my horse?" Zak asked as they left the hotel.

"I don't see why not," the sheriff said. He nodded at the deputy.

They walked over to the Company stable, the deputy's lantern slicing the darkness in front of them. Sunny stood in his stall, seemingly waiting for him as he always did. He nickered softly as Zak approached. Zak began to cry when he saw his horse.

He walked in the stall and patted Sunny on the nose. "I'm going away for a while," he said. Sunny gazed silently but attentively at Zak. He blinked twice, his long lashes meeting delicately together.

"Yeah, I'm going away for a while," Zak said again, "but I'll be back. I don't know when, but I will." He patted the horse's flank, ran his hands up and down the strong legs. "They'll take good care of you while I'm gone. I'll think about you every chance I get." Sunny shook his head, eyes wide, as if he suddenly realized what was happening. "That's all right," Zak said through his tears. "That's all right. You be a good horse and I'll be back before you know it."

Zak turned to the deputy. "I'm ready," he said.

6. There Came Hail and Fire

REALLY JUST a two-room cabin with wooden walls, the jail had recently been reinforced with brick because a couple of inmates escaped by burning their way out. Zak lay on a cot in the corner, dozing. In an hour the door slammed open and the deputy threw Dougal Black roughly into the room. Bruised and bloodied, Dougal nonetheless looked at him with clear eyes, open and alert, defiant.

They did not talk to each other, passing the night in stony silence broken only by the soft snoring of Deputy Smith, asleep in the adjoining room. Sheriff Patch stopped by once, promising to return at daybreak.

Zak woke to the sounds of pounding hooves. He listened intently: horses raced up and down the main road into town. He sat up and looked around. Dougal sat upright on his cot, alert.

Daylight streamed in through the windows. Sheriff Patch stood in the open doorway of the jail, craning his head sideways to hear. They could hear shouting above the din.

"What's happening?" Deputy Smith asked.

"Don't know," the sheriff said.

The pounding of the hooves continued. Now and then Zak heard the rattling and banging as wagons bounced over the rutted street of the town.

The sheriff turned to the deputy. "Load my guns. Get out my horse. I don't know what's going on, but I aim to find out."

"What are you gonna do?"

"I'm going into the town to see what's going on. You stay here and guard them."

The sheriff returned soon with another rider—Judge Flandrau, looking grave. He looked at the boys sternly as he dismounted in front of the jail. His features softened when he looked at Zak.

"What is it?" Deputy Smith asked.

Flandrau removed his hat and wiped his brow, rich in perspiration from the humidity. "The Sioux have attacked the Lower Agency and are raiding towns and farms. Dozens, perhaps hundreds, of people have already been killed. New Ulm may be under attack as we speak."

A stunned silence enveloped them. Finally Smith shook them out of their stupor.

"What? Attacked? Where? Who's attacking?"

"Little Crow, my old friend, has unleashed his braves upon the settlers," Flandrau said. "The whole countryside is under attack."

"Are they coming here?" the deputy asked.

"Don't know," said the sheriff. "Probably not. That's all the commotion you're hearing. The town is filling with people fleeing in front of them. We'll have to fortify the town against an attack."

Zak couldn't believe what he heard. He thought of his grandfather, of Whirlwind, of Circling Hawk. Could they be a part of that? Were they killing people? Were they dead? He found it almost impossible to fathom. But then he thought of Whirlwind, his rigid adherence to his beloved way of life, and he suddenly understood. A chill rippled down his spine.

"I can't believe it," sputtered Deputy Smith. "That can't be right. The Sioux? That ragtag collection of savages in tattered teepees?"

"Believe it," said the judge.

"What are we gonna do?" sputtered the deputy. "My mom and pop live in New Ulm." His eyes widened with apprehension.

"Easy, now," said the judge. "Panic is our enemy. We don't know everything yet. I'm organizing a militia unit to go over and relieve New Ulm. We're going to head out just after noon."

"Well, count me in," said the deputy. He looked earnestly at the sheriff. "Gibson? My mom and pop are over there."

Patch nodded. "I'm going, too."

"What about us?" Dougal Black asked.

Flandrau looked at them intently. "The sheriff and I have discussed this," he said. "I know what happened in the mercantile last night. You boys are in a lot of trouble. I don't know exactly who did what, but I have a good idea after talking with the sheriff." He looked directly at Dougal.

"There's no time for regular legal proceedings now," he continued. "With the Sioux outbreak a trial is out of the question. But I have a deal to offer you boys. I've already discussed it with Olson the store owner, and he's agreed, although I wouldn't have faulted him if he hadn't. His boys sure disagree with it."

72

"What's the deal?" Dougal asked suspiciously.

"You two join up with my militia unit and perform as expected and as ordered. At the end of the hostilities, whenever they are, tomorrow or next month, you're pardoned. Free. No charges will be pursued, and there'll never be any trial. No jail. Your liberty for your service."

Zak's mind reeled. The judge offered a deal that would keep him out of prison, something he desperately wanted. But in order to do it, he'd have to fight against members of his own family, people who'd always been generous to him. He felt twisted inside, as if two forces struggled mightily over him in a tug-of-war.

The judge took Zak aside. "Hammer, I know this is a difficult choice for you. Another in a long line of ones you've had to make. But I'm mindful of the situation. I'd put you only on scout or messenger duty. It will be extremely hazardous, out alone in front of the group. Running messages to others by yourself. But you won't officially be part of the group that I'm forming to attack the hostiles."

Zak contemplated this while Dougal spoke again.

"Let me see if I got this straight. You want me to take a deal and never have a trial."

"That's right," Flandrau answered. "Your liberty for your service."

"Well that *sounds* all fine and dandy," Dougal said, "but that's what my old man did. Took a deal when he might have beat it at trial. Gave up and left me. No way. No deal."

Zak thought quickly. What the judge asked for would be hard. But, in a natural justice sort of way, it seemed to be the appropriate penalty for the situation he'd gotten himself into. Penance, so to speak. It might even do him some good. He remembered what Sheriff Patch said about man finding his character after falling into the abyss.

"I'll do it," he said.

"Very well," said the judge. "Mr. Black, this is your last chance. I'm declaring martial law as of now. If you refuse you'll be taken up to St. Paul and held at Fort Snelling until the hostilities here are over. You will have your trial, but not for a long time."

"I guess it's the fort then," said Dougal.

"Very well," said the judge. "Sheriff, release Mr. Hammer and have your deputy escort him to the hotel so he can pack. Have him pack only what's needed for a two- or three-day excursion. Give him his horse."

He spoke directly to Zak. "Eat something and meet in the town square at noon."

As Zak packed—how does one really pack to go to war?—he struggled to control his feelings. Butterflies flew wildly in his stomach, and he felt as if someone had thrown an anvil on his shoulders. But in a strange way he also felt better, that he'd made the right decision. The whole thing would probably take only a couple of days—there didn't seem to be much of a chance the Dakota would defeat the Army once it came down from Fort Snelling.

As he cinched up the saddle on Sunny, he felt a sharp pang of worry. The possibility that Sunny could get hurt hadn't occurred to him until now.

"We'll just have to be careful," he said to his horse. "In just a few days it'll all be over. Then it can be like it was before. I'll go to school, and we'll see each other every day. We'll ride out in the wind like you like so much."

These thoughts comforted him as he rode Sunny toward the town square. But they instantly vanished when he saw the scene there. Hundreds of people choked the square. Dozens of horses and wagons stood pell-mell around the area. The noise hurt his already sore ears. Chaos reigned.

Zak leaned over in his saddle and grabbed an older man walking aimlessly, a dazed look on his face.

"Sir, what's all this?" Zak asked.

"All this?" the man repeated. "All this?" He looked at Zak uncomprehendingly, eyes wide and frightened. Zak had seen this look before—his own face in the mirror when his mother died.

The man looked around as if he was seeing everything for the first time. "It's the end, that's what it is. The end." He stumbled away.

Zak surveyed the scene. Women wept openly, some forlornly calling out the names of loved ones. Children bawled; dogs ran wildly, barking incessantly; spooked oxen and horses stood wild-eyed near their owners.

Sunny neighed nervously as they approached. "Easy, boy," said Zak quietly, patting his flank.

On the other side of the square, Zak saw Dr. Mayo walking amongst several men who were lying on the ground, bending over some as he moved. Zak rode Sunny there, working his way around the edge of the square. His stomach turned when he saw the men on the ground. Two moaned and babbled incoherently, trying in their dazed states to remove blood-soaked bandages from their heads. One man looked dead; his face was ashen and his closed eyes were sunk deep in their sockets. Dried blood encrusted the front of his shirt. Another man sat upright, staring ahead dully. He held his left arm close to his body. Zak, horrified, saw he was missing his hand.

The doctor spotted Zak and must have seen his expression. "That's what happens when you get hit with a hatchet," he said.

"Mr. Hammer!"

Zak wheeled. Judge Flandrau pounded toward him on his horse. He pointed to the other side of the square. "We're going to meet over there in a few minutes."

"Yes, sir," Zak said. He took a last look at the scene as he left.

A hundred men milled about noisily in front of the courthouse. They did not look like a militia unit—just a bunch of middle-aged men, old men; farmers. Some were on horseback, but most were not. The weaponry they possessed seemed inadequate, laughable—a few muskets and shotguns, but more pitchforks and hoes. The men looked confused, angry, and scared.

Judge Flandrau strode to the top of the courthouse stairs and raised his arms. The men quieted down.

"As of today, August 19, 1862, the Sioux are on the warpath," Flandrau boomed out in his baritone. "Our families, our friends, and our women and children are dying at the hands of the red man."

"Savages!" one man screamed from the back of the group.

"Kill 'em all!" shouted another.

The judge held up his arms again. "As you have seen, the countryside is clearing out. There will be thousands of people here in just a couple of days. Those that can make it out will come here. They will be safe here. I've sent word to Fort Snelling and requested immediate relief from the Army. Little Crow will know this and will not come this far east.

"Some have not made it out. New Ulm is under attack and is cut off from Fort Ridgely in the west. The people need to be relieved by us here in the east. In a few minutes I will send out an advance party of scouts. They will be led by Sheriff Patch and former Sheriff Boardman. The scout party will take Fort Road and will relay periodic messages back to the main unit, which will start in one or two hours. Our goal will be to repel any Sioux that advance farther east than New Ulm and to relieve that city."

The judge paused. He looked over the men. "I do not need to tell you how grave the situation is. We have expended too much energy to civilize this state to have our farms and towns burned and our children slaughtered. I expect every man here to be willing to give his life if necessary. God grant us victory. That is all."

Zak and the fifteen other men that comprised the advance party headed west on horseback at a slow trot. New Ulm lay thirty-two miles away, a good day's ride. On the western side of St. Peter they passed through the remnants of some cattle herds that had somehow been saved and were being watched by their jittery owners, all wearing the same haunted expressions as the refugees in town.

The Fort Road, an old Indian trial, was trafficked now by the Army and settlers. Spanning the distance between St. Peter and Fort Ridgely, a distance of about fifty miles with New Ulm in the middle, the road offered a path of flattened grass in the dry times and a nightmare of almost-non-navigable ruts in the wet ones. The bluestem on either side of the road stood as high as a fourteen-hand horse's flank and continued endlessly to the horizon on all sides.

Nobody spoke as they started out, each man absorbed in his own thoughts and fears. They traveled only three or four miles before they met the first of the refugees, a family of three. The man led an ox pulling a Red River cart, a U-shaped cart set upon two gigantic wheels on either side. A woman and a small girl rode in the lurching cart. The man waved at them as they met.

"Reckon yer headed out to where the Indians are," he said. "Was wonderin' when we was gonna see some relief." Tall and skinny, the man had large, almost disproportionate, callused hands. That man knows his way around a plow, Zak thought.

"Name's Johansson," said the man as they met. He shook hands with Sheriff Patch.

"I'm Patch. Where you coming from?"

"Not five miles east of New Ulm. Have a farm there."

"*Had* a farm there," corrected his wife. A skinny, frail redhead, her face and eyes looked puffy from crying. The child just stared at them with wide eyes over the side of the cart. Zak took a look inside the cart. Except for a small trunk there was nothing else. No food, no water, or other personal effects. Nothing from a house or barn. They must have fled in a hurry.

"She's right," Johansson said. "Neighbor warned us in the nick of time. We got out only a half-hour before a Sioux war party showed up. We hugged a treeline down by a creek so they couldn't see us. We waited until they'd done what they came to do, although I suppose us not being there must of made them mad. When they left they burnt down the place." He paused. "Kinda funny. Took me coupla months to build that cabin and barn, but they was smoking husks in just fifteen minutes." The woman in the cart began to cry again when the man said that.

"What's happening out there?" asked Dr. Mayo.

"Oh, it's bad," said Johansson. "There's farms goin' up like torches left and right. We seen two neighbor places same as ours. Don't know what happened to the people there, but it can't be good."

"They're scalpin' folks alive!" cried the woman hysterically from the cart. "Babies is bein' nailed to trees and womenfolk is bein' dragged off to—why I can't even think of it!"

"Now, Sadie, we don't know if that's the truth or not," Johansson said gently. He turned back to Patch. "We ran into another family who came from past New Ulm who said those things. Nobody we talked to has actually seen any of these things personally, but people have heard them and are repeatin' them like the Gospel. Doesn't seem to me to do any good unless you've seen them firsthand. Just scaring the bejesus out of everyone."

"I think you're right," said Patch. "What happened to you, though, that's real enough. I'm right sorry about that."

"Thank ye," said Johansson.

"You can rebuild after it's all over," said the sheriff.

"Oh, I don't know about that," said Johansson. "I think we're going back to New York. They ain't been any Injun trouble there since the Revolution." He sadly looked at his wife. "Don't think Sadie's cut out for it no more."

The sheriff nodded understandingly. "Well, you folks take care of yourselves. God bless you."

"Thank ye," said Johansson, and they began moving again.

People being scalped alive and babies nailed to trees! Zak thought. Gosh almighty! He couldn't believe it, didn't want to believe it. He thought of Whirlwind and Circling Hawk. Were they part of this? He didn't think they possibly could be. They weren't capable of such things, were they? Five minutes after meeting the Johanssons Zak had convinced himself it couldn't be that horrible.

But as the morning wore on the awful reality of it hit them as sure as if they'd been smacked in the face. The next batch of refugees they met were in desperate shape. The remnants of two families, neighbors from west of New Ulm, they'd been right in the eye of the hurricane.

One family, a man and his two sons, walked forlornly together on the road. A party of three Dakota had ransacked their house and burned it. The man's wife, scouting for firewood at the creek bottom behind their place, didn't return to the cabin. The man fought his sons to wait for her, but they forcibly subdued him and fled in the nick of time. The man, grief-stricken, peered at them from behind haunted, blackened eyes.

Another family rode in their buckboard, the mother prostrate in the back with anguish. Their thirteen-year-old son had died in her arms, two arrows in his back, after warning them just in time of the impending danger. They battled with the braves that swooped upon them, the father blasting three or four shots at them, running them off, but not before being shot in the shoulder. The men crowded around to see his wound. The musket ball lay in plain sight, embedded in the muscle of the man's shoulder.

After Doc Mayo worked on the man and sent the family on their way, the advance party moved on. The day grew oppressively hot as they worked their way west. The sun beat mercilessly down on them and a hot wind blasted them as they rode. The only good thing about the wind was that it kept the mosquitoes down in the grass. Dark blue thunderheads swelled ominously in the west. Zak saw ground-to-cloud and cloud-to-cloud lightning dancing above. The reports of the thunder, low and ominous, followed later. Zak timed it—miles away yet, but they would pass through it before they got to New Ulm.

After three hours the road passed by a lake to the south. The shimmering lake reflected the last of the afternoon sun. Zak asked the man next to him how far they'd gone.

About twenty-five miles, the man said. Almost there.

They stopped at the lake. Sheriff Patch told them to water their horses. He directed Deputy Smith to fill all their canteens. The deputy, a disgusted look on his face, instead shoved the canteens into Zak's arms.

"Here, you do it," he sneered. "I ain't no slave. If anyone should do it, it's you, being an Injun and all."

"An Injun?" one of the other men exclaimed, looking at Zak intently. He grimaced at him with long teeth. Zak silently dubbed him `Horse Teeth.'

"What's he doin' with us?" Horse Teeth challenged.

"Got hisself into some trouble and decided to go with us instead of goin' to jail," the deputy said. "Just like a redskin to get into trouble."

"I'm half white," said Zak.

"Don't matter none," said Horse Teeth. "Injun blood is Injun blood. Bet some of your kin is out there doin' all those things we heard about." He looked at the deputy. "I don't like it. Watch him closely. He's likely to put poison in our water or something."

When they moved out again Zak saw in the northwest—away from the building storm—columns of smoke, black pillars rising in the haze. The others saw it too, but said nothing. Zak guessed what they were—burning homes and fields. He guessed the others were giving silent but guilty thanks that they had not suffered the same fate.

"Look! A rider!" a man at the front of the column suddenly exclaimed, pointing to the northwest. Zak squinted against the haze. At first he could see nothing, but presently he made out the form of a horse, heading directly for them. The closer the horse got the more they could see it galloped wildly, out of control. A few men raised their rifles. Zak would have raised his too, if only he'd had one.

The horse approached head-on, and Zak saw it was riderless. The men who'd raised their rifles lowered them sheepishly. But as the horse got closer they could see it dragging something. The men raised their rifles again. The horse crossed the road directly in front of them, running madly, obviously spooked.

Dragging from the stirrups behind the horse was its rider. Obviously dead, his arrow-ridden body bounced loosely along the ground, his bones pulverized by the miles of pounding over the prairie.

Two men rode after the horse and stopped it. The rest of the men rode up and gathered in a circle around the body, staring silently. The horse stood nervously, eyes wide and rolling back in his sockets. It snorted twice. Frothy sweat covered its hide.

But it was the sight of the dead man that transfixed them. His clothing tattered and torn, he looked almost nude. His right arm, obviously broken, was bent grotesquely behind his head. One ear hung by a thread of skin. He stared at them with look of horror frozen in his unseeing eyes.

"Savages," one man muttered under his breath.

"Goddamned heathens. Barbarians," said another. "I'm goin' to kill every last one of them I see."

A strange sound came from the outside of the circle. A low guttural moan, starting low in the chest and working its way up the throat, rose in a man. All color had drained from his blanched face. His hands trembled. His mouth quivered, little white spots of saliva in each corner.

"I — I'm gettin' outta here," he whimpered. "I don't want no part of this. No siree, none of it." He began to blubber.

"The Sioux are gonna pay for this," Horse Teeth hissed. "I say we start right now." He glared at Zak.

Sheriff Patch's voice boomed out among them. "All right, that's enough. You," he said to the blubbering man, "Get ahold of yourself.

80

You're not the only scairt one here. And you," he said to the man who'd threatened Zak, "you mind your own business. That boy is under my direct supervision, per the judge's orders. You just watch your own hide."

Horse Teeth rode away, but he shot Zak a hateful look.

After another hour they saw smoke billowing in the southwest, darkening the horizon like a burgeoning prairie fire. Hope that's not New Ulm, someone said, but before anyone could answer, the storm hit them. Lashing winds ripped at them and hail battered them. Lightning sizzled on all sides, close, and thunder shook them to the bones. An eerie green-black darkness enveloped them.

Then, almost as quickly as it struck, the storm passed, and they regrouped in the sunshine. The smoke in the distance still billowed unabated. They approached a valley, green wooded hills rising and rolling above a river. The smoke billowed up from the valley floor, down by the river, rising high into the sky. It was terribly hot again, and the furnace-like wind from the south deposited ash and burning particles on them. It soon covered them like a fine but thick dust. Zak could taste the charcoal-like grit. The wind was acrid and stung his eyes.

When they rose over a knoll they saw the source of the smoke and sooty ash. Below them lay a sprawling town, laid out in straight and orderly streets above the river. But what should have been a peaceful scene of whitewashed houses and pleasant yards was marred by the inferno that engulfed it. Flames raged in dozens of houses and buildings. Entire blocks were ablaze. All around town, and all around the outside of town, shadowy figures raced frantically. Figures on horses raced up and down the perimeter of town. Gunshots rang out periodically. They had reached New Ulm, and it was indeed under attack. The townspeople were defending their homes, their families, against hundreds of warriors.

They had reached New Ulm, straight and orderly streets and whitewashed houses and pleasant yards, and it was burning to the ground.

"Straight out of Revelation," Sheriff Patch said, awed. "'The angel sounded, and there followed hail and fire mingled with blood, and they were cast upon the earth.'"

BOOK II:

Hail and Fire

Minnie-ha-ha (Laughing Water)

Minnie-ha-ha laughing water
Cease thy laughing now for aye
Savage hands are red with slaughter
Of the innocent today.

Change thy note, gay Minnie-ha-ha
Let some sadder strain prevail
Listen while a maniac wanderer
Sings to thee his woeful tale.

Give me back my Lela's tresses
Let me kiss them once again
She who blest me with caresses
Lies unburied on the plain!

See yon smoke, there was my dwelling
That is all I have of home
Hark! I hear the fiendish yelling
As I homeless, childless roam.

Have they killed my Hans and Otto?
Did they find them in the corn?
Go and tell that savage monster
Not to kill my youngest born.

Yonder is my brand new reaper
Standing mid the ripened grain;
Even my cow asks why I leave her
Wandering unmilked o'er the plain.

Faithful Fido, now they've left me
Can you tell me Fido why
God at once has thus bereft me
All I ask is here to die.

But not the laughing Minnie-ha-ha
Heeded not the woeful tale

What cares laughing Minnie-ha-ha
For the corpses in the vale?

—*Anonymous*

7. Overture (II)

THE SETTLERS fled. They fled wildly to the east from the slaughter, on horses, on wagons hitched with teams of horses, by oxcart, on mules. In their blind panic they pushed their animals to the breaking point, lungs heaving, nostrils flaring, eyes rolling back in sockets, hides slimy with creamy lather. They pushed them beyond the breaking point, screaming at them, whipping them, driving them until they dropped, until the prairie was littered with them, their reliable workmates, their companions, their pets lying in tangled mounds of flesh and bone swollen in the hot sun, filling the prairie with swarms of frenzied eager flies and the unbearable sweet-and-sour stench of rotting flesh.

And then they ran. They ran with terror in their eyes, extreme, utter, life-sucking terror. They ran until they could barely breathe, their lungs heaving and their clothes soaked with sweat, fleeing with the primal fear of the hunted prey, the fear of being eaten alive. As they fled they abandoned their lives as they knew them. They abandoned neat, orderly farms, sod houses and log cabins built with loving hands, their hopes and dreams caulked in the nooks and crannies with the prairie mud. The carefully-crafted and whitewashed fences surrounding neatly-mowed pastures and weedless cornfields. They abandoned hand-made quilts and trunks of hand-sewn clothes, diaries, and letters from relatives in the old countries, hand-drawn portraits of mothers, of daughters. They left memories—of bumper crops, blinding January white-outs, the birth of a son, the death of a father, a mother's soft voice. The memories of cozy mid-February nights, the family talking quietly and lovingly together in the soft, yellow light of a kerosene lamp, when all seemed right with the world, the travails of the emigration, the piercing loneliness of the empty land temporarily forgotten.

As they fled toward civilization, toward safety, they heard blood-curdling stories of massacre that were almost unbelievable, unfathomable in their brutality and savagery. Whole families butchered in their sleep. Young girls raped repeatedly before being dragged off to an unthinkable captivity. Babies cut out of their murdered mothers. Small children nailed to barn doors and used as target practice. They didn't want to believe the stories, to believe the atrocities. But as they fled they turned against their better judgment to look, and saw the smoke of a thousand farms on the plain, the smoke of the country going up as in a furnace, and they believed.

They believed.

The governor, sick in his panic, appealed for help. Good God! Hordes of the red murderous savages threatened to overrun his state! The countryside emptied as the good citizens ran for their lives! Fort Ambercrombie in the northwest under siege! Towns abandoned and burned by raiding war parties! Our women—*our women!*—violated in countless ways by the barbarians!

Contact the governor of Wisconsin! What? No arms or men to spare because they've all been shipped to southern battlefields? Well, telegraph Lincoln! This is not just *our* war, this is a *national* war with national implications. Contact the Secretary of the Army! Get horses, cannon, troops, and a general, to take back our country! Don't take 'no' for an answer. We know the Confederates threaten the capital city. But this is just as serious—the very existence of a fledgling state, the future of expansion, of our *Manifest Destiny*, hinges in the balance!

The Sioux must be exterminated or driven forever from beyond the borders of the state. The public safety imperatively requires it. Justice requires it. The blood of the murdered cries to heaven for vengeance on those assassins of women and children. Amenable to no laws, bound by no moral or social constraints, they have already destroyed every pledge on which it was possible to found a hope of ultimate reconciliation. They must be regarded as outlaws. All will have to pay.

8. Friend or Foe

"THE WHOLE town's under attack!" cried one of the men in the party. "Them's Injuns runnin' all over!"

"What're we gonna do?" asked another. "We can't go down there now! We'll be cut to pieces!"

The prospect of entering the town looked grim indeed. Although they sat on a bluff two hundred feet above the streets, giving them a good view of the panorama, they did not know what lurked in the thick timber between them and the town. The deep woods and riverbottom swamps through which they would have to cross could give cover to hundreds of warriors. "What're we gonna do, Sheriff?" someone else asked.

"I say we turn around and go back where we came from," said another. "The town's done for, anyway."

Sheriff Patch surveyed the town through field glasses.

"You men quiet down," he said brusquely. "I'm trying to think. We're not skeddadlin', that's for sure. Those people down there need our help." He lowered his glasses down. "Besides, it looks like the attack's about over. See?" He pointed to the bluffs on the other side of town. "There's Indians headed up those hills and out of town the opposite way." He put the field glasses away.

He licked his lips. "Here's what we're gonna do." He divided their force in two with a chopping motion. "You men," he said to the half on the left, "ride down as fast as you can into the town. You may draw some fire if any Indians are left down there, but you'll be going fast enough and they're not expecting you anyway. You men," he said to the half on the right, including Zak, "are gonna follow right behind. If there's Indians they'll be concentrating on the group in front and you should take 'em by surprise and make it through without drawing any fire."

"That don't sound like such a good plan," said one of the men in the first group.

"You got any better ones?" demanded Patch.

"Uh, no," said the man sheepishly.

"I'm goin' in the first group, if that satisfies you," said the sheriff. The man was silent.

"All right," said the sheriff. "Now you men remember: Don't stop. Don't stop for nothin'. Just ride as fast as you can into town and we'll meet in the square, where it looks like the townfolk have holed up. You see any Indians, you keep ridin'. There's plenty of time for killin' Indians later on. And if one of you gets in trouble, the rest of you keep goin', too. We want to get as many men into town as possible." He looked around at the men in his group. "Ready?" All heads nodded silently, grimly.

With cries of "Ha!" and "Ya!" the men in Sheriff Patch's group spurred their horses down the hillside. Dust rose behind them and soon they were out of sight, down in the cottonwoods by the river. Zak waited breathlessly, listening for the gunshots and war-whoops that were sure to follow. The other men did the same. But none came. In half a minute Zak saw Sheriff Patch's group emerge on the other side of the cottonwoods and race at breakneck speed into the town.

"A piece of cake!" one of the men near Zak cried out jubilantly.

"Don't count your chickens before they're hatched," another man said. "Let's just do as they did and hightail it down there. I want to keep all my hair."

"Come on boy, we can do it," Zak said quietly into Sunny's ear. "If ever I've needed you to run straight and true, it's now." Sunny's ears perked up. He grunted softly and pawed the ground in front of him.

"All right, let's do it," someone said. "Ya!" he shouted at his horse.

"Ha!" shouted Zak. "Go, Sunny!" He spurred his rear flank, just enough to set him in motion. He grabbed the reins tightly. Down they went, down the steep hillside. Zak's stomach lurched once and recovered. The cottonwood stand grew larger as they got closer, but Zak was so focused that he could see individual trees despite the heaving and bouncing.

Then they were in the trees. Zak kept his eyes on the back of the man in front of him. Just another half minute and they would be on the other side. It looked like they were going to make it.

But out of the tops of his eyes he saw a flash of movement. Something jumped out of the tree ahead of him, a fleeting shadowy figure, and the man in front of him was knocked out of his saddle. The two figures—the rider and the Indian who'd knocked him off his horse—were blurs as he raced by them. In a split second he thought he should stop and help—it didn't seem right leaving him there—but then he remembered the sheriff's words and he kept going.

Then they were out of the woods and into the daylight. Ahead of him lay the burning town. He raced Sunny at top speed toward the town square. In the fleeting horror before he got there he saw blazing and charred buildings, their contents strewn about the streets. He saw bodies scattered in the streets, Indians and ordinary-looking townfolk. He saw the body of a blonde-haired girl who looked about his age.

Throngs of townspeople choked the central square. A rough barricade of barrels, boxes, and overturned wagons surrounded them. Zak realized that the townspeople had cleared a path through the barricade for them to ride. Outside of the barricade Zak counted at least three dozen buildings he could see burning. Many were already burned to the ground.

On the other side of the square sat the Dacotah House, the town's hotel. Women and children emerged from it, looking around cautiously as people do when storms pass. The men in the square whooped with joy when they saw Zak's group. They went from man to man, pumping hands, their smiling teeth white against their powder-blackened faces. They cheered when they heard that Judge Flandrau would arrive later with one hundred and fifty reinforcements.

One man stepped forward, face blackened and smeared with blood, one eye swollen shut. "I'm Sheriff Roos. Who's the leader here?"

"I am, Charles," said Sheriff Patch, smiling. "Looks like you folks have been through a lot."

"Why, is that Gibson Patch?" Sheriff Roos asked, squinting at Patch. Pointing to his face he said, "I only got one good eye now, 'cept I'm afraid that it's always been my bad eye. Can't see your face too clearly."

"That's all right, Charles," said Sheriff Patch kindly. "What happened here?"

Roos sighed sadly. "We've had one hell of a time. We're goin' about our business as usual when a rider comes in and says the Sioux are killin' all the whites in the area. Some of the things he said the

91

Sioux were doin' were almost too fantastic to believe. Only a few people took 'em seriously, and left for Fort Ridgely right away. Don't know if they made it or not."

"But pretty soon we was under attack, like in a war," continued Sheriff Roos. We just these barricades up before they came." He pointed to the bluffs out of town. "We could see 'em coming out of the sun. At about a mile up there they fanned out and came on quickly, almost too quickly. When they got within earshot they took up a terrible yell and came down on us like the wind."

"This here's Jacob Nix," Sheriff Roos said, feeling around him almost blindly. A man stepped forward and put his hand on Roos' shoulder.

"Jacob was in the Army in Germany before they came over. He is our *Platzkommondant* and organized our defense. We had one squad of fourteen men who actually had rifles. Another squad of eighteen had double-barreled shotguns and another with twelve single-shots. Our reserve outfit, they had nothing but axes and pitchforks. So you see, we didn't have much."

"I guess not," said Sheriff Patch.

"When Jacob yelled *Auf euer Posten*—'to your posts,'—we erected those makeshift barricades you see out there. We put the men with rifles and shotguns behind the barricades and kept the reserve men closer to the hotel as a last resort. The women and children, they went into the hotel. Got so crowded the women had to remove their hoopskirts." He pointed to behind the hotel, managing a smile. Jacob Nix smiled beside him. Zak saw a pile of hoopskirts that looked like a small haystack.

"The Indians dismounted on top of the hill and charged into town. But it wasn't a coordinated attack, with skirmish lines and all that. They charged in one by one, sneaking from building to building, ransacking the places and setting them on fire. Luckily we'd managed to get almost everyone behind the barricades when they attacked. Little Emilie Pauli, though, she didn't make it in time."

"I saw her when I rode in," Zak said.

"Oh, you did?" Sheriff Roos asked, turning toward him. "Can you show us later where she is so we can bring her back to her parents?"

"I will."

"Thanks." He turned back to Patch. "We lost five men at the barricades and perhaps a couple dozen wounded, a couple seriously."

"We'll send the doc to look at them right away," Patch said, nodding at Dr. Mayo.

"I'd be happy to," Dr. Mayo said.

"Much obliged," said Roos.

"I'll set up a makeshift hospital in the basement of the hotel."

"Did you men lose anyone?" Roos asked.

"Yes, we lost one on the ride into town," Patch said. "We'll go look for him later, to recover his body. He's a goner, I'm sure."

Judge Flandrau and the militia arrived at about 8:00 that night, just before dark. The men elected him the leader of the town's defense and bestowed him with the honorary title of Colonel. The judge posted sentries around town for early warning against another attack and he ordered the barricades fortified with whatever the townspeople could scrounge up. Tomorrow if they were not attacked he would send out a couple of burial parties into the rest of the town and nearby countryside.

Later Zak ate sauerbraten and dumplings at the hotel. Judge Flandrau stopped in to see him. The women, after recovering from the initial shock and fright of the afternoon's attack, had set about the task of feeding the men. The judge removed his hat and sat at the table with Zak.

"Before we left St. Peter I sent a messenger up to St. Paul with the news," he said. "The messenger should get there tonight and I imagine Governor Ramsey will send an Army detachment in the morning. They should get to St. Peter in a day or two and here before the end of the week. I hope we can hold out until then. I've heard that we're getting more men in from Le Sueur and Nicollet." He paused, rolling the edges of his handlebar mustache between his fingertips. "But the Army will need to know what's happened here and what's happening in the countryside." He looked at Zak directly. "You're handy on that horse of yours, aren't you?"

"Yes, sir."

"What's his name again?"

"Sun Dance, sir."

"Ah, yes. Sun Dance." He smiled. "It's a nice name. It's terribly ironic, though, that you gave him a name from one side of your heritage and now you're in the midst of a conflict where both sides of your heritage fight each other."

"I guess it is," said Zak.

"It's that way with folks all over the state now," Flandrau said. A contemplative look came to his face. "Nobody really knows who's friend or foe. Especially the mixed-breeds like you. There will come a time, though, when all will have to declare their loyalty to one side or the other. Careful decisions will have to be made."

He waved his hand as if to dismiss the topic. "Unfortunately for you, the circumstances have dictated your decision," he said. "But as I told you I'm mindful of your situation. I'm not going to keep you here to take up arms against the Sioux when they attack again, which they will surely do. I have another plan for you." He walked over to the front desk and returned with a quill pen and a piece of paper. On it he drew a rough map. "I want you to ride out on your horse with a message for the commander of the Army, whoever that will be. It's about one hundred and thirty miles to Fort Snelling, but you should meet the Army detachment well south of there, probably at Henderson." He pointed to a town south of St. Paul on the Minnesota River.

"I know where Henderson is," Zak said. "Just a couple hours' ride north of St. Peter."

"Right. But there's no time for you to take the road all the way back to St. Peter and then north. You'll need to get there cross-country. Can you do that?"

"I think so. I know the stars well enough to navigate myself."

"Good. It's clear out so you shouldn't have any problem. When you get to the lake just point your horse north by northeast and you should make Henderson. It'll take you all night and then some to get there. I want you to deliver this message." He took a few minutes to scribble and then handed the note to Zak. It read:

To The Honorable Commander, U.S. Army Detachment From Fort Snelling:

As I have detailed in previous dispatches, the Sioux have risen in large numbers and are wantonly killing the citizens of this state. Farms and fields are burning.

Settlements, including New Ulm from where I write, have been under attack directly. I think I can hold this town until you come, if not attacked by a very large force. I am making some entrenchments, etc. I am sure everything outside the town is lost, and the people killed.

I wish you would leave from where you are as soon as you receive this message. The roads are good, and you can get here within a day or two.

Bring powder, lead, and caps. We are short.

> *Your Obedient Servant,*
> *C. Flandrau*

"The bad thing about the skies being clear," the judge said, "is that there'll be a bright moon and you'll be visible in the open, which you will be for most of the way. Keep to the river bottoms when you can. Remember, you're as likely a foe as a friend to anyone right now. Avoid contact with anyone if you can. Keep that message folded in this wax paper and put it in your shoe. Don't show it to anyone, white or non-white, until you get to the Army. Show it to them. But before you get near them beware of pickets and ride slowly, calling out well in advance." He paused. "Do you know the 'Battle Hymn of the Republic?'"

Zak said he'd never heard of it.

"*Mine eyes have seen the glory of the coming of the Lord,*" the judge sang softly, giving Zak an excerpt. "*He is trampling out the vintage where the grapes of wrath are stored.*" Zak shook his head, no. "It's what our boys are singing out east when they march into battle," the judge said. He sang the chorus. *"Glory, glory hallelujah.* It's been in all the papers. Everyone in the Army knows it, even up here on the frontier. Use that and they'll be less likely to shoot you on sight. Understand?"

"Yes, sir."

"Good." He paused and looked at Zak soberly. "This will be a most challenging night for you, something you'll not forget for the rest of your life. God be with you." He reached out and they shook hands firmly.

It was almost midnight as Zak gathered his things and paused to look at the scene behind him, the last he would see of civilization until he reached Henderson in the morning. The hotel was well-lit inside, the people having covered the windows with black tarpaulins to prevent anyone on the outside from seeing the lights. For the most part the townspeople had recovered from the day's events. Many were playing cards and there were even a few laughs. Some had even helped themselves to the draught beer.

In a couple of corners of the parlor the families of the deceased huddled together, talking and consoling each other quietly in German.

Sunny nickered softly when he approached. "I'm counting on you tonight, my friend," Zak said. "It will be a long ride, and we won't be able to rest as much as we usually do. When we need to run—*if* we need to run—I need you to run like the wind, as fast as you can. All right?" Sunny nickered again. Zak patted his flank and rubbed between his ears before he mounted him.

He rode out of town the same way they'd rode in. Bathed in the soft pale glow of the moon, the thick cottonwoods and bluffs looked nothing like they had in the daylight. The massive trees stood in front of him like a black impenetrable mass. He half expected hostile Dakota to be lurking there like they had been earlier in the day. He was sure he'd see the body of the man who'd been killed, bloody and scalped, eyes wide open, looking at him accusingly, saying, you left me. You left me here to die.

Zak spurred Sunny lightly and they flew into the cottonwoods. Zak shut his eyes tightly, expecting an arrow or tomahawk to strike him at any second, expecting the dead man to rise to get his vengeance for being left to die.

But in just a few seconds they cleared the trees and clambered up the bluffs. Zak opened his eyes and urged Sunny on, on and up, and then they were there, at the top. He pulled the reins tautly to stop Sunny and turned to look at the town. A thin haze of smoke still hung above the torched town, trapped between the river bluffs. Amazingly, he could see the soft pink glows where some of the buildings still smoldered. He looked toward the town square to see if he could see any lights in the hotel or nearby buildings, but was relieved when he couldn't. He could not see the figures of any people in or outside the town.

He turned Sunny toward the prairie. It spread out before him in all directions, silent—a white, sinister ocean. He had to cross *that*. He turned to look at the town again. Did he really have to do it? How would they know if he didn't? He could just wait around on the periphery of the town, out of sight, for a day or two. They wouldn't see him. He could ride into town and report he had successfully delivered the message and was back. They wouldn't know the difference.

Yes, they would, he said to his mind. Judge Flandrau would certainly ask him some questions and would want to know if the Army commander had a message for him. Besides that, he didn't think he could pull it off. It would show on his face.

He turned back to the waiting prairie and took a deep breath. "Well, here we go, Sunny," he said quietly. "It's now or never." He pushed his knees gently into Sunny's side and they moved out.

9. Trampling Out the Vintage

THE PRAIRIE grass whispered as they waded through it. It was if all of the occupants of this vast sea talked amongst themselves conspiratorially, deciding whether to let these intruders pass. But nothing—not a living animal or soul—could be seen anywhere in the pale moonlight. If they'd made a decision, Zak didn't know it.

He decided to avoid the road altogether—no sense in making himself more available as a target than possible. He and Sunny set out in an east—northeast direction, a mile or so north of the road. The lake they'd passed yesterday was a huge landmark they wouldn't miss and then they could veer off northeast to Henderson and the Army.

After a half-hour of riding Zak saw the dark silhouette of a stand of trees ahead. Must be a marsh or slough there, he thought. Trees grew only around water on the prairie, much like a desert. Zak realized he was in the open and probably in plain sight. Hostile Dakota probably waited in that stand of trees for just this opportunity to ambush and scalp some prey. He was ripe for the plucking!

He struggled to see anything in the trees, opening his eyes as wide as he could in the pale light. There—was that some movement? He swore he saw the black figure of someone on a horse. He saw the horse's head bobbing up and down. There it was again! It was a brave, just waiting to pounce! He was a dead man!

Zak panicked and put the spurs to Sunny. He had no real escape plan, he just panicked. Sunny bolted, and they flew forward to the grove of trees. In self-defense Zak tried to pull the pistol Flandrau had given him, but it stuck in his waistband. He almost screamed in fright as they passed the stand, not even an arrow's-flight away.

Then in the moonlight Zak saw he had been tricked. Or, rather, he'd tricked himself. The deadly brave on horseback was nothing more that a small cottonwood, bobbing up and down in the wind.

He breathed a sigh of relief. But his relief turned quickly to embarrassment, then shame. Soon he was angry with himself. He was just starting the ride; he'd make himself crazy before morning if he kept this up. He tried to remember the song Judge Flandrau had told him about, the song that the Army would recognize and then would recognize him as non-hostile. "*Mine eyes have seen the glory of the*

99

coming of the Lord," he sang softly to himself, only a whisper. *"He is trampling out the..."* What were the words again? *"He is trampling out the vintage where the grapes of wrath are stored."* He knew what "vintage" was, but he wondered what they meant by "trampling out the vintage." He wondered what they meant by the "grapes of wrath." He knew that there was such a thing as God's wrath—that must be what they meant. God is coming, and he's angry about the world's hatred, the world's wars. He will trample people like grapes in his anger. Is that what they meant?

He remembered once that a trader had brought red grapes with him on the steamboat and had given some to his father. They had never seen nor eaten grapes before. Zak thought they were the greatest delicacy he'd ever tasted. He and his mother had eaten them slowly, savoring them, taking tiny bites so that it took three or four to each grape. They had giggled with each as if enjoying the biggest luxury in the world.

Suddenly Zak started awake. He sat upright in the saddle and rubbed his eyes. How long had he been asleep? Sunny had stopped and was alert, his ears pricked up. Just ahead he saw a farm—a tiny tarpaper shack with an attached stable, a small fenced-in corral, a pigsty, and a small corn patch in the back. It was not too different from the place he'd lived in near the Lower Agency.

A sudden surge of hope ran through Zak. Maybe these people would have some food. No light came from the windows but they probably wouldn't mind being woken up. People opened their homes to travelers at all times of the night all the time. He would eat and gather some strength for the rest of his ride. It would be nice to have a little company as well. The last couple of hours had been some of the loneliest he'd ever experienced.

Zak tied Sunny to the rail outside the stable. When he looked behind the house he saw that the fence and pigsty had been torn apart and the cornpatch flattened, as if someone had trampled it. A chicken wandered aimlessly, pecking for food, as if it had not been fed in a while.

Something just didn't seem right, didn't feel right. A little voice in Zak's head told him to ride away as fast as he could. But something he couldn't control made him go to the door and knock.

No answer. He knocked again. This time he thought he heard a little grunt and some rustling sounds. Perhaps the owner was just rising from bed. He knocked one more time—this time the door swung open a bit on its own.

"Hello?" he called into the house. "Is anyone in there?" There was no answer, but another grunt came. Somebody was definitely inside the house. Perhaps they are hurt and need help, Zak thought. He opened the door and stepped inside.

Moonlight shone through the windows, illuminating the inside with a soft light. The house was a mess. Dishes lay in scattered pieces. The tattered curtains hung limply from their rods. The wood stove lay on its side, black soot spilling out onto the floor. The table and chairs were smashed, splinters protruding like broken bones.

Someone had ransacked the place.

He heard it behind him, a low snuffling sound. He wheeled and froze. The door swung shut in the wind, revealing the owner of the home, flat on his back. A hatchet protruded from his chest. Blood, black in the moonlight, soaked his shirt. He had been scalped.

Standing over him was his hog, smacking its lips.

It was eating his face.

When it saw Zak it looked up, a hunk of torn flesh in his jaws, the black blood dripping thickly from its jowls. It snorted, once, as if to warn Zak away from its prize.

Zak turned and bolted out the door. He almost screamed, but resisted. The Dakota that had killed the man might be nearby. He hopped on Sunny, spurred him and they raced away. He did not look back.

Avoid all people if you can, the judge had warned. He had been right. Avoid all people. Avoid everything.

He rode for a while in the moonlight. He did not doze. He did not dare.

Soon he saw a solid treeline ahead. He was almost at the lake. He had made it this far! This would be a good place to rest for a while—Sunny could drink and rest and he could climb out of the saddle and stretch his legs, which ached. His back throbbed from the jostling.

The lake gleamed in the moonlight, a shiny silver, and the tops of the small waves glittering as they sloshed against shore. Bullfrogs croaked and crickets sang. Swarms of fireflies greeted them, blinking on-and-off with short yellow flashes. Cattails rustled restlessly in the breeze. Zak dismounted and led Sunny to the water. He sat on the shoreline, his feet in front of him and his hands behind him. It was very pleasant. The breeze kept the mosquitoes down.

I wish I could sleep here, Zak thought. To sleep, to dream, to escape the cruel war if only for a little while.

A horse nickered not far behind him. Zak stared at Sunny. He had heard it too and his head was up and looking behind him, ears pricked up. Zak looked back, careful not to make any sudden movements that might be seen or heard.

Out on the prairie, within shouting distance, four Dakota braves rode silently, stealthily. The moonlight framed their silhouettes perfectly. Two braves wore single feathers in their hair and one had a full headdress—a chief or a medicine man. All carried rifles.

Zak tiptoed down to Sunny and placed his hand reassuringly on his flank. Sunny was quiet. Zak took his reins and held tightly, looking around him. There wasn't much to hide behind. There was a clump of bushes a few steps away, but they wouldn't get there in time. Besides, the braves would hear them if they moved. And they couldn't go into the water to hide in the cattails; the splashing, even a little, would betray them. The best thing to do was to remain completely still and hope that absolute stillness would shield them.

The next few seconds seemed like hours to Zak as they stood, frozen. Sunny seemed to understand what Zak wanted and he made no movements. Zak hardly breathed as they watched the braves pass. He wondered if he'd made the wrong choice back at St. Peter yesterday—was it only yesterday?—and if Dougal Black had made the right one. Dougal may be on his way to prison, but he would be safe. He wasn't out alone on the prairie with death stalking him at every turn.

The braves were almost out of sight when Sunny moved, just a little, a hoof grazing the pebbles on shore. But to Zak it seemed to split the night like thunder. Paralyzed with fear, he focused on the braves.

102

Three of them still moved forward. But the one in the back had stopped. Zak could tell by his silhouette that the man had turned on his horse, peering into the darkness behind him—directly at them, it seemed. His body was taut, listening intently. Zak summoned all of his concentration to remain still, wishing, *willing* the brave to move on.

They sat like that for what seemed like an eternity, the hunter and the prey. The tense silence roared in Zak's ears like a cyclone.

Finally, apparently satisfied nothing was out there, the brave turned forward again and rode to catch up with his group.

Zak waited, petrified, for what seemed like a full hour before moving on again. He wondered what time it was—the moon was already in the southwestern sky and there was a faint glow in the east, so he guessed dawn to be only another hour away. When the sun rose he would be in a precarious situation on the prairie. He would be more visible in the open, so he would have to find more treelines to hide in. But with any luck he would run into the Minnesota River again near Henderson and he would be almost completely safe in its tree-lined bluffs. Despite the dangers the upcoming morning posed, Zak longed to see the sunrise. He'd rather see the danger and react to it than be ambushed blindly.

At dawn he came upon another farm. Hugging the shoreline of a huge marsh, he darted in and out of thick cottonwood stands near the farm. When he emerged from the last stand before moving out into the open again, he was at the edge of a small cornfield. On the other side of the field sat a small house, a stable, and a corral. Two Dakota men hauled items out of the house—clothing, food, personal items. Two others stood with torches at the edges of the roofs on the house and stable. All of them whooped and shouted while they plundered.

Without thinking Zak drove Sunny into the marsh. Immediately they were in among the cattails and reeds, which rose over Zak's head. The water came up to Sunny's flank and was cool on Zak's legs. The reeds whipped him as they waded. slicing not deeply but very painfully on his neck and arms. They found a spot in the thick reeds, which concealed them. Through a tiny opening in the reeds he could see what was happening on the shore.

The house and stable now spewed huge flames and smoke, which drifted over the entire area. The carcasses of slaughtered cattle, chickens, and a cat lay scattered about. The two Dakota ransacking the house now had only rifles in their hands, prowling around the edge of the marsh.

They must have heard them going into the water! They were looking for him! Zak held absolutely still and Sunny, sensing the danger, did the same.

"We know you in there," one of the Dakota called out in English. The voice chilled Zak to the bone. He wasn't going to make it out of this one. He couldn't even ride out of the marsh and tell them he was half Indian, for they would shoot him on sight. Besides, if they didn't shoot him, what could he really tell them? That yes, he was half Indian, but that he was on a mission to the U.S. Army? Even though his militia servitude was somewhat against his will, the Dakota would hold it against him and wouldn't hesitate to kill him.

"Come out, we know you there," the one Dakota called out again. Now they were at the edge of the marsh, poking into the reeds and at places pushing them aside with their rifle barrels. They looked fierce and terrible. One had his head shaved on one side, the long hair from the other hanging over his shoulder. His face was painted blood red, with white circles around his eyes. The other wore cut hair, like a white man, and he wore a straw hat, which seemed ridiculously out of place. Probably stolen off a dead settler. He wore a frilly white shirt smeared with dried blood. Someone else's blood. His face was painted green, with little yellow dots on his cheeks. He called out again in English.

"We can play game. Not a nice game, you not want to play." They poked around the reeds at the edge for a couple of more minutes and then looked at each other. Cut-Hair looked at his partner, smiled, and raised his rifle. The shot rang out, startlingly loud. They were shooting randomly into the marsh! He would be hit for sure!

That was the most difficult time for Zak. He could barely contain the crushing fear that squeezed his stomach. In a moment of almost blinding panic he drifted away from reality. In his mind he rose above it all, undetected, a little bird able to wing away freely. He flew up and up, farther into the blue sky, far away from the certain death below.

104

Sudden gunshots jarred him back to reality. Two or three more shots rang out—and then Zak realized they were not shooting in his direction! They were not even looking his way! Someone, probably the owner of the farm, had also fled into the marsh. They couldn't see that person, but they shot in the direction he must have gone.

They didn't even know he was here. All he had to do was wait it out, just as he had done earlier at the lake.

The Dakota shot into the marsh five more times before giving up. Smoke from their rifles and from the burning buildings lay thick over the marsh. Zak barely contained his coughing. Through the slit in the reeds he saw the Dakota finally mount their horses and ride away, their dirty work completed.

The buildings burned quickly, much like the description given by the settler Johansson. Zak wondered if the owner in the marsh could see his hard work going up in flames.

As the buildings burned out and the smoke began to clear, the mosquitoes rose thickly, biting him repeatedly on his arms and the back of his neck. He resisted the temptation to swat for a while, but then he couldn't stand it any longer. They drove him crazy! Sunny was bitten, too, and began to stir anxiously. Zak looked through the slit again. No sign of the Dakota.

Zak dismounted and they waded to the shore. He cautiously stuck his head out of the reeds. Still no sign. The coast was clear.

He heard a rustling in the reeds to his right, in the direction where the Dakota had been looking and shooting. Someone stuck their head out of the cattails, searching frantically for the Dakota. Zak gaped.

It was a girl.

She looked about his own age. Her long blonde hair lay matted against her head. Mud caked her sopping blue calico dress. She craned her neck, looking fearfully toward the burned buildings for any sign of the Dakota.

Zak stepped out of the reeds. "Hello," he called out.

The girl rolled terrified eyes toward him. When she saw him she screamed and plunged back into the marsh, splashing frantically into the water.

"Wait!" Zak called out. "Wait! I'm not one of them!"

105

"I'm not one of them!" He called out again and led Sunny out onto the land. "Wait here," he said.

He ran over to the area where the girl had entered the marsh. "I'm not one of them," he called out a third time. He peered into the reeds and cattails, but couldn't see her. "I'm coming from New Ulm! I'm delivering a message to the Army! Honest!" Still nothing.

"Look," he called out. "If I was one of them I'd have left with them. I'm going to the Army!" Still nothing.

Finally a voice whispered tensely, "I don't believe you!"

"But it's true," he said. "I can show you the message I'm delivering. I even know an army song." He began to sing. "*Glory, glory, hallelujah. Glory, glory, hallelujah.*"

There was a pause. Then there was rustling.

The reeds parted and the girl came out.

She was the prettiest girl he'd ever seen, even in her condition. She stood a little taller than he was. She tried to straighten her hair and her dress, but quit when she looked down at her muddied clothing. She looked at Zak with deep blue-green eyes.

"I suppose anyone who sings to me isn't going to kill me," she said shakily, and smiled.

Zak couldn't help smiling back. He was speechless. This was the last thing he expected to see on his journey. They looked at each other.

"I'm Hannah," she said. "Hannah Smith."

"Hello," he said.

She paused, and then smiled again. "Do you have a name?"

Recovering, Zak grinned and gave his name sheepishly.

"Are you really coming from New Ulm?" she asked. "What is happening? I don't understand." She looked at the burned out buildings with sad eyes, but she did not cry. "Is this happening all over?"

"I think so," he said, and recounted the previous day and night's events. "You're lucky," he said. "But your folks?" He held his breath as he asked the question.

"Mother's not here, thank goodness," she said. "She's in St. Paul visiting my aunt."

"Your pa?"

Hannah turned to Zak. "He died a couple of years ago. Consumption."

"Sorry," Zak murmured.

"Oh, it's all right," she said. "Mother and I get along fine. I'm just so glad she wasn't here. She's not in good health and I don't think she could have taken it."

"What happened?" Zak asked.

"It was all so sudden. My neighbor, Mr. Allen, rode by and said they were coming. I didn't believe him at first, but when I went out to look I saw them coming. I barely had time to run. I didn't think they saw me, but they must have."

She looked back at the marsh and then back at the burned-out buildings. "That one with the hat. I know him. I think his name is White Dog. Mother and I have fed him and his family before when they've passed. We never asked for anything in return, but this is how we're paid back?" She sighed. "Oh, well. They're just buildings. I'm still alive and so is mother, thank goodness." She turned back to Zak.

"You're kind of young to be doing things for the Army, aren't you?"

"I'm sixteen," he said, a little stronger than he'd intended.

She laughed. "So am I."

"It's a long story," he said, embarrassed at his defensiveness.

"I see."

He thought for a moment. "You can ride with me. I'm going to Henderson."

Tears welled in her eyes for the first time. "Thank you," she said. "They won't come back, will they?"

"I don't know. But if we get out of here we should be all right. It's not far to the town."

He helped her onto Sunny and then he got up in front of her. They were still both wet.

"A fine pair we make," she said as they moved out.

"We'll dry out as we ride." Then he remembered. "I forgot to show you the message I'm delivering."

"I believe you," she said. She put her arms around his waist. "After all, you've saved me."

107

They rode in silence for a while. Eventually they warmed to each other, providing small details of their lives. Zak's dual heritage fascinated Hannah. She was sympathetic with his plight.

Hannah just plain fascinated Zak.

The town of Henderson sat abandoned. As they rode in from the south nobody greeted them. There were no people walking in the street or on the boardwalk that lined both sides. The false-front buildings advertising "Lawyer" and "Barber" and "Saloon" and "Potions and Elixirs" were empty, their blinds down and doors locked tightly. It was like a ghost town.

And worse, there was no army.

"I don't understand," Zak said as they moved up the dirt street. "Judge Flandrau said they would be here by now." He looked around. What do we do now? he thought.

"Are you hungry?" Zak asked.

"Yes," Hannah said. "I haven't had anything to eat since last night."

"Neither have I," Zak said. "Look," he said, pointing. "There's a mercantile. I'm sure it's locked just like the other stores are. But we have to get some food."

"How are we going to get food if it's locked?"

"Break in," Zak said. He shrugged and spoke over his shoulder to Hannah. "It's not like there's anyone to see. Besides, it's a necessity. I'm on army business. The owner would understand. I'll leave a note and bill it to the Army."

"That might work, I suppose," Hannah said.

The mercantile was indeed locked.

"How are you going to do it?" Hannah asked.

"Just watch," Zak said. He remembered Dougal Black's tricks. "Here, tear off the bottom part of your dress," he said.

"I do declare," Hannah said, smiling.

Zak felt his face flush. He knew his ears were turning red. He looked up at her. "It's just for—"

"I know," Hannah said, still smiling. "It was a joke. You know, a joke?"

Zak, embarrassed, wanted to laugh but instead said, "This is serious business."

"Oh, I see," Hannah said mockingly. "Serious business." But she ripped a piece from her dress.

"Look—" Zak said, wrapping the cloth around his fist, intending to punch through the window. But was cut off by the sound of a hammer cocking on a gun.

"Hold it right there, you two," boomed a voice from behind them.

10. A Dirty Redskin Trick

"PUT YOUR hands where I can see them," said the voice. "Now turn around, slowly."

When they did they saw an older man with a long white beard pointed a shotgun at them. He squinted at them in the sun. "Now just what do you think you're doin'?"

They were silent for a moment. "I asked you a simple question," said the man. "You speak English? What are you two doin'?"

Zak cleared his throat. "We were just gonna look for some food," he said.

"Food? By breakin' and enterin'?" challenged the old man.

"We didn't see any choice," Zak said.

"Neither of us have eaten since yesterday," Hannah chimed in.

"There's lots a people hungry nowadays," said the old man. "What gives you to the right to break into somebody's place a business?"

"We were going to leave a note," Hannah said.

"A note? What good's a note gonna do to the owner? A note won't pay for a new winda."

"The Army would," Zak said. He began to remove his boot where the judge's message was. "Here, let me—"

"Just hold it right there!" yelled the old man. "Don't you move another muscle!"

Zak stood straight again. "I can explain. I come from New Ulm, which is under attack by the Dakota. Judge Flandrau there—he's the commander of the militia—says he notified the Army at Fort Snelling yesterday and that they should be moving out today. He sent a message with me for the commander of that detachment. He said the Army should be here today. Which they're not."

"No, they're not," sneered the old man. "You're a messenger for the Army? How old are you? Fourteen? How am I suppose ta believe that?"

"It's the truth!" insisted Hannah. "He saved me from some warriors that would have killed me! They burned my mother's farm!"

"I'm sixteen," Zak said to the man. Then he turned to Hannah. "I didn't really save you," he said.

111

"I think you did," said Hannah, smiling.

"All right you two, enough!" said the old man. "Prove it!" he said to Zak.

"I have to remove my boot," said Zak. "I'll show you the note."

"All right, then," said the man grudgingly. "But you try any funny stuff and I'll fill your hide full a buckshot!"

Slowly, Zak removed his boot and pulled out the note. It was still dry just like it was when he'd checked back at Hannah's farm. He unfolded it and handed it to the old man, who inspected it closely. After a long time he lowered down his shotgun and handed the note back to Zak.

"I'm afraid I owe you youngsters an apology," he said. "Ever since the town's cleared out I been kinda watchin' over the places for 'em."

"Where is everybody?" asked Zak.

"They all went to St. Peter or St. Paul as soon as they heard of the Injun trouble. Guess everybody figgered this town was too small to hold if attacked."

"How come you're still here?" Hannah asked.

The man waved his hand. "I'm too old to go runnin' around," he said. "I came here and built my place all by myself. Swore it was the last place I was gonna be before I cash it in." He looked around. "No, this town ain't much, but I ain't leavin'. C'mon," he said, beckoning to them. "Come over to my place. I'll fix some vittles for ya and feed'n'water your fine horse there."

They followed him to his house, which was down below the town near the river bottom. It was small but sturdy, obviously built by knowing and caring hands.

"This is a fine house, sir," said Hannah. "You must be very proud of it. I can see why you don't want to leave."

"Why, thank you, young lady," he said. "Name's Grady. Took me nigh six months to build this. Slept in a tent the whole time, just like in the Army."

"You were in the Army?" Hannah asked.

"Yessiree," he said. "War of 1812. I was present when the British invaded the capital city and burned the White House. We got whipped then. Only thing that saved us was a tornado that reared up and chased them redcoats outta town."

It turned out that not only had Grady been in the Army, but that he had then sailed the seven seas on a merchant marine before hunting big game in Africa. He had contracted malaria twice and scurvy three times. He'd come out west to "see the frontier before it was gone." He'd been a buffalo hunter and had almost died when the horse he was riding had collapsed and the thundering herd had trampled him.

"Lost one of my family jewels that time," he said, pointing to his groin. Hannah blushed. Grady had laughed uproariously at his joke and her discomfort. But he'd made amends when he brought out a trunk and produced a beautiful new dress.

"Was my wife's," he said, his eyes moistening. "Looks about your size. Go on, put it on. It's of no use to me any more." But when Hannah put it on and brushed her hair they could see that it still meant something to him.

When they left Grady's they felt refreshed, having eaten a full meal of venison and corn and having washed up with water from his rain barrels. Even Sunny seemed refreshed, and they started north towards St. Paul and, hopefully, the Army.

The countryside was empty as they worked their way north along the Minnesota River. The farms and tiny settlements had not been burned or attacked; in fact, there seemed to be no evidence of the uprising here. But the word had spread, and the people had fled, to the north and the safety of the cities, or to the south and the relative safety in St. Peter and Mankato, where there was strength in numbers. Fields stood neglected, some ready for a harvest that wouldn't come; cows stood unmilked and hogs unfed, although most had taken their livestock with them when they could. It was all very unsettling.

Zak had not been this far north since they'd moved west. But he knew that all travel went south from Minneapolis and St. Paul along the Minnesota River, be it travel or land or by water. When they had moved, steamboat travel on the river had been high, and they had seen dozens of the ships navigating the winding passageway. On this day there were none. The judge had said the Army would probably move south toward Henderson by steamboat, so Zak figured he and Hannah would wait on the shore and hail any ship that passed. He would take off his white—well, it was now a dirty cream—shirt and wave it so that any landing party would see his intentions were not hostile.

As the afternoon moved toward dusk Zak thought they should be getting close to Shakopee, the small river town named for the father of the departed chief. There would most likely be a steamboat landing there and they could wait until the Army landed, staying overnight. As the sun went down the land was cloaked in long shadows. The moon hung low in the east and the stars winked. It will be nice to get some sleep, Zak thought. His odyssey would end tonight if the Army was indeed at Shakopee, and would certainly be over in the morning. He looked over his shoulder at Hannah. She dozed.

In that instant he heard the unmistakable *crack* of a rifle and felt the bullet *whiz* by his ear. Frantic, he wheeled Sunny into a grove of trees. Hannah had heard it too and together they leaped off the horse. Who was shooting at them? They were behind cover, but for how long? Zak held his finger to his lips and Hannah nodded.

Who could it be? There hadn't been any sign of Indians. Then Zak remembered the judge's words about the Army—that there would be sentries on the periphery of the main force. That had to be it. He decided to take a chance. It was better than waiting around to be shot.

"Don't shoot!" he called out. "I'm a friend!"

It was quiet a moment and then he heard some fervent whispering from the trees where the shot had been fired. He strained to listen, but couldn't make out the words. Something about "Injuns" and "trick." Another voice *shushed* them savagely and Zak could tell they were being scolded. Must be an officer there, he thought.

"Don't shoot!" he called again. "If you're from the Army, I'm a friend! I bring a message from New Ulm!"

Again, fervent whispering. The three voices were arguing and were not successful being quiet about it. Finally the third voice, the one who had quieted the other two, called out.

"How do we know you're a friend?" it asked.

Hannah whispered in his ear. "Sing your song."

Of course! He definitely needed sleep, for he had forgotten all about the judge's suggestion. *"Mine eyes have seen the glory of the coming of the Lord; he is trampling out the vintage where the grapes of wrath are stored."* He paused. More whispering, but louder.

"I say it's a trick!"

"A trick? What kind of Injun knows that song? That's our song!"

"They're crafty! I say it's a dirty redskin trick!"

"But he speaks pretty good English!"

"You two shut up, and that's an order," said the third voice. "I'll handle this."

"Glory, glory, hallelujah," Zak continued singing. *"Glory, glory, hallelujah . . ."*

"All right, *friend,* knock off that singing. Come out and show yourself," called Third Voice. "Keep your hands where we can see them."

Zak and Hannah stepped out into the near-darkness.

"Come forward."

They stepped toward the voice. After about ten paces Third Voice said, "That's far enough."

Immediately three uniformed soldiers surrounded them. Two came from behind trees on both sides and the third from in front. The ones on either side pointed rifles at them. Zak saw the remaining daylight glint off their bayonets, inches from their chests.

The third was a big man. His silhouette loomed large in front of them. "Why, it's just a boy and a girl," he said quietly in his deep voice.

"Who are you?" demanded the soldier on their left. He was not much taller than either Zak or Hannah.

"Shut up, Gilby," hissed the big man. "I'll ask the questions. You just watch them. Carver, you keep a lookout." He stepped closer toward them. "Who are you?"

"My name's Hammer," said Zak. "This is Hannah. I come from New Ulm with a message for your commander. I rode all last night and today to find you."

The big man said nothing.

"I don't like this," Gilby said at their left. "They may be distracting us while the rest of them work their way around us and into town."

"I said shut up!" hissed the big man.

"But Sergeant . . ."

"Shut up!" He paused. "All right, let's see who you are. Carver, light a match in front of their faces. Block it with your body so's no one can see it nowhere else. Gilby, keep watchin' 'em."

In the dim matchlight Zak could see the blue uniforms of Gilby and Carver, but he didn't look at their faces. He concentrated his attention on the big man in front of them. He wore stripes on his sleeve and was in control. He seemed at least reasonable. He had a bushy beard, thick eyebrows that protruded from his pulled-down cap. His bulbous nose stuck out at them. Zak could not tell the color of his eyes.

"Looks Indian," said Gilby. "'Cept for her. Maybe he's got her captive and she can't say nothin'."

"I'm no captive," said Hannah. "The Indians burned my farm. This boy saved me and took me here. My mother is in St. Paul. She knows the governor."

"Gilby, I told you not to talk no more," the big man said. "I'm puttin' you on report later."

"Yes, sir," Gilby said sullenly. Out of the corner of his eye Zak caught a glimpse of Gilby giving him a dirty look, as if he blamed him for the reprimand. He'd made an enemy.

"Gilby, don't call me sir. Only call commissioned officers 'sir.'" He looked at Zak and Hannah. "You two look harmless enough," said the sergeant. "Let's see that message. Carver, light another match."

"It's from Judge Flandrau," said Zak.

"Never heard of him," said the sergeant. But he read the note twice, carefully, and handed it back to Zak. He nodded. "Snuff out that light now," he ordered. "Carver, let's you and me get these two back to Sibley right away. Gilby, you stay out here. I'll send another man to join you. And for God's sake, keep your eyes peeled. This country's liable to be swarmin' with hostiles lookin' to lift our hair."

"Yes, sir," Gilby said sullenly.

"Don't call me sir!" he bellowed. He turned to Zak and Hannah. "I'll lead through the woods. You two follow."

"Yes," said Zak.

"And no talkin' unless I talk to you. You'll have plenty a opportunity to do that when you get to Sibley."

So Henry Sibley was the commander, Zak thought as they wound their way through the woods. Henry Sibley, the fur trader and politician who was his father's old boss!

They traveled on a narrow path that probably had been cleared only that day. He could not see farther than the sergeant's back in front of him, but as they walked on he could hear the buzz of activity. Soon he could see bonfires through the trees. In a minute they emerged into a huge clearing and into the Army camp. The camp sat on the banks of a river. On the other side of the river was a town, Shakopee probably. Three large steamboats floated at the dock.

In the Army camp, tents and horses and wagons and cannon sat amongst the greatest hubbub Zak had ever seen. In the bright orange light of a thousand torches uniformed soldiers moved everywhere—a group marching together in perfect formation; a line of them at the chow wagon; another group listening to a preacher giving a service by a huge bonfire at the riverside; soldiers in groups of three and four around small campfires, drinking coffee, singing songs, laughing. In the midst of the Army roamed several dozen civilians, sutlers probably, selling tobacco and other assorted goods, whiskey when no officers were near, opportunists even in the young state's moments of greatest crisis.

"You been in the town?" the sergeant asked over his shoulder to Carver.

"Not yet."

"It's as crowded as this. Civilians from all over have moved in. Hotels is full up. Some of the townfolk have opened their homes to them, but most of 'em are sleepin' outside, in makeshift shelters, tents, under their wagons. Can't hardly move through the town for all the livestock. Whole town smells like a barnyard." He chuckled.

"Carver," he continued, "go find someone to go out and relieve Gilby. My orders. Any man questions 'em, you bring 'em to me. I'll be over at Sibley's." He nodded in the direction of a set of four large tents. "You two come with me. I'm gonna turn ya over to the Colonel."

"Sibley the colonel?" Zak asked.

"Yeah. You heard a him?"

"My pa knew him way back when."

"That right? Your pa in politics?"

"No, he was a trader up near St. Paul."

"A trader? A trader? One of those shysters? They're one of the reasons we're in this mess." He looked at Zak. "Your ma's Sioux, ain't she?"

"She was. She died."

The sergeant's features softened. "Sorry, lad," he said. "You've had a rough time of it lately. That must have been some ride last night."

"It was, sir."

When they got to the tent the sergeant went inside briefly and came out. "Colonel will see you now," he said. Then he spoke in a low voice to Zak. "Name's Keegan. My friends call me Buff. You look me up if'n you need a little help."

"Thanks," Zak said. Keegan winked and was gone.

They stood there for a couple of minutes until a voice called out of the tent, "Come in now."

They entered the tent. Sitting behind a large field desk was Henry Sibley. Zak had seen him a few times before they'd moved from St. Paul, and he looked basically the same—a little older, heavier, but still fit. He looked dashing in his blue dress uniform. His dark brown hair swooped down over his forehead. He wore a well-manicured goatee. His dark, penetrating brown eyes gave Zak and Hannah the once over, quickly judging them and deciding for himself what they were about and what they'd been through. When he was satisfied with his quick conclusion he beckoned them to two chairs seated opposite the desk from him. He bowed slightly to Hannah and held her hand while she sat. "Thank you," she said.

"Sergeant Keegan said you have a message for me from Judge Flandrau," he said to Zak, getting to the point crisply, immediately.

"Yes, sir," said Zak, handing him the note.

"What's your name, son?" he asked.

"Hammer. Zak Hammer."

Sibley made no acknowledgement of recognition as he read the note. "Hmm," he said a couple of times as he read. "Hmmm. It sounds like it's worse than I thought. The reports coming in from the countryside must be true after all." He folded the note and look pensively at his field desk, upon which a large map of the state was laid out.

He cocked his head at Zak and raised his eyebrows. "What did you say your name was?"

"Hammer. Zak Hammer."

"Any relation to Brandt Hammer, the trader?"

"He is my father."

"He was one of my first employees," Sibley said. "What was it? Eight years ago? Ten? When he came here he could hardly speak English. When he got off the steamship the first thing I had him do was to get a Sioux wife. Your mother, I suppose?"

"Yes, sir," said Zak.

"How is your father? He moved west with the others, didn't he?"

"Yes he did. But he's gone."

"Gone? I hope you don't mean he's deceased?"

"No sir, just gone. He left me after my mother died."

Sibley considered this for a few seconds. "You have any brothers and sisters? Aunts or cousins that are taking care of you?"

"No brothers or sisters. All my kin are at the Agency."

"Of course." Sibley considered this. "You're in a difficult situation," he said matter-of-factly, not questioning. "I do not envy you. How is it that you've become a messenger for Charles Flandrau? I expect he's taken a shine to you if he entrusted you with this sort of duty."

"As to how I got into this situation, it's a long story, sir," Zak said. "But I'm flattered that the judge trusts me. He seems like a good man."

"Charles Flandrau is indeed a good man, the salt of the earth. I've known him as long as I've known my wife. I respect and admire him greatly."

Sibley folded his hands on the desk in front of him. "The situation facing this state is the gravest of its young life. Charles Flandrau and I helped this territory become a state, and I do not intend

119

to see our efforts wasted by hordes of screaming savages. I traded with the Sioux and lived amongst them. They have betrayed us. Governor Ramsey put me in charge of the Army division at Fort Snelling, appointed me as Colonel and gave me orders to quell the uprising. That is exactly what I intend to do." He looked at Hannah. "My regrets about your farm, but thanks be to God for the safety of you and your mother. If you wait outside my tent for a few minutes I will have someone take you into town to see to it that you are taken care of properly as a lady and that you are taken to St. Paul to be reunited with your mother."

"Thank you, sir," Hannah said. Sibley bowed his head slightly.

"Hammer," he said, turning back to Zak, "for tonight you may take shelter with Sergeant Keegan in his squad. You may relay my order as such. In the meantime I will figure out what role you are to play from now on. Since you are not officially part of the Army, I need to examine my authority on that issue. I will want to know the exact circumstances of your servitude and I will see into what niche you fit, if any. I will send for you in the morning. We will be moving out after that. That is all."

"He likes you," Hannah said as they left the tent.

"How can you tell?"

"I just can. I think he was impressed that the judge sent you. That sergeant, too—Keegan—he likes you. I think you have a friend there."

"Yeah, I wonder why," Zak said.

"Don't wonder," Hannah said. "Just accept it."

"You're right," Zak said. "I'll need it. I don't know anything about army life. Hopefully the colonel won't put me in the infantry. I don't want to fight against my own relatives."

"The colonel seems aware of that," Hannah said.

Soon a corporal arrived, one of Sibley's assistants. He bowed to Hannah. "Miss, I've been ordered to take you into town, to a hotel owned by a lady the colonel knows. Do you have any personal effects you wish to take along?"

She laughed resignedly. "Just what I'm wearing, sir."

DANIEL W. HOMSTAD

"Very well. If you will come with me we will go in my wagon."
He started away.

Hannah turned to Zak. She had tears in her eyes. She looked at
him directly and took his hands in hers.

"I'll never forget what you've done for me," she said. "Thank
you again for saving me. I don't know what I would have done had
you not come along."

Zak didn't know what to say. He blushed and looked at his
shoes. Hannah put her hand under his chin and pulled his face up to
hers.

"You be careful now," she said. And then, "Will we see each
other again?"

A sudden rush of emotion flooded over Zak. He'd never felt this
way about someone else before, let alone a girl—a *lady*—he'd just met.
He was embarrassed. But when he spoke, his words came out clear and
strong.

"I'll find you."

Hannah leaned forward and kissed him once, lightly, on his
cheek.

And then she was gone.

11. Talk of Glory

"YOUNG FELLA, I'm happy to have ya," Sergeant John "Buff" Keegan bellowed, slapping Zak on the shoulder when he reported. "Happy to have ya. You can tent it with me for the time being, if'n you can stand it."

"The sarge does not possess a strict hygiene regimen," the man named Carver explained. The rest of the squad laughed. Keegan, standing by the fire, sniffed under his arms proudly. Around the campfire, the camaraderie was loose and the stripes on his arms were ignored by all. All, that is, except Gilby. Still bitter at being put on report, he sulked on the periphery of the group. He glared at Zak periodically, his ugly face framed in the flickering light of the campfire. He did not accept Zak into the squad as the others had readily done after hearing of his exploits. Keegan commanded the center of attention around the fire, something he appeared accustomed to. He was huge, loud, garrulous, and obscene.

Zak liked him immediately.

"I don't need no hygiene out here in the wilderness," Keegan bawled. "It's not like I'm gonna find any dancing partners out here. Bears, mebbe, but I imagine I'll smell downright sweet to them." Laughter cascaded over the fire.

"No bear in the right mind would touch you with a ten foot pole," another soldier said. "You're hairy, and fat, and a drunk."

"You watch your mouth!" Keegan brayed. "I'm hairy, and a drunk, but I ain't fat." He patted his enormous belly with both hands. "I'm fit as a fiddle. Just . . ." he paused and winked at Zak, "stout, that's all!"

"Stout? Stout?" There was a chorus of incredulity around the fire. Someone threw a piece of hardtack biscuit at Keegan. It bounced easily off his ample belly.

"Speaking of drunk," whispered Keegan conspiratorially, "Anyone meet up with that sutler that was prowlin' around earlier?"

"Yeah, I did," said a soldier, and from out of nowhere appeared a whiskey bottle.

"Oh," Keegan said, taking the bottle from him gingerly as if it were a piece of antique china. "Oh. I do like the feel of a liquor bottle." He pulled off the cap and took a huge gulp without flinching. "That's better'n mother's milk, too." He took another huge swig and gave the bottle back. It made its way around the circle to Zak.

"No, thanks," said Zak. Liquor had gotten him in enough trouble already.

"C'mon, what's the matter? Won't hurt ya none," said one soldier.

"It'll do ya some good," said another.

"What's the matter?"

"I think he's chicken," said Gilby from the outside of the circle. The men were quiet at this challenge.

"I ain't chicken," replied Zak in a controlled tone. "I just don't want any."

"The boy don't want none, he don't have ta have none!" bellowed Keegan. "He don't need no whiskey to prove he ain't chicken!" He winked at Zak, and then shot Gilby a hard look. "Why, Gilby you're one ta talk. You're so chicken you got feathers comin' outta your scrawny rear end. And that thing on your face! You gotta beak that'd put the gnarliest ol' cock ta shame!" He roared at his own joke, and the rest of the men howled with him. Gilby slunk off into the darkness.

"Say," one soldier said. "We gonna move out tomorra? Ah want to see some action!"

"Yeah, I'm gonna line 'em up and mow 'em down," said another soldier, pointing his revolver off into the darkness at imaginary Indians. "I'm gonna get me a medal. My pappy, he got one in Mexico in '46 and I'm gonna get my share!"

"Wonder if them savages are gonna put up a fight?" asked another soldier.

"Nah, they started it, but we're gonna finish it," said another. "Few days, some action, and we'll be back to choppin' wood and drillin'."

"Maybe if we do good they'll send us down south, ta help out the boys down there."

"We was supposed ta go down south, but then the savages rose up. Figures."

"I got a brother, he's in the Army of the Potomac down there. I'd like ta see him," said another.

"Whattaya think, Sarge, we gonna move tomorra?" asked Carver.

Keegan was quiet for a few moments. Then he spoke somberly. "You boys listen to me." He took a drink from the whiskey bottle, which was nearing empty. "All this talk of glory, and fightin', it don't mean nothin'." He paused, looking at the men around the fire. "There ain't no glory no more. Maybe back in the days of the Revolution, when we was fightin' to be free a the British, there was some glory. But no more. Our boys fightin' in the south now—on both sides—they know that. They said this war between the states was gonna be over before it started. But you see the papers. They're dyin', and they're dyin' thick, in the thousands. Gonna be in the hundreds a thousands before it's over. Brother fightin' brother. Famblies broken up. There ain't no glory in that."

The men sat silently. A couple hung their heads.

"Don't be in no rush ta get your piece a glory here," Keegan continued. "People are sayin' that we're gonna crush the Sioux, that this little tin-pot conflict'll be over in no time. But there's people dyin' and there's gonna be more dyin'. The Sioux, they know how to fight. It's in their blood. They got their backs to the wall, got nothin' to lose. They've lost it all almost already." He took another drink. "This little tin-pot conflict is gonna make or break this state, and the land's gonna be plenty bloody before it's over."

He stood. "I hope we move out tomorrow. I ain't itchin' to fight the Sioux, 'cause I got ties to 'em, but the best thing Sibley can do is get us out there and get the thing over with as fast as possible. For everyone's sake."

Colonel Sibley listened without comment while Zak gave him the details of his induction into the militia by Judge Flandrau, nodding from time to time. When Zak had finished Sibley thought for a moment and then spoke.

"As I said yesterday, I don't envy your position. You're really in a no-win situation. It's a no-win situation for this fledgling state." He stood and paced around the tent. "I have always been friends with the Sioux. I have traded with them and lived with them. They called me 'Walker in the Pines,' for I would go among them, alone, unafraid, and do business with them. We trusted each other. That is the way it was

125

all over." He paused. "But the Sioux have betrayed the trust of the people. We made a good-faith effort to civilize them and live the proper modern way. But try to cultivate them, to Christianize them as you will, and the sight of blood will in an instant call out the savage, wolfish, devilish instincts of the race. There are a select few, like Bishop Henry Whipple, that insist it is not so. Whipple says it's our fault, that we've cheated the Indians and tried to make them live our ways against their will. That they have their own civilization that is in danger of being extinct. But Whipple's wrong. I have lived among them. They are heathen. I know."

He waved his hand as if to dismiss the thought and sat down. "Forgive me for my digression. I have decided to keep you on as a scout and a messenger. You're in the Army, so you will receive normal pay. You will not be in uniform, of course, which may save you if you get into a precarious position with the natives. But I will honor the agreement you made with Judge Flandrau and will send him periodic reports on your progress. I take personal responsibility for your rehabilitation and expect you to conduct yourself as a gentleman and a soldier at all times."

"Yes, sir," said Zak.

"Good."

"Sir? May I ask a question?" Zak said.

"Certainly."

"Are we moving out today? The men want to know."

A look of consternation flashed over Sibley's face, just for a second, and Zak realized he'd stepped out of line.

"No, we are not moving out today," Sibley said curtly. "I am short the necessary supplies and men to move against Little Crow. I take my lessons from General McClellan, the Commander of the Army of the Potomac. He does not move until he has the necessary supplies and men. He is often criticized for it, but he has never been defeated." Sibley turned and looked out of his tent. "No, we are not moving yet. It will be dress parade as usual. You may go."

"Dress parade? Dress parade?" Keegan bellowed unbelievingly when Zak told him what Colonel Sibley had said. "Again? We're out here in the wilderness and he wants dress parade? There's people

126

dyin', for cryin' out loud!" His face went beet red, almost matching the redness of his beard. His eyes, already a little glazed from a liquid breakfast of whiskey, shone fiercely. "What is it about an Army uniform that screws up a man's thinking? You take a sensible man like Henry Sibley, put him in blues and put a bird on his shoulders, and you turn him into a fathead! A half-wit! God almighty!"

"He thinks he's like General McClellan," Zak said.

"Little Mac? Little Mac?" Buff huffed. "You're damned right he's like him! Little Mac's as slow as molasses too! He ain't moved against the Confederates with any more speed than a turtle with four bad legs! Lincoln's gotta be pullin' his hair out, tryin' to get him to fight. If Henry Sibley's like McClellan, we're in for a long haul and them people on the prairie ain't gettin' no help nohow soon! Dress parade!" He snorted.

But dress parade it was, and Zak watched as the companies were called out and assembled into formation on the prairie, just past the edge of the big woods: Sixth Regiment, formed of mostly new recruits who were supposed to go south, ten companies, the companies each with their one captain, two lieutenants, five sergeants, eight corporals, forty privates, drummers, fifers and buglers, tramping up and down the prairie, practicing in full dress, maneuver after maneuver, wheeling, spinning, bidding the gay marching tunes and the barking calls of the officers. They did this for over two hours in the midday sun, and when they were done they were ordered back to camp for target practice with their .58 caliber Springfield muskets—"buck and ball" guns because the bullet and three buckshot was the regulation load for them.

No orders to move out were given. The men grumbled.

"Why do they call you 'Buff'?" Zak asked back in camp.

"Nickname. Because when I was a youngster I was bigger'n all the rest of the boys. My mama said I was big as a baby buffalo, and that's what it got shortened to—'Buff.' Been known that way ever since. How 'bout you, young fella? You got any nicknames I can call you by?"

Zak thought. "You can call me Horse Dreamer if you want."

"Horse Dreamer?" Buff pulled on his beard, thinking it through. "Horse Dreamer? I kinda like that. Well, Horse Dreamer, let's just keep that between us, our little secret. These men in the Army, they ain't in no mood to have nothin' remotely Sioux in amongst them now." He winked at Zak. "But ol' Buff, he likes that name. Now let's go get some a that chow. I hear that sorry excuse for a cook callin' us." They walked off together.

They ate their lunch—hardtack biscuits and boiled pork—back by their tents. There was debate among the men about Sibley's tactics. Some of the men sided with Buff, believing Sibley moved too slow. Others sided with Sibley, saying they had no desire to move against the Sioux unprepared. The debate grew raucous and loud. Zak didn't participate, sitting on the edge of the circle and listening absentmindedly. Soon all the voices blended together as he dozed in the sunlight after eating.

He heard a voice behind him he recognized instantly.

"Well, looka what we got here." The cold, flat voice made the hair on the back of his neck stand straight.

He turned slowly toward the voice. His stomach lurched queasily.

Dougal Black.

Black stood silently, grinning wickedly. Gilby stood next to him, also grinning. It didn't take long for them to find each other, Zak thought. Two peas in a pod. Two rotten peas.

Dougal wore infantry blues, the uniform sparkling new. Zak was confused. "What are you doing here?" he asked.

"They were taking me up to St. Paul to await trial," Black answered haughtily. "The Army stopped the wagon I was in and took it for their use. They told me to suit up and join, for they needed every man jack in the field. Was good, for I had done some thinkin' on the way up, and decided I didn't want ta go to prison." He grinned again, eyes triumphant. "Ain't gonna be no trial now, no prison." He ran his hands over his uniform. "I'm in the Army now."

"I'm not sure the Army knows what it got," Zak said.

"They probably don't, do they? That's even better." Dougal looked Zak up and down. "How about you? You ain't got no uniform, just the same rags you had on before. Thought you was all fired-up to join?"

128

"I'm on scout duty, and a messenger," said Zak. "But I get pay, shelter and food just like the regulars."

"Is that so? Well, ain't that special? An Injun bein' sent to scout other Injuns." Dougal grinned at Gilby next to him. "That's rich, ain't it?"

"It's rich, all right," Gilby said conspiratorially.

"This guy a friend a yours?" Buff asked, suddenly behind Zak. Zak shook his head, no.

"No?" Dougal cried, in mock incredulity. "Aw, c'mon. We go way back. We're buddies."

"We ain't buddies," Zak said, more to Buff than Dougal. "Not any more."

"Aw, that's too bad," Dougal said. He feigned sadness. "That breaks my heart."

"You don't have a heart," Zak said.

Dougal clutched the area where his heart was as if stabbed by an invisible knife. "Now that hurts. That hurts."

Buff eyed Dougal suspiciously. "You in this company?"

Dougal turned his attention completely to Buff, as if gauging a new enemy, weighing the threat posed. Zak could practically see the gears working in Dougal's head.

"Nope," he finally said.

"Well," Buff said. "You in the wrong place. I suggest you shove off."

"What if I don't want to?" Dougal sneered. He clearly had no regard for the stripes on Buff's arm.

"I said shove off," Buff said, moving toward Dougal. "And that's an order."

"All right, all right," Dougal said, putting his hands up in front of him defensively. "Yes, sir."

"Just see that you do," Buff said, turning back to the squad, casting a concerned glance at Zak.

Dougal turned to leave, but then turned back and walked to Zak.

"I got some unfinished business with you," he whispered in Zak's ear, "regardless of your new protector. I'll just bet you told the sheriff about what happened in the mercantile. You're the reason I'm in

Dutch, in this rotten army." He grinned. "But now that I am, there ain't room for both of us," he said, and left.

"Who was that?" Buff asked Zak when he returned to the squad.

Zak told him the story.

"Well, you're damned right in wantin' to stay away from him," Buff said. "That's a bad egg. A rotten apple. Dangerous. I seen lots a men like that, and they have a nasty habit a draggin' people down with them."

The next morning reveille blared a half hour early, setting Buff off, who let loose a string of epithets that made Zak blush. "We don't move out right away, and when we do, they cut short our sleep," he said after his outburst. "Man's gotta have sleep."

But they did not move out. It was dress parade, again. This time Sibley kept them at it for almost four hours. It was almost noon when they returned to camp, but not before being informed they would have afternoon parade as well.

"The man's a coward and a rascal," Buff complained to anyone who would listen as they ate lunch. "I ain't seen such towheadedness and tomfoolery in my life. This keeps up and we won't get out west until I'm dead and buried, pushin' up daisies on the prairie." Some men murmured their agreement.

Reveille came even earlier the next day, but when they were assembled they were informed they were moving out. Their first destination: St. Peter.

If the situation in St. Peter had been chaotic on the first day of the Dakota attacks, it was sheer madness now. Before they entered the town they waded through thousands of cattle, watched by their traumatized owners who warily guarded their little fiefdoms. Refugees choked the town—tents and makeshift shelters occupied every square foot. The townspeople and refugees met them with relief, although a few appeared angry with Sibley's slow progress. Zak heard Sheriff Patch, who'd returned to St. Peter from New Ulm, inform Colonel Sibley that ten thousand people were now in the town. The hotel was being used as a hospital to treat the considerable number of wounded. But there were problems feeding all the people. Sibley ordered the establishment of a bakery and slaughterhouse, and ordered that five thousand loaves of bread and fifty sides of beef be produced each day. The cattle owners would be later compensated by the government, as would the people whose wagons and horses were to be commandeered for the Army's use.

Sheriff Patch told Sibley that New Ulm was in dire straits and that Flandrau would probably be forced to abandon it. Fort Ridgely had been attacked twice but had held out. Immediate help was needed. Zak also heard that another scout, Jack Frazer, had told Sibley that the Sioux had at least fifteen hundred mounted warriors in the vicinity of the Lower Agency alone. He told Sibley that the entire Sioux nation was united to defeat them and that there were at least five thousand total braves they would have to fight. When Zak told this to Buff he snorted and said Frazer was a known drunk and the only way he saw five thousand braves was in a drunken delirium. Buff said Sibley was a fool to listen to such rubbish and that they should move out at once if they were to get this war over with any time soon.

But Sibley didn't move the Army for four whole days.

They traced the same route Zak had taken just days before. When they reached New Ulm it indeed sat abandoned. Sibley sent scouts to the south to see if Flandrau and the townspeople had moved toward Mankato. When they arrived at Fort Ridgely they found it still standing as Sheriff Patch had said, but the beleaguered defenders were almost at their wits' ends after repelling numerous attacks.

In the evening after their arrival at Fort Ridgely some soldiers dug up an Indian who'd been killed in one of the attacks. They urinated on the dead man and used it for target practice. Zak, like all the rest, couldn't suppress his curiosity and stole his own look at the mangled corpse.

He barely suppressed his gorge. It looked like his uncle, Whirlwind.

12. *The Broom of Death*

THEY LANGUISHED at Fort Ridgely for a full week before Sibley sent his men into the countryside. Restlessness stalked the men, and they amused and occupied themselves in the way bored soldiers do—sleeping, playing cards, fighting, and drinking any and all whiskey that could be found. Sibley issued an order strictly forbidding drinking, but it was enthusiastically ignored. They bought whiskey on the sly from cunning peddlers and sneaked off in the middle of the night, braving the dangers of the open prairie to raid farmhouses that had already been raided by the Dakota.

"Dress parade" consumed the mid-day hours, and the men grumbled through drills they'd already done dozens of times. The consensus among the men was that Sibley was either scared or slow, or both, and even his staunch defenders were changing their opinions of him. Shouting could be heard from his quarters, and the men learned through the soldiers' grapevine that Sibley stubbornly resisted the earnest suggestions of his junior officers to move out.

So they bided their time, waiting for the orders to come. Zak often thought of Hannah, trying to remember every detail of what she looked like—her hair, her soft eyes, the way her eyes crinkled when she smiled. He closed his eyes and tried to remember the sound of her voice. His head spun and his hands were always wet when he did this. What was going on? Could he be in love with her? He'd never loved a woman in his life—except for his mother, of course—and he wasn't sure what he was supposed to feel. But all he knew was that he'd never felt this way about any girl before. He wondered if she felt the same way about him. He tried to remember the way they talked, the way she looked at him. She *did* smile a lot at him and, criminey, she had kissed him! She must have some feelings for him. But he wasn't sure. He just *had* to see her again!

On the fifth night another squad challenged Zak's to present its biggest man to wrestle their biggest man. They heartily nominated Sergeant Buff Keegan, and he heartily accepted. He and his opponent, a gargantuan German named Otto Bremen, locked hands and threw each other around in the grass by the campfire light. No punches were thrown, no eyes were gouged, and there was no kicking or

133

kneeing—just straight, honest wrestling, each man attempting to trip the other man or throw him down and go for a pin. For a half-hour they did this before Buff pinned Bremen for the three-count. After the match Buff, slightly drunk, slightly bloody and weary, staggered off to his tent. Men shouted to other challenges came forth, and matches raged for another hour before calm settled in.

"I challenge that Injun Hammer," someone suddenly called from the back of the group. The group parted and there stood Dougal Black, grinning wickedly, holding a whiskey bottle. He swayed slightly on his feet. His slurred his words. "I challenge him an' bet I can get him down in two minutes."

"What do you say, Hammer?" came a voice from the crowd.

"Go on, do it!" called another.

"Unless he's yella!" called a voice. Zak turned toward it—that weasel Gilby, also holding a whiskey bottle, also grinning wickedly.

Zak pondered it for a moment. He hadn't wanted to wrestle anyone, but here was his chance at his nemesis. Dougal couldn't pull any fast ones in front of all these other fellows, he thought. It'll be fair and square.

The men formed a circle around them and in the middle Zak and Dougal locked hands. Zak had already planned his strategy—he would hand-wrestle with Dougal for a while and make a few feints with his right leg. This would make Dougal think he was right-legged and he would be watching for it. But after a few feints he would whip around his left leg, his strong leg, catching him unawares, and put him down. He'd go for the pin quickly. He had no desire to prolong this.

That was not the way it went.

"You're protector ain't here no more," Dougal sneered as they locked hands, and Zak suddenly knew this wasn't going to be just a wrestling match. But before he could get himself into a defensive posture Dougal pulled him close and kneed him in the stomach. Zak grunted as the air was forced out of him. He attempted to get his knee up to deflect the next blow but he was too late and Dougal kneed him again, this time in the ribs. The force of the kneeing caused their hands to unlock, and Zak fell to the grass and rolled over twice, to the edge of the circle. He shook his head to clear it, but as he was getting to his hands and knees he saw Gilby out of the corner of his eye, his leg in motion, and he felt the kick before he could stop it, the blow to his face stunning him. He collapsed to the ground on his stomach.

"Get up!" Dougal screamed at him.

"Yeah, get up, you stinkin' Injun!" Gilby yelled in his ear.

Zak stayed on the ground. Amidst the pain he did some quick thinking. Dougal is smarter than I gave him credit for. He saw Buff leave and saw this as his opportunity to get him. Dougal must have figured, correctly, that the other soldiers would not intervene if the match turned into a fight, for there was nothing more entertaining to soldiers than a knock-down, drag-out brawl. He had to get up and fight Dougal. On the other hand, if he stayed on the ground nothing more would probably happen, for soldiers' etiquette would not let a man kick another man to death while he was on the ground.

But he had to get up. Suddenly he was enraged, all of the insults and wrongs by Dougal filling him with an anger that swelled in him. The pain in his abdomen was almost forgotten as he got to his feet and wiped the blood from his mouth on his sleeve.

"Come on," he said to Dougal in a low voice. There was an excited murmuring among the crowd of soldiers.

"You want some more?" Dougal asked in mock incredulity, feigning a surprised look and looking at the circle of soldiers around them. "Sure about that? This is your chance ta end it. Back down like a good little redskin and I won't whup on you no more." The soldiers behind him laughed.

Zak bull-rushed Dougal and caught him with a shoulder in his midsection. He heard a low *oomph!* come from him as he landed on top of him. Zak got immediately to his feet and Dougal, tough and quick, scrambled up right away. He swung with his right fist but Zak ducked, feeling the glancing blow on the top of his head. Immediately he swung upwards with his own right, feeling the blow land solidly on Dougal's ribs. Before Dougal could react or curl into a defensive position, he landed another right in the same spot. He tried a third but Dougal pushed him away.

Dougal came at him again, attempting a kick to his groin. But Zak grabbed his foot and flung it upwards and out, sending Dougal to his back, where he lay momentarily.

"Get on him!" someone in the crowd screamed.

135

"Stomp him!" cried another. So much for the soldiers' etiquette.

But Zak did neither. He waited, his fists up in front of him, while Dougal got to his feet. Dougal was wary now, sensing defeat but proud, and he came at Zak with a rage that was almost visible. Zak slipped backwards on the dewy grass and Dougal instantly had him in a headlock and clawed at his face, searching for his eyes. But Zak got hold of his fingers and twisted them back, releasing the headlock. Dougal screamed but before he recovered Zak punched him twice in the chest, and he stumbled backwards, falling down again. But Zak did not pursue him. He wanted the defeat to be complete.

"Come on!" he screamed at Dougal, waiting with his fists up. Dougal stayed where he was for a few seconds, touching his nose gingerly and looking at the blood on his fingers.

"Get up!" someone shouted at Dougal.

"Don't let him do this to you!" Gilby screamed at him.

Dougal came at him again, but he was slow and the confidence was gone from him. As he stumbled towards him with his head down, Zak deftly stepped aside, getting in two quick but hard blows to Dougal's ribs as he passed. Dougal grunted and almost went down, but the automatic stubbornness in him prevented it and he turned again towards Zak. The look in his eyes showed he knew what was coming, but he was powerless to defend against it. Zak punched him in the face twice. Dougal went down and did not get up.

Zak, his chest heaving, looked up and found Gilby's face in the throng. He stumbled over there and grabbed Gilby by the front of his shirt. He pulled his face to within inches of his own.

"You're next," he growled at Gilby. "You want to mix it up too?"

Gilby, eyes wide, put his hands in the air, whiskey bottle still in one hand, to indicate he did not.

The circle of soldiers cheered as Zak made his way through them. He felt them slapping him on the back in congratulations, but he scarcely felt them or heard them. Exhaustion washed over him and all he wanted to do was sleep.

"Wake up, youngster. There's gonna be some action."

Buff shook Zak awake. He looked outside the tent. It was just after dawn, and the sun had crept over the eastern horizon. He'd slept soundly, the best he had since he could remember.

"What? What's happening?" he asked.

"Dunno," Buff said. "Just know there's gonna be some action. Get your britches on. Sibley's gonna address us in a half-hour on the parade ground." He peered at Zak's bruised face in the dim light. "What in tarnation happened to you?"

After some coffee and a quick breakfast of pork and potatoes, Zak rushed out to the parade ground. The officers congregated in the middle of the parade ground. The bugler sounded "Assembly." Several dozen troops stood in loose formation. Several volunteer citizen soldiers stood there as well. Sibley addressed them after a five-minute wait.

"This day, August 31st, 1862, we are close on Little Crow's heels," he began. "I have heard from my sources that he intends to make a stand sometime soon. I certainly hope he does not change his course, for revenge is to be ours. We will sweep them with the broom of death.

"But until then we must get ourselves to the point of readiness. That is why we continue to train before moving out. Also, I await shipment of more ammunition supplies from St. Paul."

"We ain't used any ammunition yet," Buff Keegan muttered under his breath. "We should await him removing his skirt and pantyhose, that's what." Zak and those immediately around them chuckled quietly.

"I have been informed," Sibley continued, "that we will soon be joined by the Third Minnesota Regiment, which was surrendered, disgracefully I have heard, to the Confederates in Tennessee. Without going into the particulars, for I fear to slander its commander without knowing all the details, the regiment was surrendered without a fight, the officers were taken prisoner and the infantrymen were pardoned and sent north. They are experienced troops and will be of valuable service. We will have almost two thousand men to face Little Crow.

"But there is a task that needs doing immediately. I have decided to dispatch a detail into the countryside to locate and bury as many victims of the massacre as possible. Then the detail will examine the site of the Lower Agency and determine the damage there, as well as ascertaining the present whereabouts of the Indians if possible.

"Captain Hiram Grant will take Company A, Sixth Regiment..."

That's us, Zak thought.

"... and Captain Joseph Anderson will take a company of cavalry on the burial detail. Accompanying them will be the twenty citizen volunteers and seventeen teamsters with teams and wagons. The totals for the party will be seventy-five infantry, fifty-four cavalry, and the rest, for a total of 149 men. Captain Grant will command the entire detail, with advice from Major Joseph Brown, who has knowledge of the area and the Indians as their former agent."

Sibley paused, parading back and forth in front of the men. "Those are our citizens, our relatives, our family members lying unburied on the prairie. They deserve decent Christian burials. I expect every man to comport himself as a soldier in the U.S. Army and to carry out his duty with seriousness and due respect for the deceased."

"All right, you heard the Colonel," Buff Keegan told his assembled squad before they joined the ranks to move out. "Every man'll get forty rounds of ammunition and two days' rations. In the wagons there are 2,000 extra rounds.

"We'll follow the Agency road to the ferry, stopping to bury the dead. Some of 'em been dead for ten days or more, and some may be recognizable to you or t'others. But y'all gotta keep hold a yourselves. Crying can come later. I want every man jack to carry out his duty. Any questions?" Nobody spoke. "And keep your eyes open. The Sioux are still around, for sure."

Buff grabbed Zak as they prepared for the march. "You're on scout duty and I'm afeared on the burial detail," he said. "It won't be none easy, 'cause I knowed you used to live in the area. But at least you're not marching in the infantry. You stick close to me and I'll watch out for ya." Zak nodded.

"Zak Hammer?" someone called from behind him. Zak turned. Running to catch up was Joe LaCroix, the father of his friends Mirna and Minnie.

138

"Mr. LaCroix!" They shook hands warmly. "It's good to see you again."

"Always the polite young man," LaCroix said, smiling. "If I've told you once, I've told you a thousand times, you can call me Joe. How are you? What are you doing here?"

"It's a long story as to how I got here, but I'm here."

"How're your parents?"

Zak gave him an abbreviated telling of the whole tale.

"I'm so sorry to hear about your mom," LaCroix said. "Your pa . . . ," he searched for respectful words, "well, he had his demons. But I'm sorry about that, too."

"Thanks," Zak said. "What are you doing here? Where's your family?"

"That's why I'm here," LaCroix said. "The night before the outbreak we got warning. It was the strangest thing. I was asleep in my bed when a hand touched my shoulder and someone, a woman, whispered in my ear, 'Big trouble coming. Tomorrow warriors kill all the whites and mixed-bloods who act like whites. Go now, before too late and tell no one else or you, and I, will die.' That was it. I don't know how that person slipped in and out of my house without waking my wife or my dog.

"All of us, including my daughters Mirna and Minnie, my baby son and the dog, Duta, were going to slip away. We walked down to the river to cross it and start for Fort Ridgely. We heard shots coming from the Agency, so we knew the warning had been true. I hurried to ferry my wife, son, and dog in my canoe to the other side of the river. I told my daughters to wait in some bushes until I came back across for them because we all would not fit in the canoe. But when I got back there they were gone. I searched up and down the banks for a long time but couldn't find them. I couldn't call their names loudly because for all I knew the warriors were close. Then I heard my dog barking from the other side. Sick with grief, I paddled back over, figuring I should save as much of my family as I could. The dog kept barking. I had to strangle him with my belt to silence him or we'd have been discovered."

LaCroix's eyes watered from the painful account. "I left my daughters, and they disappeared. I'll never forgive myself if I don't find them. That's why I'm going on this here detail—to find them, one way or the other. I only hope to God that they're hiding somewhere, or, at worst, in captivity. If it's some other thing . . . ," his words were choked, " . . .I don't know what I'll do."

Zak's eyes watered, too, at the thought of the possible fate of his two friends. "I think you'll find them alive," he said. "They're smart, and tough. I can't tell you not to worry, but you need to concentrate on finding them first."

LaCroix wiped his eyes with a blue handkerchief from his pocket. "Thanks, son," he said. "Doin' the best I can."

The bugle sounded.

"Well, we're movin' out," LaCroix said. "I've been assigned to burial detail and scout duty because I used to live in the area."

"Hey, so have I," said Zak.

"Well, I'll be," LaCroix said. He patted Zak on the shoulder. "Well, let's watch out for each other, all right?"

The little force set out on the Agency road, banners unfurled in the wind, the drum and fife corps playing *Yankee Doodle*. The sun shone on them, pleasantly warm, but Zak was apprehensive about what they would find. He guessed the others felt the same way, for the officers rode silently and conversation in the marching ranks was muted. The men were subdued as each privately pondered his fate.

But for the rest of his life, when he looked back at this day, Zak realized that no matter what they individually did to confront their fears and steel their emotions, nothing could have prepared them for the horrors that unfolded.

13. They Were Shooting the Horses

ZAK'S EYES burned from the wind-borne ashes. Throughout the countryside the charred remains of houses, cabins, barns, sheds, and even outhouses stood blackened, sooty shells. Blinking, he stared beyond the buildings at acres and acres of scorched earth. Once heaving seas of green and gold, the vast grain fields now stood as motionless stubs, with not enough left for even locusts to scavenge. Thousands of feet had trampled the corn patches into useless mulch. Dead pigs and cattle randomly littered the land, tongues and bellies swollen hideously to the bursting point in the blazing sun. Wolves had gnawed on some of the carcasses, leaving only bits and pieces of the rancid meat for the crows to pick.

Captain Grant sent Zak forward on scout duty with Joe LaCroix, Buff Keegan, and two other men. They found the first family only a half-hour into their ride.

Nestled into a lush, green valley, the farm stood in ruins. Just a stone's throw from a pleasant, babbling brook, the blackened shell of the house marred the scene. Nothing stood—no walls, struts, or beams. Somehow the stable, just south of the house, had survived an attempted torching. But on one of its whitewashed walls facing the house, a giant blue-and-yellow painted flower—obviously the work of a child—was smeared with blood. Slaughtered chickens and cattle rotted outside the stable in the heat.

As the family had lived together, so had they died. The mother lay just outside the foundation of the burned house, struck down perhaps while trying to warn her husband and daughter, who lay together under the painting of the flower. The father had been scalped.

Zak stared unbelievingly at the bodies for a long time. Choked with grief and revulsion, he finally flung himself off Sunny and bolted for the brook. As he bent over the water nausea washed over him in waves. His head swam and his gorge rose acridly in his throat.

How much could he take? he thought once he controlled himself and drank from the cool brook. How much death and destruction do I have to see in this life? Those poor people! All they had wanted to do was live their lives the best they could. That's all anybody deserves, is to live their lives the best they can. These people had nothing to with

141

the conflicts between the Dakota and the U.S. Government. They had nothing to do with policies made by greedy politicians in far-off places.

Sudden hatred filled him. Hatred for the government agents who cheated the Dakota. Hatred for the Dakota for their horrifying retribution. For the first time he comprehended his own uselessness. As with all wars, this conflict was nothing more than a cauldron of fear, destruction, waste, grief, loss, and death. And he was powerless to do anything to change it, to stop the madness. He was caught in the middle—literally—and the maelstrom threatened to suck him down, down, into a darkness of despair and hopelessness.

The others stood silently when Zak returned. LaCroix looked at his tear-streaked face and said nothing. But Buff spoke.

"That's all right, youngster," he said, gently. "It's all right to let it all out. Don't worry none about that. It's when you can't let it out anymore that you start worryin'."

"She ain't any older'n my oldest daughter," LaCroix said.

"What should we do?" one of the men asked Buff.

"You and Mahoney," he pointed to the other man, "go back and tell Grant what we've seen so far and that we've found three bodies. Tell him to meet us here. Meantime, we'll start buryin' 'em. They're broiling in this hot sun."

They laid the family to rest on the banks of the brook, working silently in the sunshine. The flies buzzed thick and bothersome, frenzied by their macabre feast. After they were through they kneeled at the side of the brook to drink.

"This ain't right, all this killing," LaCroix said, wiping his mouth and leaning back on his haunches. "The Sioux were starvin', I know, but it still don't make it right. Fight the Army, yes, and maybe the traders. But not innocent people. Not like this."

"It's the only way they know how," Buff said. He filled his cap with water and placed it on his head, licking the drops that came down his face. He looked at Zak and LaCroix. "Sioux war is total war. Women and children included. It's what they honestly believe. Don't make no never mind where a scalp comes from, they're all honored the same. To them, this . . . ," he pointed at the graves and at the scene of destruction, " . . . is all fair game, proper 'n' all. The whites, we don't understand, never will. That's why, when it's all over, and the Sioux

142

lose, which they will, there'll be big trouble for 'em all. Not for just the warriors who did this. But for 'em all, women and children included."

"Most of my kin is Dakota," Zak said. "I can't believe they would do all this. It doesn't seem like them." Except for Whirlwind, he thought. He's entirely capable of this. How would he ever be able to face his relatives again after all this?

"It's a hard thing, youngster," Buff said. "It's a hard thing for all of us. All three of us have had Sioux kin at one time or another. Hardly nobody in this state—Sioux, white, mixed—is gonna be spared some heartache, I can tell ya that."

The remainder of the detail arrived then. Captain Grant told them they'd buried a half-dozen others that had been found by some other scouts to the north.

They buried over a dozen more people on their way to the Agency, some at their farms, some along the road, some in the fields. When they spotted a dead woman one of the citizen volunteers cried, "Oh my God, oh my God, my wife," and he leapt from his horse to her side. In a stab of recognition and pity Zak saw it was the man they'd met in the advance party on the way to New Ulm, the man with black eyes who'd been subdued by his two sons and evacuated while his wife was still missing.

He'd found her at last.

By the time they reached the ferry near the Lower Agency it was early afternoon. The men rode in sullen silence. When they reached the ferry their mood swung to shock and smoldering anger. Lying about the crossing were the remains of thirty men. Decomposing, hideously swollen, their bodies emitted a stench that sent two of Grant's soldiers to the ground, vomiting on their hands and knees in the grass.

"It's Captain Marsh's command," Captain Grant said through gritted teeth. "They left Fort Ridgely on the morning of the first day and were never heard from again, although it was rumored they'd been ambushed." He surveyed the scene, took off his hat, and rubbed his face. "I guess that's what happened."

"They're in neat ranks where they fell," Buff said. "Didn't have no time to even shoot back."

Grant sent Zak, LaCroix, and Buff across to scout the opposite banks and the nearby Agency while the dead soldiers were buried on the riverbank. Together they pulled on the rope that spanned the river, pulling the ferry with them. Zak pulled in numbed silence. He wondered if he'd have been killed had he still lived out here. Deep down, he felt guilty he was still alive. He tried to tell himself that was a ridiculous thought, but he couldn't shake it.

They were not surprised to see the Agency in almost total ruins. Flames had consumed almost all buildings. Two dozen dead people—men, women, and children—lay strewn about in varying degrees of decomposition and horror. Gunshots had caused most deaths, arrows others. A spear impaled one woman to the ground. Several bodies were burned beyond recognition.

Zak recognized one man, though. Andrew Myrick, the trader who'd said the Dakota could "eat grass" before he'd release food on credit, lay face up where he'd died. He had not been scalped or mutilated, but lay as an example for others to view. His mouth was stuffed with grass.

After burying Myrick, a sudden urge gripped Zak.

"I'll be back in a minute," he said to Buff and LaCroix.

"Where ya goin'?" Buff asked, eyebrows lifted.

"Just gotta do something," Zak said.

Buff looked at him. "All right," he said cautiously. "But be back soon. We're gonna start buryin' the rest of these folks. Watch yer back. If there's trouble, hightail it back here right away."

Zak walked Sunny down to the site of his old house, the place he'd spent part of his unhappy youth. There it stood, but someone had tried to destroy it. The roof lay caved in. The only occupant appeared to be either a badger or a woodchuck. Zak poked around for any of his mother's things that had possibly been left inside, but there were none. The stable was in similar disrepair. The corn patch where his mother had died was overgrown with weeds. Nobody had lived here after he and his father had moved out.

Zak stared at the ruins for a long time. Raw emotion boiled in him like water in a teapot. In a few minutes, though, the rage passed, replaced only by a sad resignation. He calmly took out some matches and ignited a small pile of kindling just inside the broken-down doorframe. Soon the flames spread to the doorframe, and then out on the walls, creeping quickly upwards onto the roof. In minutes the entire structure blazed, gray-black smoke billowing into the air. Zak watched until the walls fell in, and then he mounted Sunny and rode away.

They bivouacked that night near Birch Coulee, a tributary of the Minnesota River just downstream from the Agency. Just before they arrived at the coulee Zak spotted a man in hiding. When the man saw Zak he ran, but soldiers pursued and caught him. They dragged him, kicking and screaming, before Captain Grant. The man was badly sunburned and his clothes were in rags.

When the soldiers released his arms he whipped out a small knife and, to the horror of all watching, tried to slit his throat. Soldiers quickly subdued him and Doc Mayo rushed to give aid. The man muttered and thrashed about while the doctor worked. After a few tense minutes Doc Mayo announced the man would live. The wound had only been superficial.

"But he's delusional," Doc Mayo said. "He's been out here by himself for too long. Thought we were the Sioux. Poor devil's so disturbed, he can't tell friend from foe."

"Will he be all right?" Grant asked.

"Yes," Dr. Mayo said. "He just nicked the windpipe. Physically he will make it, but I'm not sure mentally."

Zak stared at the crazed man. Burrs choked his matted hair and gnarled beard. His eyes jerked wildly from side-to-side, peering at them suspiciously. He rocked back and forth in the back of a wagon, holding his knees, muttering to himself.

"You men," Captain Grant said to Zak, Buff, and LaCroix, "go back to where that coulee flows down to the Minnesota. There's an area of smooth prairie some two hundred yards from the timber of the coulee. We are going to camp there tonight, for it has the advantage of furnishing wood and water. But I want you to scout around there to look for any hostiles and to give me a report as to where I should place the pickets."

145

Watching carefully for any raiding war parties, they surveyed the area around the coulee. Zak didn't know exactly what to look for, be he watched and listened to Buff and LaCroix intently.

"Don't look like such a great spot after all," Buff said as they reviewed the area from a knoll after their observations. "Look there—," he said, pointing, "the coulee flows down that wooded ravine to the river. Plenty of cover for the hostiles. It's only a gunshot away from where the captain wants ta put the camp, which, by the way, is right out in the open." LaCroix nodded. "And looky that," Buff continued, pointing to another area. "There's a high spot on the west side which overlooks the camp. They can sit up there all day and lob arrows and musket balls down on us like acorns from a tree. I don't like it none."

LaCroix nodded again. "It ain't good," he said, "and I got a bad feelin' about it. I saw some fresh footprints and hoofprints in the sand down by the coulee and little piles of kinnikinnick, too." Zak knew the Dakota mixed kinnikinnick bark to smoke with their tobacco, having seen his grandfather do it. LaCroix was deducing, correctly, Zak thought, that some Dakota had been here recently.

"Could just be a small party," Buff said.

"Could be," LaCroix said. "But I saw many footprints. More than a few men and horses watered themselves down there. Like I said, I got a bad feelin' about it. Plus everthin' you said is true."

"Plus the long grass down there gives them a screen they can use to creep up on us from the woods," Zak said.

LaCroix nodded. Buff cast an approving look at Zak. "That's rightly so, youngster," he said, smiling. "Better watch it—yer gonna make yerself into a soljer before ya know it."

"Not if I can help it," Zak said. Buff guffawed and LaCroix smiled.

But their observations fell on deaf ears.

"That's just evidence of a raiding party," Samuel Brown, the former agent, said when they reported to Captain Grant. "We're going to camp out on the open prairie, for God's sake—we'll see them coming for miles, if they're even in the area, which they do not appear to be."

"But . . . ," Buff began.

146

"Don't worry about the Indians," Brown said, cutting him off. "There are none within a hundred miles. You're just as safe as if you were in your mothers' feather beds."

"But . . . ," Buff began again.

"Sergeant, I have heard your opinion," Captain Grant said, putting his hand up in front of him to stop any further opinion. "Mr. Brown is from the area. He knows the Sioux. If he says it's safe to camp near the coulee, it's safe to camp near the coulee. Now that's it. That's my order."

Grant ordered the wagons placed in a half-circle around the north part of the camp. Their teams were tied loosely to them, allowing ample room to graze, but also there in case of need at a moment's notice. The rest of the horses, including Sunny, were kept in a makeshift corral in the southern part of the camp. The soldiers pitched their tents in the middle of the camp. Grant dispatched pickets just outside the camp perimeter. Buff Keegan suggested that pickets be placed even further out, but Grant disregarded the idea.

Grant assigned Zak to horse-watching duty, to prevent them from being stolen by any braves that may be in the area and to prevent stampedes in case of disturbances. After midnight Zak went and spent an uneventful seven hours guarding the horses, watching alertly, convinced from their earlier observations that something was going to happen.

Just as the sun rose Zak heard footsteps behind him. He wheeled quickly and saw Buff coming towards him with two tin cups with steaming liquid in them. "Horse Dreamer. Brought some coffee fer ya."

"Thanks," Zak said, and took the cup gratefully.

"See anythin'?" Buff asked.

"Naw. Been quiet. Maybe nothing's going to happen."

"Mebbe," Buff said. They were quiet for a couple of minutes.

"Can I ask you a question?" Zak said.

"Sure, youngster. Shoot."

"Why're you looking out for me?"

Buff was silent for a long time. Then he spoke. "Had myself a Sioux squaw some years back. She was a fine woman, as hard

147

workin' and industrious as any man'd want. Could carry the load a two squaws on her back."

"So that's the kin you were talking about before?"

"Yep. Now you see why this little conflict is hard on me, too. I don't look forward to fightin' the people my wife came from. But I'm in the Army, and I gotta do what I gotta do. Someone shoots at me, I'm shootin' back in self-defense."

"Her name was Horse Woman," he continued. "That's why I like your name. It's close ta hers. She could ride better'n any warrior I ever seen." His wiped his face with a huge paw. "We had us a little papoose. Brownest, cutest little thing you ever seen. Named him Buffalo Horse. Kinda tied in his ma and pa's names. He growd up quick and was ridin' his own pony in five years." He took a long drink from his coffee.

"We lived in a little shack down by the Mississippi, not far from Pig's Eye's. Wasn't much, but it was ours. Wore my hands bloody building it. Had me an ox and a plow and we lived off the land. Had my own lil' fambly." He took another drink of his coffee. "Flood of `51 took 'em. I was off huntin' for coupla days. Rained to beat hell and current rose up faster'n you could shake a stick at. They didn't have a chance. When I got back they was gone. House was gone. Got swept downriver, I reckon. Never did see hide nor hair of `em again."

Zak was stunned, deeply saddened. "Gosh, I'm sorry," he finally said. It seemed like so little to say. But he knew from his own experiences with death that there really wasn't any more to say.

Buff nodded slowly, drained his cup and wiped his mouth on his sleeve. He looked off into the rising sun. "My boy'd be your age now, if he was alive," he said. "Reckon you and me gotta connection that way."

"I'm sure he and I'd have been friends," Zak said.

Buff looked at him with liquid eyes. But they were bright liquid eyes. "Reckon ya would have," he said. He looked off into the distance again.

Suddenly he grabbed Zak's arm. "What's that?" he asked, whispering harshly.

"What?" Zak said, confused.

"Sshh," Buff hissed. He pointed to the treeline of the coulee, a couple hundred yards away. "I thought I saw somethin' down there!"

Zak squinted, trying to see between the trees. "What? I don't see anything," he whispered.

"Dunno. Just thought I saw somethin'. Keep yer eyes peeled."

They stared for a few seconds, but nothing moved. "My eyes mus' be playin' tricks on me," Buff said. He shook his head violently. "But I thought I saw somethin' movin', low ta the ground."

"Have some more coffee, maybe that'll clear your head," Zak said.

"Mebbe so," Buff said. He shook his head again. "You done with yours? I'll go back and fill us up." He turned to go, but froze when a horse whinnied, and then another. There was a stirring in the horses. Zak and Buff watched them intently. The horses, previously grazing contentedly, were now looking in the direction of the treeline, ears pricked up. Zak picked Sunny out of the crowd of horses. He held his head higher than the rest, more alert, and Zak could see his raised ears twitching. Sunny turned once in the direction of Zak, saw him, and looked back at the treeline.

"Somethin's down there, all right," Zak whispered. "Sunny's picked it up." From their right they saw the stray abandoned cattle they had picked up yesterday. They now moved nervously toward camp.

"They've picked it up, too," Buff whispered. "You go on back inta camp and alert the captain. Tell 'im there's somethin' gonna happen and that the men should be mustered. Go on, now. I'll stay here and keep an eye out."

Zak stole back into camp and found the captain's tent. "Can I help you?" The captain's adjutant, already awake and prepared to screen out any irrelevant business from his boss, looked at Zak suspiciously.

"I was down on horse duty," Zak said. "Me and Sergeant Keegan think something's happening out there and that the men should be mustered."

"You do, do you?" the adjutant half-sneered. Zak could see he clearly did not take him seriously. "What exactly did you and our colorful sergeant see?"

"Well, the sergeant thought he saw some movement in the treeline down by the coulee. Then the horses pricked their ears up and looked that way and the cattle came into camp. They sense something, or somebody, is moving down there."

"That's it?" the adjutant said, a hearty sneer this time. "You two thought you saw something and you think the animals can sense it? I'll tell you what," he said, leaning toward Zak. "Ol' Sergeant Keegan is still probably drunk and hallucinating again. He didn't see nothin'. He imagined it, and now he's got you into it, too. I'm not going to bother the captain with this."

"But my horse is down there, too," Zak said imploringly. "I know when he senses something. And when he does, he's right. I'm telling you, there's something going on down in those woods. It could be a force of warriors. The captain should be alerted!"

"What did I say to you?" the adjutant said. "Was there any part of it that you did not understand? As Mr. Brown said yesterday, there aren't any Indians within a hundred miles of here. The captain is scheduled to sleep for another half an hour and I intend to see that he does just that. Now take your childish imaginations and go back to your post before I put you on report." He wagged his index finger at Zak as if dismissing a naughty schoolboy.

"But . . . ," Zak began, but sudden gunfire from the direction of the horses drowned him out. Zak wheeled. Buff was running back into camp, bawling like a branded bull, stopping once to fire his rifle in the direction of the treeline before running again.

"They're in the trees!" he shouted. "Hundreds of 'em! I seen 'em!" More gunfire erupted, now from the pickets. Zak saw the smoke from their rifles starting to drift toward the treeline. He strained his eyes at the treeline. He could see puffs of smoke like exploding balls of cotton bursting from behind trees, from up in trees.

Buff bawled breathlessly at the adjutant. "I seen 'em!" He shouted again. "Get the captain! Get the captain!"

"What are you shouting about?" cried the confused adjutant. "You saw who? What is going on?"

"The Sioux! They're down in the treeline! There's gotta be hundreds! We're under attack!"

The adjutant's face blanched. "But . . . ," he began.

150

"Don't just stand there, you idiot!" Buff grabbed and shook him. "Wake him up! We need to muster the men!"

The adjutant wheeled to go into the captain's tent. But the captain was already awake, pushing aside his tent flap and stepping out. He had only his pants and suspenders on, and was bending over to pull on his boots.

"We're under attack!" the adjutant shouted in his face.

"I'm aware of that," said Captain Grant dryly. "We need to form a skirmish line facing the trees. Bugler!" he called out, looking around.

"Right here, sir," said the bugler, appearing out of nowhere.

"Bugler, get the men in line. You," he pointed to a man who'd just come in from the pickets, "get those pickets back in. We'll . . ."

"They're dead!" cried the soldier. "All of `em have been overrun. I was the only one to get out!"

"Very well," said Grant, color draining from his face. "Get in the skirmish line with the rest. We've got to form it right away or we'll be overrun as well."

Buff spoke up. "Sir, I don't think a skirmish line will work. They'll be too exposed. The Sioux are behind cover and will pick off every man that stands up. We ought to make some barricades and dig ourselves in. They'll hear the shootin' at Ridgely—all we got ta do is hold `em off until they get here with their cannon."

The captain mulled this over, stroking his chin. Buff snorted impatiently.

"No," Grant finally said, shaking his head. "I'm not going to dig in like animals and cower from them. We'll stand and fight like the trained soldiers we are. They'll be no match for our discipline. Get your squad down into the line."

"The fool!" Buff fumed as they ran down toward the line that was forming. "A skirmish line! A skirmish line! We ain't fightin' the British at Bunker Hill! We'll be cut to pieces like Swiss cheese!" The soldiers scrambled from their tents, throwing on their uniforms and loading their rifles while running. Suddenly Zak stopped short.

"Sunny!" he cried.

"What?" Buff shouted at him over the roar of the gunfire.

"I've got to get Sunny! The horses are all exposed down there! He'll be killed!"

"You'll get yer tail shot off!" Buff screamed right in his ear. "You stick close ta me up here!"

"I've got to get him!" Zak shouted.

"No time!" Buff screamed, pawing at him. "You stay with me! That's an order!"

"I can't!" Zak shouted. "I can't! I'll be back!" He broke away and ran to the horses.

But Sunny was not there. Zak tried frantically to find him, running up and down the makeshift corral. Where could he have gone? he thought. I just saw him a few minutes ago!

Then the horses began to fall as if struck by lightning. Zak heard the sick *thwack* of musket balls tearing flesh. The horses whinnied—screamed—terribly.

They were shooting the horses.

Something bounced off Zak's boot. He looked down—a musket ball had hit him and rolled away. Soon balls rained down all around him, striking the ground and bouncing like hailstones. One by one the horses went down in tangled masses of torn flesh and broken bone. Their screaming was heart wrenching. Balls bounced off fallen horses' bellies, and one whizzed over Zak's head. He took one more frantic look for Sunny. Nowhere. Grief-stricken, he bolted back toward the camp.

The skirmish line faced the menacing treeline. Figures darted around in the grass between the camp and the treeline—braves keeping low, firing into the camp and rolling to different positions. The soldiers fired but could not hit the moving targets. Suddenly from the south side, where the dead horses lay, a withering blast of gunfire raked their ranks. Warriors had circled around and were firing in on the camp from behind. The skirmish line wavered, shuddering, and then broke as soldiers dropped in tangled clumps like rag dolls.

"Overturn the wagons! Form a circle!" Buff yelled. Captain Grant was nowhere to be seen. Frantically the men unhitched the wagons from their dead teams and dumped them on their sides. Equipment, provisions, personal effects crashed to the ground chaotically.

"Dig a hole!" Buff shouted into Zak's ear. "Here! Behind this dead horse!" He shoved a spade at Zak, who tore at the earth furiously, flinging sod away in panic. In between his rasping breaths he sobbed.

"Hammer! Are you all right?" Someone yelled over the din. He turned. It was Joe LaCroix.

"Yeah, I am! Here, dig yourself in!" he shouted, throwing the spade to him. LaCroix dug a crude hole in minutes.

Buff and the other soldiers did likewise. "This'll give you some added protection!" he shouted at them.

"Return fire at will!" rang a command. Captain Grant was back in charge.

The next few hours were interminable. The Dakota never charged the embattled camp, but their cover in the treeline and in the grass was so complete that they fired at will without detection. The soldiers shot back, but they shot at phantoms. The men huddled in their holes, behind wagons and dead horses, only heads and shoulders above ground. Occasionally a man braved the murderous barrage and stuck his head and rifle over a carcass to fire a random shot. Three holes down from Zak a man rose up to do the same but he jerked back immediately, his head snapping smartly back. He hung limply over the hole, his face toward him. Zak stared, horrified. The musket ball had penetrated his left eye and had blown out the back of his head.

Suddenly shots came from overhead, killing two soldiers in their holes. Zak and LaCroix peered over the animals in front of them.

"There's a sniper in a tree real close," LaCroix said. "He's shooting over the horses. He'll kill us all if we don't get him first."

LaCroix loaded his musket. He reared up out of his hole, balanced the gun on the horse in front of him, and took aim. Zak peered cautiously up. The blast from LaCroix's gun deafened him. A warrior dropped from a tree no more than two hundred feet from them.

There was a lull in the shooting. The rest of the warriors must have seen what had happened. In a minute a voice called out of the tall grass in English.

"LaCroix," the voice called, "we know it is you that shot. You have killed the son of Chief Traveling Rain. Now we will kill your little girls."

LaCroix sat silently for a moment. "Thank God," he finally said, more to himself than anyone. "They're alive." Then he quieted again. Zak could guess what he was thinking. He was now overcome with fear at what may happen to his daughters in captivity.

The stifling heat scorched Zak's throat. Acrid smoke stung his eyes and polluted his nose. The constant barrage of gunfire pounded his brain like a sledgehammer. His head felt like it was filled with mortar and someone was chipping at it with a hammer. He just wanted to crawl down as deep as he could into his hole and sleep, to put all of this out of his mind. In his worry about Sunny he almost forgot his desperate thirst. He thought of Hannah. I promised to find her again, he thought. That's one promise I might not be able to keep.

Curiously, another lull then settled in. The men glanced at each other uneasily. Out of the smoke in front of them rode a solitary Dakota brave on horseback. He carried a white ribbon on his lance. When he was only a few dozen yards from them he halted his horse and called out to them in English.

"We are as many as the leaves on the tree! Soon we come down and kill all the soldiers. We do not want to kill our brothers. All in camp who have Dakota blood come out. We will not harm you."

Zak thought quickly. Maybe they wouldn't harm him if he came out! He'd certainly live another day and would have a better chance of seeing Hannah again. But when he looked at Buff and Joe LaCroix they shook their heads slowly, seriously. Zak got the message. *No. Don't even think about it.*

LaCroix yelled back at the Dakota messenger. "Fah! Cowards! You do not dare! Every man in this camp has five guns to shoot! You fight like the Chippewas! Go back and stay with your squaws!"

The brave's face twisted in rage at this ultimate insult. But before he could respond a hail of gunfire from the camp made him wheel his horse around and tear back for the treeline at top speed. The men continued to fire at his back as he rode away, but if he was hit, he didn't show it, sitting tall all the way back.

This must have enraged the Dakota, for they renewed their attack with a vengeance. The fury of the assault overwhelmed Zak, and he drifted away in his mind briefly. Wild screaming from his right jerked him back to reality. Down the line a soldier scrambled from his hole, yelling incoherently. His hair was on fire. He rolled around on the ground, slapping his head in a panic until the fire was out. He rose to his feet and began stripping out of his uniform.

"I can't take this any more!" he screamed. "Oh, God, I can't take it any more!" He was out of his shirt and trousers before someone attempted to subdue him. But it was too late. He ran, almost naked, past the defensive line and into the open field. He got ten steps before bullets from a hundred guns mowed him down. He fell slowly, first to his knees, where he stuck his arms in the air as if he was imploring God to save him. Another volley of shots blasted him onto his back where he twitched for a few seconds before he died.

It was almost too much to see, too much too bear. Zak drifted out of reality again. He left his own body, and again he was a little bird, only a bird, hovering freely over the scene, looking at all the little people down below, the strife, the death. In his wonderful freedom he circled the scene once or twice from his safe vantagepoint, and then he winged away, up into the currents of the prairie wind, the fresh air and blue sky surrounding him, away from the mayhem and destruction.

The massive form of Buff Keegan filled his vision. Buff's face was blackened from gunpowder. Zak barely heard his hoarse screams.

"Youngster," he tried to yell once, but all that came out was a grating squeak. He licked his lips and tried again. "Youngster," he croaked, "we all outta water. You gotta go down to the coulee and fetch some."

"Me? Why me?" Zak asked.

"You ain't got no uniform on. You kin crawl on yer belly through the grass and they might not even see ya. If'n they do, they might not shoot atcha, thinkin' yer one a them."

"You want me to go?"

"I'm sorry, little buddy, but we're dyin' here." He put his hand on Zak's shoulder. "You kin do it, Zak. You got it in ya. I'll be waitin' for ya."

Zak fought his panic, panting heavily. Why me? he thought again. He could have refused. They couldn't court martial him, for he wasn't a soldier.

But at the same time, he didn't want to let Buff down, let the men down.

He crawled along the line of soldiers to where the group of dead horses lay. He lay in the midst of the carcasses for a few minutes, steeling himself for his mission. Then, craning his neck to make sure there were no warriors nearby, he set out on his hands and knees towards the coulee, two hundred yards away.

The tall grass concealed him for the first few dozen yards. So far, so good, he thought, crawling and dragging the ten canteens Buff had given him to fill. But halfway to the coulee, the grass thinned out. He lay on his belly and slithered forward like a snake, expecting to feel the impact of a piercing arrow or exploding musket ball at any time. But they did not come. In a few minutes he made it, unscathed, to the banks of the coulee.

He filled three canteens with the murky water and started on a fourth when he heard a soft sound, a slight footfall, behind him. In terror and dread, he turned slowly. Three Dakota warriors stood menacingly behind him.

One raised his arm. In the fleeting moment before he felt the pain of the club, Zak thought he recognized one of the warriors.

And then, only blackness.

14. Shadows on the Prairie

WHEN HE awoke he was on his back, his hands tied behind him. He looked up to see unfamiliar faces staring at him, Dakota faces.

He had been captured.

He lay there for a few minutes while more unfamiliar faces appeared. They gawked down at him, looking at his face, scrutinizing everything about him. They were all men, and Zak guessed he was not too far from the battlefield. His suspicions proved correct when he heard the sound of gunfire in the distance. He tried to judge how far away he was, but couldn't possibly know. A half-mile, a mile perhaps.

The tips of his fingers tingled as the bindings restricted the blood flow to his hands. He heard the sound of pushing and shoving as someone was trying to get through the crowd around him. In a moment he looked up to find two familiar faces staring down at him.

Whirlwind and Circling Hawk!

Whirlwind growled something to another warrior, who shrugged his shoulders and bent down behind Zak. He felt the blood rush back into his hands as the warrior cut his bindings. He sat up and looked around him. He was in the middle of a Dakota camp. There were no teepees or lodges, so it must be a day camp. Women huddled around campfires, feeding warriors that sat, cross-legged. This must be the camp of the force attacking at the coulee, Zak thought. Their position in the treeline and tall grass was so secure, so protected, that part of the force could keep the Army pinned while others retired back to this camp for food and water. With chagrin, Zak thought back to Captain Grant's disregard for their suggestions about where to bivouac. He rubbed his wrists and then looked up at his kin.

Whirlwind grunted something. He frowned at Zak.

"Whirlwind says hello," Circling Hawk said. "So do I." He smiled.

Whirlwind pushed Circling Hawk and spoke harshly to him. The smile disappeared from Circling Hawk's face, but Zak saw he was clearly happy to see him. Whirlwind growled again, gesturing to Zak and then back in the direction of the gunfire.

"What are you doing with the long knives, Whirlwind wants to know," Circling Hawk said. Whirlwind spoke again, emphatically, stabbing an index finger into Zak's breastbone. "Your mother was Dakota, your uncle gives you a horse, and you show your respect and thanks by fighting against them?"

Another warrior spoke harshly behind Zak. He turned to see a warrior gesturing at him with a tomahawk. Before him stood the ugliest man he'd ever seen, with a scarred face and the flattest, crookedest nose he'd ever seen. Looking closer, Zak saw he was missing part of his nose. The nostrils emerged from only a lump of scar tissue.

"That is *Mahpiyaokinajin,*" Circling Hawk said. "or Stands in the Clouds. Some call him Cut Nose because of his face. He says he should kill you right here, right now. That you are a friend of the long knives even with your Dakota blood. He should tear the scalp off your head and place it on his highest lodgepole."

Whirlwind growled at Cut Nose, who became silent. Whirlwind spoke again to Zak.

"He says he will wait for your explanation, to see if it is satisfactory. If it is not, he would agree with Cut Nose."

Zak breathed deeply. He chose his words carefully, for his fate hinged on his story. He told it, trying to remember every helpful detail. When he was through, the men around him were silent, contemplative. Circling Hawk smiled again, nodding, obviously approving of Zak's explanation. Whirlwind still frowned, but the anger had left his eyes. Only Cut Nose remained belligerent, speaking in harsh tones.

"You cannot be believed," Circling Hawk translated. "You were not forced into the Army. You chose it and could have left it. You are trying to save your neck by saying you had no other choice. You should still be killed."

Whirlwind spoke, gesturing at Zak and at himself and Circling Hawk. "Whirlwind says he believes your story to be true," Circling Hawk translated. "You had no choice but to obey the judge. You did not willingly join the long knives and take up arms against your own people. You have respect for the gift horse Whirlwind gave you, even though it is missing now. He says not to worry, for all things work out."

Zak breathed a sigh of relief. He might be saved after all.

Cut Nose spoke to Whirlwind again, as harsh as ever. Whirlwind stood silently as if considering something. Then he looked inquiringly at Circling Hawk, who nodded.

"What is it?" Zak asked.

"The matter must go before the Soldiers' Lodge tonight, and they will determine your fate. You will tell your story again and the chiefs will discuss it, giving their opinions on what should happen to you. Little Crow will go with the opinion of which he is convinced."

Zak's heart fell. So it wasn't so clear after all. But when he looked imploringly at Whirlwind, his cousin nodded at him once and seemed to smile. Cut Nose muttered to himself and stalked off after glaring at Zak.

"He has hot blood," Circling Hawk said. "Even hotter than Whirlwind's. Some will speak against you, others for you. Little Crow will listen closely to both sides, but he will agree with Whirlwind. His words are greatly respected by all."

Whirlwind spoke again. "He says you are to stay here until the battle at the coulee is over," Circling Hawk said. "Then you will come with us to the village."

"Where is the village?"

"A couple of hours' ride past the Agency. Everyone is there, our soldiers, our women and children, our horses, our dogs."

"And all the captive whites?" Zak was thinking of Mirna and Minnie.

"They are also there."

Zak mulled this for a moment. Then he asked, "What are you doing here? I thought you were learning the white man's way at the mission school. Your English is much improved."

"I was at the mission, but I saw the starving of my people. I felt bad that I got more food and better shelter than they did just because I was there. When the people rose Whirlwind came for me. He spoke to me in words that showed I would betray my ancestors and my family if I did not join. Whirlwind, he is one of the leaders. He is not a chief, but he is brave and has fought well."

"But all that killing," Zak said. "Women, children, families. Have you been a part of that?"

"That is the work of those with the hottest blood," Circling Hawk said, "and the work of those that took up the white man's farming ways. Those with the hottest blood want vengeance against the whites and those that took up their ways do bad things to make up for their guilt."

"And you and Whirlwind?"

"I cannot say that we have killed no whites," he said. "I am not sure. But if we have, it has only been against soldiers and armed citizens and only in fair, open fights. We have butchered no innocent people. We do not want to kill all the whites like those with hot blood. We only want the war over soon and a peace that will keep us on our land forever."

Zak breathed in relief. He still thought the killing of innocent citizens was reprehensible, but he understood what his relatives and others like them wanted and for what they fought, and he respected it. Whirlwind and Circling Hawk were not much different than men like Sergeant Keegan, he thought. They did not relish conflict and only wanted it over quickly. They only did their duty and what they thought was right.

A booming sound from the battlefield abruptly ended their conversation.

"What is that?" Circling Hawk asked. He looked in the sky. "There is no storm now."

"Cannon," Zak said. He'd heard them test the cannon before leaving Shakopee. "The rest of the Army from Fort Ridgely is probably here now." That would change the nature of the conflict. The army could train the cannon on the treeline and drive the warriors back. He guessed the Dakota would fall back soon.

He was right. Soon the warriors streamed into camp. Whirlwind appeared on horseback, looking as dour as ever. He spoke to Circling Hawk and motioned for them to follow.

"He says it was a victory but an incomplete one," Circling Hawk said. "The bluecoats from the fort brought cannon and forced the Dakota out of their positions. Whirlwind says they should have charged the camp when they had the chance. Now they do not, and what is left of the long knives' force will now be saved."

160

Zak thought of Buff and LaCroix. He wondered if they'd made it.

"What about my horse?" Zak asked. "Have you seen it?"

"I have seen many horses," Circling Hawk said.

"But you remember the one Whirlwind gave me," Zak said. "I went to get him in the middle of the battle but he was gone. Could you have seen him?"

"We shall see. Many things happen in battle." Apparently that is all he would say. He was being very mysterious.

A warrior rode through the camp. *"Puck-a-chee!"* he called out. *"Puck-a-chee! Puck-a-chee!"*

"It is time to leave," Circling Hawk said. "You may ride with me."

They rode back through the same country in which Zak had been just a couple of days before, over the ferry, past the ruins of the Agency. But then they were into new territory. As they made their way westward along the Minnesota River they passed the last of the white villages and farms and moved onto barren prairie, inhabited only by the Dakota. After a couple hours' ride they were at the village.

It seemed more like a city, a city of teepees. When Zak had been to Shakopee's village after his mother's death he had seen perhaps a few dozen teepees. But if Shakopee had a few dozen in his village, this city had ten dozen doubled. There could be a thousand of them, Zak thought. They sat facing the center of the camp, and the cattle and horses and wagons were in the center. By the time they got to Whirlwind's teepee it was dusk, and the camp was illuminated by a dozen huge bonfires in the center.

"We will wait in Whirlwind's teepee until the Soldiers' Lodge is called," Circling Hawk said. "We will eat now and they will come for us when they are ready."

After a meal of boiled beef and potatoes, Whirlwind entered the teepee and motioned for them to follow. Zak felt overwhelmed by his change in fortunes, and the ordeal at the coulee left him exhausted. On top of it all, his nervousness about his fate preoccupied him. Although Whirlwind and Circling Hawk had given him not-so-subtle hints that he would be spared, he still didn't feel completely sure. It seemed like he was always on trial, with someone else always deciding his fate.

The Soldiers' Lodge was convened in Little Crow's teepee. Along with Little Crow, chiefs Shakopee, Wabasha, Medicine Bottle, Red Middle Voice, Mankato, Big Eagle, Cloud Man, and Red Legs were present. All would listen to Zak, ask questions if they wanted, and voice their opinions as to what Zak's fate should be. Little Crow himself would make the final decision.

They entered Little Crow's tent and into a cloud of tobacco smoke. The chiefs sat, cross-legged, in a circle around the fire, smoking their pipes and talking in low tones. They made room for the three of them and were silent, scrutinizing Zak as he sat between Whirlwind and Circling Hawk. Little Crow nodded formally at Zak when he looked up. Circling Hawk translated the proceedings.

"You are the son of Wounded Hand's daughter and a white trader," Little Crow said. Zak wasn't sure if he should reply. He looked at Circling Hawk, who nodded.

"Yes, sir," Zak said.

"What is your Dakota name? I want to hear you say it."

"Horse Dreamer. My esteemed relatives call me *Sungahamdes'a.*"

"That is because why?"

"Because the horse is my spirit helper."

"The two men on either side of you are your relatives."

"Yes, sir."

"You are close to them."

"I have been over the years. I consider *Cetan Okinyan* to be a brother, almost."

Circling Hawk smiled when he translated this. Little Crow nodded. He took a puff from his pipe.

"You were found aiding the long knives in their war against the Dakota," he said.

"Yes, sir."

"What is your account of why you were found in such a state?"

Zak gave virtually the same account he'd given earlier in the day, expanding on many of the details. When he was finished the chiefs were silent, smoking their pipes and contemplating his words.

"If you would not have joined, you would have been sent to a prison?" Little Crow finally asked.

Zak nodded. "Most likely, after a trial."

"What would a trial be like?"

Zak spread his arms out in front of him. "A proceeding much like this. The facts would be stated and a jury—people sitting in judgment of the facts—would determine whether I was guilty of the crime or not."

"They would determine your punishment?"

"No. A judge would have. If the jury found me guilty, a judge would hand down the sentence, possibly prison."

Little Crow nodded again. "So we here are like both a judge and a jury?"

"I think so," Zak said.

"When you joined, did you make any oath of loyalty or service to the long knives?"

"No. Colonel Sibley . . ."

"Ah, Walker Among the Pines," Little Crow interrupted. "It is ironic that my old friend is now my enemy." Zak was silent. Little Crow indicated for him to continue.

"Sibley abided by the judge's recommendation and will—was to—give him a report when my service was over."

"Why did you not accept the punishment of the white man and refuse to fight your own people?" Shakopee suddenly asked him. He stared coldly at Zak, as he'd been doing the whole time. "Is that not what a man of principal would have done?"

Be careful, Zak thought. Shakopee is clearly not on your side, and he is powerful. "Shakopee's question is most thoughtful and relevant," Zak said, thinking ahead of his words before saying them. "It was a difficult decision for me to make. I did not particularly fear the thought of prison itself." He stopped himself. "No, that is not true," he said. "I did have a fear of prison, but my greater fear was being separated from my horse, the only friend and companion I had. I was told I would not actually take up arms against the Dakota, but would serve in other ways. I believed that I could serve with courage and distinction and redeem myself without doing direct violation to my heritage and to the Dakota. I believed it to be an appropriate arrangement. Whether or not it was a correct decision, I do not know. But I made the decision myself."

"So you decided what was best for yourself instead of subjecting yourself to the system that was in place?" Medicine Bottle asked. Darker than the rest of the chiefs, his white teeth pierced the dim light with his sneer. "You are above the white man's law?"

Zak's stomach turned. This chief was against him also.

"The judge is the one who had decided what was best for him," Whirlwind interjected angrily, fixing a hard stare at Medicine Bottle. "Did you not hear his words? The judge acted on behalf of the law. The judge gave him a choice between the two things he thought were right."

Medicine Bottle looked at Little Crow. "It is all right, Whirlwind may speak," Little Crow said. "He has knowledge of this young man's family and character." He pointed at Zak with his pipe. "I believe you have answered the question of Shakopee and Medicine Bottle already. But I want to know whether you actually took up arms at any time against the Dakota."

"Never," Zak said. "I have never fired a weapon at the Dakota."

"Did you ever carry a weapon?" Shakopee asked him.

"Yes."

"Why is it then that you say you never took up arms against the Dakota?"

"I carried a weapon for self-defense only."

"You would have fired your weapon at a Dakota?"

"If my own life was threatened, yes."

"Self-defense is different," Wabasha spoke for the first time, looking at Shakopee. "It is by instinct that people defend themselves. It is a human right."

"It is still the taking up of arms," Shakopee said defensively.

"What would you do in such a situation?" Wabasha asked Shakopee. "Let the other man shoot and kill you without protecting yourself?"

Shakopee sat back, smoking his pipe. He clearly did not intend to answer the question. *He's already made his decision,* Zak thought. *He made some good points. I only hope the others have open minds like Wabasha.*

"May I say something?" he asked.

"Of course," Little Crow said.

"I have made mistakes in my life," Zak said, "and I continue to make them every day. But I am trying to atone for the past, and to make the right decisions and live a life my mother would be proud of. That was my motivation when I chose between the two things the judge proposed. In no way did I ever intend to disrespect the Dakota. But I did have to make a choice, and I am comfortable with it, although I know not all of you are." He paused, letting the words sink in. All except Shakopee and Medicine Bottle were listening to him intently. "I understand why the Dakota have gone to war, although I do not agree with the killing of innocent people. I respect every one of you and know you are doing what you think is right for your families and for the Dakota. I have not had the luxury of a family to think of, and so I have done what I have thought will be best for me, right or wrong. I leave the decision of my fate to you. I have spoken."

Whirlwind, Wabasha, and Little Crow nodded. The others sat silently. Zak tried to read their faces, but they were of stone. Little Crow looked up at him.

"Very well," he said. "You may go back to Whirlwind's teepee now and await our decision. You will know what it is shortly."

Zak waited on pins and needles for an hour before Circling Hawk returned for him. They returned to Little Crow's teepee and entered. Little Crow sat alone at the fire. He motioned for Zak to be seated and, after he was settled in, spoke. Circling Hawk translated.

"I listened with an open mind to your account," Little Crow began, "and I listened with an open mind to the chiefs. Some spoke in favor of you, others did not. Shakopee and Medicine Bottle were particularly against you, and they made persuasive arguments." He took a puff from his pipe.

"But my chiefs have selected me as spokesman of our nation, and so the decision falls only on me. Wabasha, Big Eagle, and the others voiced their opinions that, while they do not approve of your service to the long knives, you made a hard decision that took courage. They believe you that you did not take up arms against the Dakota. They believe you did what others may have done in your position. I listened

165

to them closely, and was impressed with their arguments. But I was most persuaded by your uncle, Whirlwind, who spoke highly of you. He spoke of your character and your bravery in dealing with your mother's death and your valor in the battle at the coulee, and he believes you have a good, if sometimes misguided, heart.

"Therefore, I have decided that your life will be spared. Further, you will not be placed in captivity with the other whites and those with mixed blood who have lived like the whites. You will remain with the Dakota and will be of service to us in the same manner you were to the long knives."

Zak sat motionless, stunned. He knew he was being saved, but he was overwhelmed by Little Crow's decision that he would be of service to the Dakota now. He was going to be on the Dakota side now! Is that what Little Crow meant? Surely they wouldn't make him fight against the whites now!

As if reading his thoughts, Little Crow said, "I will not force you to shoot any of the trespassing settlers or the long knives, since you have white blood in you. Instead, you will serve as a scout and a messenger for me." He looked at Zak slyly. "You may go now, Horse Dreamer."

"Does he really mean that?" Zak asked Circling Hawk as they left the teepee. "Did I hear what I just thought I heard?"

"It appears to be so," Circling Hawk said. "Now you will see the conflict from that side of you which is Dakota. You will see it as Horse Dreamer. It is not often that a person is allowed the opportunity to see both sides at the same time."

"I guess not," Zak said. "But I wish I didn't have to see it from either side."

"It is something I am sure many people wish for," Circling Hawk said.

Zak, now in good standing, roamed freely about the camp. Activity permeated the entire camp—women skinned and dried cattle the men had captured and slaughtered; dogs ran everywhere, yapping incessantly; children, oblivious to warfare and death, played the games children did, the girls shooting dice and the boys shooting the hoop and wrestling. The men came and went, some in war parties, some to

DANIEL W. HOMSTAD

scout, some to hunt. Some of the men frolicked in their plunder, parading gaudily in the clothing and jewelry they'd confiscated from settlers' homes. They made a motley crew, dancing in their hoop skirts, calico dresses, and furs, wearing earrings and necklaces as nose ornaments. Some were drunk on whiskey.

Zak never thought of escape. He knew the risks of being alone on the prairie, with nervous soldiers and hot-blooded warriors prowling about. He would be liable to be shot by anyone. Besides, he wasn't even sure he wanted to escape. It was true he was still horrified by the wanton slaughter of innocent citizens, but that was undoubtedly the work of men like Shakopee, Medicine Bottle, and the awful Cut Nose. White men he knew, men like Dougal Black and Gilby, were no better. There were rotten apples in every barrel.

He returned to Whirlwind's tent and stepped into it. When he got inside, he realized it was the wrong teepee. As he turned to leave he saw two girls cowering in the corner.

Mirna and Minnie LaCroix. They were alive!

During a short, tearful reunion, they told Zak that since their capture they'd been treated quite well, although rumors ran rampantly that the captives would all be killed. Zak told them he'd do his best to ensure they would return safely to their father.

When he arrived at Whirlwind's teepee, he stopped short. What he saw made him almost drop to his knees with joy and relief. Tied just outside the teepee, grazing casually, was Sun Dance! His horse, his companion and friend, was alive!

He ran to Sunny and threw his arms about the horse's neck. Sunny recognized him immediately, snorting and bobbing his head, pawing the ground with his front hooves. When Zak stepped back he could barely see Sunny for the tears of happiness in his eyes.

"You're alive!" he exclaimed. He could hardly believe it. Having seen the way the horses had been killed at Birch Coulee, he'd thought Sunny was a goner. But there he was, in front of him, and Zak felt life anew.

Suddenly a rush of concern flooded over him. Was he hurt? Surely *something* had to have happened to him. Zak remembered the way the musket balls had fallen like hail.

"If something has happened to you, I don't know what I'll do," he said to the horse. He inspected him up and down—his face, ears, neck, flanks, belly, legs, hooves, and even the tail. But there were no injuries. There was not a scratch on his horse. Relief surged through Zak like lightning. He could not believe his good fortune.

He heard two boys laughing behind him. Turning around, he saw Circling Hawk and a warrior, no more than a boy, that he did not know. They giggled and pointed at him. The boy Zak didn't know spoke first.

"He says he bets, by the look on your face, you never thought you'd see that horse again," Circling Hawk said. "He says you look like you've seen a ghost."

"Uh, no, I mean yes," Zak stammered. "Yes, I didn't think I'd see him again. Did you . . ." He pointed at the other boy. "What is your name?"

The boy spoke.

"Tatanka Wanagi," Circling Hawk translated. "Buffalo Ghost."

"Did you bring him here?" Zak asked.

Buffalo Ghost giggled again, covering his mouth with his hand. He spoke again. "You might say that."

Zak was confused. "What? How? Tell me!"

"Buffalo Ghost was in the force that pinned the soldiers down at the coulee," Circling Hawk said. "He wanted to count coup . . ."

"Count coup?"

"Yes, a warrior gains glory and receives honor when he touches the enemy, either by killing him or touching him. It is the same with horses, too."

"So Buffalo Ghost counted coup by killing the horses?" Zak was still confused.

"No. You count coup by *stealing* horses. Stealing a horse from the enemy in his own camp is one of the bravest things a warrior can do. And that is what Buffalo Ghost did, before the rest of the horses were killed."

"He stole my horse? Sunny? From the camp? But I was watching them the whole time."

Buffalo Ghost spoke.

"He says he knows," Circling Hawk said. "He saw you sitting there for the whole night. He says you watched the horses very well,

168

made his job difficult. He says he stole your horse when the gunfire started and you and the other soldier had turned your backs and gone to the camp."

"Did he know it was my horse?"

They laughed. Buffalo Ghost spoke again.

"He says of course not," Circling Hawk said. "He says it was just a coincidence."

Flabbergasted, Zak marveled at this turn of events. A coincidence! It was more than that! What were the chances that, out of all the horses there, Buffalo Ghost had decided to steal Sunny? It was a miracle! Zak was almost speechless. *Thank you, God,* he prayed silently. In whatever form you are.

"Gosh, I never thought I'd thank anyone for stealing my horse," he finally said. "But thank you. Thank you for my horse Sun Dance."

Buffalo Ghost said something. "He finds it odd you name your horse," Circling Hawk said. "And he says he finds it odd that you name it Sun Dance."

"Why is that?" Zak asked.

"Buffalo Ghost says you should have named it `Luck.' Because that's what you both have."

Zak was silent. He couldn't speak any more. Suddenly he realized just how tired he was. He needed sleep, badly. But not until he'd ridden Sunny, just for a little bit.

Buffalo Ghost spoke again.

"One is fortunate to get a second chance," Circling Hawk translated.

"I know," Zak said. "Believe me, I know."

That night, a huge feast turned the camp into mayhem. The women slaughtered dozens of captive cattle and roasted them over gigantic fires. After the feast the entire village participated in the war dance. Several warriors started the dance by shooting arrows into the air. Aimed at evil spirits, the arrows were trampled by the dancers upon their fall to the ground.

The dancing transfixed Zak with its unearthly, eerie quality. As the flames grew higher so did the pitch of the dancers. All had their best costumes on. Men wore buckskin jackets and leggings, adorned with fringes and brightly-painted images of eagles and bears and deer. One man wore a full-sized wolf hide, the empty shell of the animal's head resting on the top of his. Little Crow, Shakopee, and Mankato wore headdresses of eagle feathers that reached the ground. The women and the children wore their finest too, and they jangled from the sound of attached bells whenever they moved.

The whole village seethed in a swirling mass of frenzied humanity, people in fervent religious ecstasy, praying to their gods for victory and deliverance, for their way of life, for their pasts, their futures. What began as low singing amongst the throng soon elevated into chanting and howling, utterly mesmerizing rising and falling tones that battered and subdued Zak. He sat hypnotized by the whipping bodies, by the hypnotic flickering firelight, incapable of comprehending the full scene and unable to move or speak.

Suddenly someone grabbed both his hands. He looked up and saw two warriors he did not know. Then he squinted and recognized them—Whirlwind and Circling Hawk! They stood before him in identical black buckskin jackets and leggings. They wore black moccasins. Their long black hair flew freely in the hot wind of the fire, whipping wildly. Their faces, necks and hands, painted a stark white, seemed to glow in the eerie light. They looked subhuman. They looked like skeletons.

They pulled Zak up and out of his stupor. Whirlwind dipped his fingers into a small sac, and they emerged with a dripping red substance on their tips. Circling Hawk held Zak's head steady as Whirlwind daubed the red dye on his face, under his eyes, on his nose and chin. Zak wondered what type of monstrosity he looked like. Then they pulled him into the surging throng. For a moment Zak stood there, still. But Whirlwind and Circling Hawk pushed him from behind and soon he was moving, letting his mind wander and his feet move as he, too, danced, slowly at first, then faster, and faster, frantically, wildly, his lungs heaving, his body gyrating and contorting, moving almost instinctively, urged on and on and on by his innermost primal voices.

The dance lasted most of the night. Toward the end, they engaged in a purification rite through a sweat bath. Whirlwind had built a dome-shaped frame out of willow poles, placing buffalo-hide robes over the frame to make it airtight. In the center of the lodge Whirlwind dug a small pit, into which he placed scorching hot stones. Whirlwind, Circling Hawk, and Zak stripped off their clothes and sat around the pit. Whirlwind poured water on the hot stones, filling the lodge with steam. Whirlwind passed around a pipe and they smoked, paying homage to their spiritual aides.

"To the wind, which aids me to fall upon my enemy like a cyclone," Whirlwind said.

"To the hawk, which circles in the sky and helps me locate my enemy," Circling Hawk said.

Zak didn't know what to say, but they looked at him expectantly.

"To the horse, which helps me through difficult times," he finally uttered. Apparently that satisfied Whirlwind and Circling Hawk, for they nodded solemnly.

Zak left the lodge exhausted and wandered out of the camp circle, onto the moonlit prairie. He intended only to get some air and clear his head before returning to camp. As he walked the light played funny tricks on him. The firelight from the camp behind cast one shadow ahead. The moon above him cast another, smaller shadow, to his side.

That's fitting, he thought. Two shadows. Two shadows for the two parts that are me. One shadow for my white heritage, one for my Dakota side.

"I wonder which I really am?" he wondered aloud to himself. "Who am I?" He thought of Hannah. "Can you help me?" he asked, as if she was walking beside him. "Hannah, who am I?"

But of course no answer came. The land lay silent, unyielding any secrets it may have.

Zak walked faster, changing directions, moving this way and that. But, try as he could, he could not make the two shadows merge into one.

15. *Ghosts Over the Earth*

ZAK AWOKE with a start, shaken out of slumber. He rubbed his eyes and looked up. Circling Hawk shook him again. Zak looked around in confusion—he was out on the prairie just beyond the village.

"What happened?" he asked. "What am I doing out here?"

"You must have slept out here," Circling Hawk said. "I saw you wander off last night and thought you just needed some room to breathe. When I awoke in Whirlwind's teepee this morning and you were not there, I came to find you."

Embarrassed, Zak rose to his feet. "Sorry," he said. "I was exhausted and the night breeze was cool."

"I often leave the teepee to sleep under the stars," Circling Hawk said. "Come now. We are leaving in a little while."

"We are? Where are we going?"

"We are going out on a war party. Little Crow is leading some of the men to attack the settlements in the north."

"You're going? Am I going, too?"

"Yes, to both questions. You are to come with and scout ahead of the main party, and to relay messages from Little Crow back to the village, if necessary."

"How do you know all this?"

"Whirlwind visited Little Crow's teepee this morning," Circling Hawk said.

Three hundred painted warriors, gathered on three hundred painted horses, presented an impressive and formidable sight. Circling Hawk said the force consisted of half the total warriors in camp. The other half would remain to guard the camp. Zak rode Sunny alongside of Whirlwind and Circling Hawk to the front of the group to confer with Little Crow. Looking at the stern, proud faces that he passed, Zak wondered how Sibley, with his unimpressive leadership and unimpressive tactics, could ever defeat such a force. The only way the United States Army would win on the frontier would be to have more men and supplies, he thought.

Little Crow waited for them. He greeted Whirlwind and spoke directly to him. Whirlwind listened silently until Little Crow was done, seemed to ask a couple of questions, and then nodded. He rode ahead and motioned for Zak and Circling Hawk to follow. From the side Zak saw Little Crow motion toward two other men, who rode out of the main force to follow as well. When they got about a hundred yards ahead of the main force, Whirlwind stopped, turned his horse to the four of them, and spoke.

"He says we are to ride ahead and search for any sign of trespassers or of the long knives," Circling Hawk said. "If we see them we are not to fight them in any way, only send a messenger—you, Horse Dreamer—back to Little Crow while the rest of us keep our eyes on the long knives. We are not to attack, for to do so may alert the target of our main force, which is following. The main force will be attacking the town the whites call Hutchinson, which we will scout for them."

Zak nodded. It seemed simple enough. He wouldn't be forced to shoot at anyone and they wouldn't be part of any coordinated attack. He breathed a little easier.

Whirlwind spoke again.

"Whirlwind says it is good to know with whom you ride," Circling Hawk said. He pointed to the other two men that had ridden up with them. That one there . . . ," he said, pointing to a small man with a pinched face, "is *Hitunkada*, or The Mouse." Circling Hawk spoke in Dakota. The Mouse nodded at Zak. Circling Hawk spoke again. "That one there . . . ," he pointed to the other man, "is Godspeed."

"Godspeed?" Zak asked. "Just `Godspeed?'"

"Yes," Circling Hawk said. He spoke in Dakota to Godspeed. Godspeed did not acknowledge Zak, staring at him sullenly. He looked different than the rest of the Dakota—curly black hair, darker skin, black facial hair.

"His mother was Dakota and his father was an escaped black slave from the south," Circling Hawk said, as if reading Zak's thoughts. "His father's name was Godspeed. He was re-captured by white slave hunters and taken back to the south. It is said he was never heard from again. So the mother just called the child Godspeed, perhaps in remembrance." Circling Hawk paused. "It is best that you stay away from him," he said. "He hates the whites worse than any of the warriors with the hottest blood. It does not matter that you have Dakota blood in you as well. The only reason you are safe is because you are Whirlwind's nephew and he fears Whirlwind like everyone else."

Whirlwind muttered something and turned his horse. "We go now," Circling Hawk said. They set off at a slow trot, Whirlwind in the lead, singing an ominous-sounding song in a strong baritone voice:

Maka opta wau,
Maka opta wau,
Akicita wau.
Maka opta wanagi hemaca.

"It is the Dakota chant of defiance," Circling Hawk said. "'Over the earth I come; over the earth I come; a soldier I come. Over the earth I am a ghost.'"

Zak watched Whirlwind—truly a ghost over the earth. He missed nothing, his head moving from side to side as he constantly scanned the horizon. He continuously looked at the ground for signs that people had passed through. He sniffed the air, testing for things of which only he knew. He muttered constantly to himself.

"What was it like with the long knives?" Circling Hawk asked after a while as they rode.

Zak thought for a moment. "It was confusion," he said, "and fear. They feel betrayed by the Dakota and believe the Dakota are out to kill them all."

"Betrayed?" Circling Hawk asked incredulously. "We are the ones who have been betrayed. Can they not see that?"

"They cannot see past their own ways, their own religions. They do not understand the Dakota way of life and never will."

"Then there is no hope for living together."

Zak considered this. "I don't think so," he finally said.

Circling Hawk rode quietly for a while. Then he spoke. "Did you have friends with the long knives?" he asked.

"There was one," Zak said, thinking of Buff Keegan with a sharp pang of separation. He wondered what the garrulous sergeant was doing right now.

175

"Friends like you and I are?" Circling Hawk asked.

Zak thought for a moment. "Yes," he said.

Circling Hawk considered this. "Then this is hard for you, this war," he said.

"Yes, it is."

Whirlwind turned on his mount, giving them a hard look. Zak and Circling Hawk looked at each other sheepishly and were quiet.

A couple of hours later they rose over a knoll and Whirlwind motioned for them to stop. He dismounted, motioned for them to stay, and then he was over the knoll on foot. Zak and the men looked at each other questioningly. Whirlwind must have seen something, Zak thought.

He did not have to wait long for an answer. In just a few minutes Whirlwind returned. He motioned for them to follow, and they turned and rode back a hundred or so yards to a grove of trees they had passed earlier. They could speak there with no one hearing them. Whirlwind motioned for them to dismount and then he spoke.

"There is a settler's farm just over the rise," Circling Hawk translated. "There is a family of three whites—a man, a woman, and a girl."

"Three whites? They're still there?" Zak asked incredulously. Circling Hawk nodded.

What are they doing here? Zak thought. Criminey! Hadn't they heard of the war? Why haven't they packed the wagon, grabbed old Bessie and hightailed it back east? He suddenly had a bad feeling, a very bad feeling, about this situation.

Whirlwind spoke again. "We are not to attack them," Circling Hawk said. "Remember Little Crow's words. We will go around them as stealthily as we can. We will all ride around together. Should they not see us, you . . . ," Circling Hawk pointed to Zak, "are to ride back to Little Crow and inform him, riding well around the farm."

Godspeed spoke.

"Why do we not attack?" Circling Hawk translated. "It is a small family and it is a good day to count coup."

Whirlwind spoke harshly. "It is Little Crow's wish. That is all you need to know. Is that understood?" Godspeed nodded sullenly.

176

They rode back to the knoll and followed Whirlwind's directions, hugging a treeline that shielded them. Zak looked down on the farm—it looked remarkably similar to the one he'd seen on their first day out of Fort Ridgely, the same style house, the same stable, and the same corn patch. The man and woman worked in the yard, shucking corn. The girl chopped wood.

Zak looked ahead. Whirlwind's route along the treeline would take them very close to the farm, almost too close, but there was no other way. On the other side of the farm flowed a river. Crossing it would put them in plain sight.

They rode slowly, Whirlwind first, followed by Circling Hawk, Zak, The Mouse, and finally, Godspeed. Just as they almost left the farm behind, a shot rang out behind Zak. He wheeled in his saddle just in time to see Godspeed pointing his rifle in the direction of the farm and firing another shot. Zak heard screaming and when he looked down on the farm he saw the man and the woman both on the ground, writhing in pain. The girl saw them and took off toward the river. Whirlwind called sharply to Godspeed. Godspeed, eyes blazing defiantly, looked at them and kicked his heels into the side of the horse, galloping away from them and onto the farm.

Whirlwind spoke sharply to them and they rode down after Godspeed. Zak realized they'd have to catch the girl, for she could easily sound the alarm throughout the countryside if she escaped. Zak fervently hoped that they could catch her before Godspeed got to her. She could be sent back, alive, to be with the other captives.

When they got near the house, Whirlwind, Circling Hawk, and the Mouse sped off to the north. Zak spurred Sunny past the house's south side.

Neither Godspeed nor the girl was in sight. He heard the hoofbeats of the others as they rode around well on the other side of the farm, searching. He'd have to look for them down here by himself.

Zak slowed Sunny to a walk and listened. At first he could hear nothing but the wind in the trees and the gurgling of the river as it moved over some rocks. But then, as he strained his ears, he could hear something off to the side, away from the river and back up in the direction from which they'd originally come. He turned Sunny and walked him slowly, cautiously, as he listened. There! He heard it again. He could hear the sounds of a struggle and a muffled cry.

Suddenly they were through a patch of thick scrub brush and into a tiny, open meadow. Directly ahead of them were Godspeed and the girl. He was on top of her, pinning her to the ground. With his left hand he covered her mouth. With his right he tore at her clothing.

"Godspeed!" Zak shouted. "Godspeed!"

Godspeed wheeled and appeared startled at seeing Zak. For an instant he paused, as if uncertain. But then he grinned wickedly.

What happened next seemed to take place slowly, sluggishly, as if all the movements were under water.

Zak watched, horrified, as Godspeed took his hatchet from his belt, raised it over the helpless girl, and chopped her head off.

Zak wheeled Sunny about and they bolted back the way they had come. Dizzy from fright and shock, he barely saw the house and stable of the farm as they flew by them. Sunny scrambled up the hill and past the treeline but Zak pushed him out onto the open plain. They raced through the grass, over the grass, until he heard the thunder of racing hooves beside them and saw a hardened hand reach and grab Sunny's reins firmly and expertly. They slowed to a run, and then a trot, and then a walk. When they stopped Zak looked up to see Whirlwind hand him back the reins, looking at him questioningly.

Circling Hawk arrived on his horse at that moment, followed closely by the Mouse. They had the same looks on their faces.

"He killed her!" Zak shouted. He still couldn't believe what he'd seen. His voice was choked and strained. "He killed her!"

When Circling Hawk translated this, Whirlwind looked at him somberly, silently. Then he turned his horse around, back toward the farm. Zak and the rest followed.

Godspeed was waiting for them at the treeline. He did not look at Whirlwind directly, his eyes shifting around between Zak, Circling Hawk, and the Mouse. Whirlwind spoke to him, shortly, curtly. Godspeed replied, gesturing to himself and then back at the farm. Whirlwind spoke again, and Godspeed replied again. Whirlwind shrugged, turned and spoke to Circling Hawk and then rode off at a walk. Godspeed followed him.

"Godspeed said that the white man saw him and fired at him first," Circling Hawk said.

"But that's a lie!" Zak said. He looked hard at Godspeed, who did not turn around to look back. "There were only two shots total! The man and the woman both went down! One bullet from Godspeed's gun couldn't hit them both at the same time!"

"Whirlwind said the same thing to him," Circling Hawk said. "But Godspeed repeated what he said."

"And he believed him? He couldn't have! Isn't he going to do anything?"

"It was not a matter of believing or not believing. Whirlwind, when he turned to me, said there is nothing to be done about it now. We have more pressing duties." Circling Hawk paused. "And he is right. What happened back there was not right, but what can we do?"

"We could at least bury them."

Circling Hawk looked at him. "It is not the Dakota way to bury the enemy dead," he said.

"But . . . ," Zak began.

Circling Hawk cut him off. "Including the settlers," he said. "Look. There is no time to do it anyway. We need to get to the town and scout it for Little Crow." He sighed. "If you stay, you may still be here when Little Crow arrives and he will not be pleased."

Zak shook his head. "I don't care. They didn't deserve that. The girl," he said. "At least the girl. I'll catch up to you, I swear." He thought of Hannah. The girl was about her age. "But I'm not going to let her lie out there and bloat in the sun and get torn apart by wolves."

"As you wish," Circling Hawk said resignedly. "You will need to ride hard to catch us."

For a minute after he buried the girl, Zak considered mounting Sunny and heading east, away from there, away from the death and destruction, away from everything. He could make St. Peter or Henderson in two days' ride. Assuming he wasn't shot by some Indians mistaking him for a soldier or some soldiers mistaking him for an Indian, that is.

"I'd just be running away from myself, anyway," Zak finally said to Sunny. He could no more abandon the Dakota now than he could have left the Army, even though he'd had plenty of chances.

After a couple of hours of hard riding he caught up with the rest of them. Circling Hawk smiled at him when he pulled alongside of them. Whirlwind acknowledged him with a grunt. Godspeed and the Mouse didn't look at him.

"We are almost there," Circling Hawk said. "When it gets dark we will steal into town. We will see how many people there are, if they have put up any defenses, and if there are any long knives there."

"We're going right into the town?" Zak asked.

"Everyone but you," Circling Hawk said with a rueful smile. "My brother says you are brave and strong, but you are not accustomed to the Dakota way of moving around quietly. He intends no disrespect but he doesn't want you giving them away with a wrong step."

"No disrespect taken," Zak said. Secretly, relief filled him. He'd had his share of dangerous missions. For a lifetime.

"But what will I do?" he asked.

"You will watch the horses," Circling Hawk said.

That sounds familiar, Zak thought.

When darkness fell he waited with the horses while the rest of them slipped off toward Hutchinson. Zak tried to keep his head empty—he was tired of thinking—but he couldn't, and soon he was reliving the events of the last few days. Haunting images seared his brain—the burning buildings, the unburied dead on the prairie, the surreal war dance in which he'd been. Over and over he saw Godspeed raise his hatchet over the cowering girl. Finally, distressed, he convinced himself to stop thinking and he sat with the horses in a state of wary half-sleep.

The scouts came back a couple of hours later, just about the time the bulk of Little Crow's force arrived. The men that camped outside the town that night were mostly silent. There were no fires, no war dances, no singing, and barely any talking above mere whispers. By the moonlight Zak saw the warriors lying pell-mell around the area, most asleep, some chatting quietly with those nearby. Whirlwind and Little Crow talked quietly and then they, too, stretched as if to sleep.

Circling Hawk slipped up next to him.

"What's happening?" Zak whispered. "What did you see?"

"There's a stockade around the center of the town," Circling Hawk said. "It is a square of four walls of heavy timber driven into the ground. Looks new. The town is abandoned all around it. Everyone must be inside the stockade."

"Is Little Crow going to attack?"

"Yes, at dawn. Whirlwind tried to talk him out of it, saying it is too well fortified, but Little Crow would have none of it." Circling Hawk paused. "He is getting desperate, I think."

"Why?"

"What you do not know is that except for our victory at the coulee, things have gone badly. I have heard Little Crow attempted twice to take New Ulm but it did not fall. The same with Fort Ridgely. Little Crow believes, I think, that if he does not win again soon that the chiefs will be displeased and he may lose the loyalty of his influential chiefs."

"Have there been any troubles about that?"

"I have heard there are those, like Wabasha, who want peace immediately and are attempting to negotiate secretly with Sibley. There is bad blood among some in the camp."

"What do you want to happen?" Zak asked.

"Like I told you before, I want peace, too, but not until we have some of what we have lost. I fear that is the division amongst us will defeat us, not Sibley and the long knives."

Zak watched the attack from a copse of trees on top of a low hill just outside of Hutchinson. As the sun rose Little Crow and the warriors descended upon the town with a fury, quickly setting the abandoned houses and businesses ablaze and surrounding the stockade. Warriors launched dozens of flaming arrows into the stockade, but the citizens inside raced about frantically putting out the fires almost as quickly as they started. He could hear their frenzied shouts above the din of thundering hooves and yelping warriors. Throughout the battle only one building inside the stockade was actually destroyed.

The citizens fired upon their attackers from holes carved out of the stout logs of the stockade. If the Dakota had cannon, Zak thought, they could lob balls down into the stockade. But the citizens were well protected from mere gunfire. Zak could see the Dakota grow frustrated with their lack of progress, resorting to launching an arrow attack that fell upon the inside of the stockade like a deadly rainfall. But those citizens that were repelling the attack were too close on the inside of the stockade wall to be hit, and those that were not participating the defense, the women and children mostly, stayed inside buildings and were unharmed. As the Dakota grew more desperate Little Crow ordered two or three wide trees cut down and they attempted to use them as battering rams to bash down the stockade doors. But the citizens had barricaded the doors well with wagons and the Dakota were denied entry.

About noon Little Crow called off the attack and the warriors withdrew, filing past Zak with defeated faces full of anger and frustration. Two warriors, including the Mouse, had been killed in the attack. The town outside the stockade had been heavily damaged, but the stockade itself still stood with its defenders largely unharmed. No scalps or captives had been taken. They rode silently, subdued, with many braves casting heated glares at Little Crow as he rode toward the head of the mile-long column.

The sour mood of the returning warriors infected the entire camp, and its inhabitants went about their business silently, the women tidying the teepees and cooking without acknowledgement from their sullen husbands, the children playing quietly without the normal attention from their fathers. An air of defeat hung like thick fog over the camp. Circling Hawk wondered aloud to Zak if the Dakota would spend the coming winter starving on the prairie, fleeing from a pursuing, vengeful army that would stop only when they were destroyed.

"The whites are as many as the stars in the sky, the branches on the trees," he said. "Now that our defeat is certain they will come down on us like wolves on a lame deer."

Shortly after arriving back in camp Whirlwind found Zak and motioned for him to follow him.

"He says Little Crow has sent for you," Circling Hawk said.

What did Little Crow want with him? Circling Hawk had told Zak that the camp was rife with rumors about Little Crow wanting to kill all the white and mixed-blood captives before the next battle. Surely he wouldn't revoke his clemency on Zak and toss him in with the mix, too. Or would he?

They entered Little Crow's teepee. Once his eyes adjusted to the dim light Zak saw Little Crow seated by the small fire, smoking a pipe. One side of him sat Mankato, on the other a boy who looked white, with sandy hair that covered his ears in curls. He looked a year or two older than Zak. They sat opposite the fire from Little Crow, who held up a piece of paper and spoke.

"He says he has a letter in English," Circling Hawk said to Zak, "that has been translated by several. But he wants to be sure what is in the letter, so he sent for you. Now read it to him and tell him what it is."

Little Crow handed Zak the letter. He squinted in the dim light and read aloud:

If Little Crow has any proposition to make, let him send two half-breeds under a flag of truce and they will be protected from harm.

Col. H. Sibley

Zak translated this for Little Crow, who nodded and spoke afterwards.

"He says others have translated it the same way," Circling Hawk said. "He says now he knows he can trust you. Sibley placed this note on a stick in the ground after the battle at the coulee. Little Crow is going to answer it. You are to take his Dakota words now and put them down in English," Circling Hawk said. "Then you will take them to Sibley at Fort Ridgely today." Little Crow gestured to the boy next to him. "You and this boy will go together, and you will return together," Circling Hawk said. Zak nodded at the boy, who nodded back.

Little Crow handed Zak a pen and inkwell and a piece of paper, and began to speak. As Circling Hawk translated, Zak wrote:

183

Dear Sir,

For what reason we have commenced this war, I will tell you. It is because we made a treaty with the government, and beg for what we do not get and then can't get it till our children are dying for hunger. It is the traders who commenced it. Mr. A. J. Myrick told the Indians they would eat grass or dirt. Then another told the Dakota they were not men. Then another was working with his friends to defraud us out of our moneys. If the young braves have pushed the white man, I have done this myself. So I want you to let Governor Ramsey know this. I have a great many prisoners, women and children. It is not all our fault. The Winne-bagoes were in the engagements, and two of them have been killed, too. I want you to give me an answer.

Yours truly

Friend Little Crow

Whirlwind handed Sunny's reins to Zak when he emerged from the teepee. He gripped Zak's shoulder and spoke.

"He says this is a dangerous task for you," Circling Hawk said.

"I know," Zak said. "But I am only a little afraid."

Whirlwind nodded when Circling Hawk translated and he pulled out a small sac, into which he dipped his fingers. When he removed them they were covered in blue paint. He daubed some on Sunny's face, little lines under and over each eye.

"That is to keep all evil spirits away," Circling Hawk said. "And to protect you on your journey."

"Thank you," Zak said, climbing into his saddle.

Whirlwind patted Sunny's flank. He spoke again.

"He says he will personally ensure the safety of your two young female friends," Circling Hawk translated.

Whirlwind grabbed Zak's left hand with his own right and squeezed it hard. They looked hard into each other's eyes. When Whirlwind released his hand he turned and strode off without looking back.

Zak and Circling Hawk clasped hands.

"Let us hope that your mission brings us better circumstances," Circling Hawk said.

Zak nodded. "I hope so," he said.

Circling Hawk pulled a knife from his belt. In one swift move he slit his palm. Showing no emotion, he grabbed Zak's hand and slit it. Zak winced, but did not cry out. He was taken by surprise, so it didn't hurt that much. Removing a rawhide loop from a sack on his belt, Circling Hawk tied their bleeding hands together tightly.

They were blood brothers.

And then he, too, was gone.

Zak could have no idea that when he next saw him, it would be under the most dire of circumstances.

16. *Awful Things From the Frontier*

"DO YOU speak English?" Zak asked the other boy as they rode side-by-side away from the camp.

"Yes," the boy said.

"What's your name?"

"Campbell, Tom Campbell. What's yours?"

"Zak Hammer," he answered. Or is it Horse Dreamer? he thought. He looked at his palm, which had stopped bleeding. The pain had come now, throbbing. He flexed his fingers.

"You from around here?" Zak asked Campbell.

"Yeah. I lived up at the mission at the Upper Agency."

Zak looked at him, again thinking he looked white. "Your father was a missionary?"

"Not really. He was just the superintendent of the mission."

"Is he white?"

"Yes. He is from Scotland."

"Scotland? Is that in Great Britain?"

"I think so," Campbell answered.

"How about your mother?"

"She is mixed, too. We were captured and held captive by Little Crow."

"Your father, too?" Zak asked.

"My father was killed," Campbell said.

"I'm sorry." Again, it seemed like so little to say. They rode silently for a while. Campbell did not ask about Zak's life, and Zak did not offer to tell of it. He'd done enough thinking and talking about it recently.

"Do you have the message Little Crow wrote?" Campbell asked.

Zak tapped his breast pocket. "Right here," he said.

Campbell looked as if he wanted to say something else, but didn't dare. "What?" Zak finally asked.

"What?" Campbell responded, shrugging.

"You want to say something else," Zak said.

Campbell was quiet for a moment. "I'm carrying another message," he finally said.

"Another message?" Zak asked. He was confused. "From Little Crow?"

"No. From the 'Friendlies.' It's a secret."

"The 'Friendlies'? Who are they?"

"The Sioux that want peace right away, without using the captives as trade like Little Crow wishes."

"Are you joking?" Zak asked, incredulous. "If Little Crow would have found out, you'd have been dead!"

"I know," Campbell said. "I couldn't wait to leave the village." Campbell paused. "While we are away the Friendlies are going to break away from the main camp, and take the captives with them for safekeeping until Sibley arrives."

"What!" Zak said. "They'll fight each other! Little Crow won't allow that!"

"Maybe not, but there are a lot who will be in the Friendly camp. And I am glad. My mother can be saved then."

Zak pondered this for a moment. So they carried two messages, one from each of what will be two opposing Dakota camps. Zak shook his head. Just when he thought things couldn't get any stranger, and when he'd thought he'd seen it all, came this bizarre development.

"Well, we'd better have our stories straight then," Zak said. "Sibley is going to have a hard time deciding whether to believe us both. He may think it's a trick. But if we share the same details about the camp, and about our missions, we'll be credible and he just may believe us both."

"All right," Campbell said, and they discussed what they remembered. Soon they had it boiled down to a few critical details and facts to which they would stick, no matter what the question would be.

After a while they passed the ruins of the Lower Agency, crossed the river, and were only a few miles from Fort Ridgely. Zak began to get nervous. There were bound to be trigger-happy army pickets as they got closer. He tried to heighten his senses, increase his wariness. I didn't come this far and for so long to get shot now, he thought.

"We need a flag of truce," he said to Campbell.

Campbell nodded solemnly. "I've been thinking the same thing." They looked at their clothing, as well as each other's. Neither of them wore anything white. They rode in silence, thinking.

"There!" Zak suddenly exclaimed. Just off the road a hundred yards or so was a Dakota burial scaffold, over which was stuck a pole with white sheeting fastened to it. As they rode closer, however, Zak saw that dead in the center of the sheet was painted a blue circle.

"That won't work," Campbell said. "I've never heard of a flag of truce with a blue circle. That'll get us shot at for sure."

"Maybe, maybe not," Zak said. "But it's all we got for now. I'll do some thinking about it as we get closer."

He tried but could come up with no alternatives until they got to an abandoned farm. He had a thought. "Let's go inside," he said.

Everything in the house had been taken or destroyed, but when they went in the cellar they found a keg of soft soap. "There!" Zak exclaimed. "There's our answer!"

Campbell understood, nodding silently. He stooped to pick up the barrel and hoisted it on his shoulder. "There's a creek about a mile and a half from the fort, and we can try it there," he said.

It was easier said than done. At the creek they scrubbed and scrubbed the sheeting with the soap, but the blue circle stubbornly fought them. After a while the circle grew faint, but the otherwise white sheeting had taken on a somewhat bluish hue. They looked at each other.

"It'll have to do," Campbell said.

Zak nodded. "We have no other choice." He mounted Sunny. "Here, give that to me," he said to Campbell. Campbell handed him the sheeting and mounted his own horse. Zak raised the sheeting over his head and together they rode for the fort.

The pickets met them before they even saw the fort. Four soldiers emerged from a near-hidden redoubt of logs and dirt and called for them to stop. Two, a private and a corporal, came from behind the redoubt. The corporal pointed a pistol at them while the private trained his rifle on them.

"Who're you?" said the corporal when they were within a few feet of each other.

"We've been sent by Little Crow with a message for Colonel Sibley," Zak said.

"That's *General* Sibley to you," said the corporal, not too politely.

189

"Oh, I am sorry," Zak said. "Has he recently been promoted?"

"Lincoln's own order," said the corporal.

The corporal must have been briefed about Sibley leaving a message for Little Crow, for he said, "We've been expecting someone like you." He put his pistol down. "Let's see the message."

"I'm afraid I can't do that," said Zak. "It's to be delivered to the general and no one else."

The corporal measured him coolly. "All right, you stick to that until you get to Sibley," he finally said. "Follow me." To the remaining soldiers in the redoubt he said, "You two stay here. We'll be back out in a few minutes."

A detachment of soldiers soon escorted them past the outlying buildings and into the quadrangle of the fort. The soldiers inside stared at them with cold hatred, and Zak guessed they viewed anyone from Little Crow's camp as a hostile and a murderer. Soldiers searched Zak and Campbell roughly and took their horses from them. Then Zak and Campbell were separated. On his way to Sibley, a booming voice resonated behind him.

"Youngster! Damn, is that you?"

Zak and his escort, a young corporal, turned at the exclamation. Zak's heart leapt as he saw Sergeant Buff Keegan bounding towards him. Before he could react Buff had him in a bear hold, and Zak could barely breathe as the life was nearly squeezed out of him.

"Youngster! I'll be dipped in sheep dung!" He pushed Zak away to arm's length, squeezing his shoulders. He looked at Zak, beaming, as if he'd been gone for years. It sure felt like years, Zak thought.

"It *is* you, by gum!" Buff continued. "I thought fer sure you were a dead duck! When you didn't return from gettin' water at the coulee I figgered yer hair'd been lifted! I been beatin' myself up over it, since it was my call sent ya down there!"

"Hello, Buff," Zak said, grinning widely. "You're a sight for sore eyes. You sure are."

"Well, ahm glad ta hear it," Buff said. "It just ain't been the same around here since you been gone. Yer pal Dougal Black's been mighty uppity and there ain't been nobody to whip his tail and keep 'im in line like you done. Besides, it's been boring, *boring*, settin' here at this fort doin' nothin'. Man can only drink whiskey and sit on his thumbs for so long `for he itches ta do *somethin'*."

"C'mon, let's go," the corporal said impatiently. "You two can chew the fat later."

Buff shot the corporal a murderous look, but held his tongue. "All right," he said coolly. He turned smiling eyes back to Zak. "You catch up with me later, lil' buddy, ya hear?"

"I hear," said Zak.

Sibley sat eating dinner in his quarters. Zak saluted. When Sibley saw him a shadow of surprise passed over his face, but only for a moment. He saluted back and motioned for Zak to be seated opposite him at the table.

"Well, young Hammer," he said. Zak was surprised he remembered his name. "We thought you'd been killed at Birch Coulee. They told me you never returned from your canteen mission."

"I was captured, sir," Zak said.

"Indeed!" Sibley said. "That's unusual. The Sioux normally don't take male captives."

"I was recognized by some of my kin," Zak said. He didn't feel he needed to elaborate further. Something told him to be cautious.

"Fortunate for you!" Sibley said. "What did they do with you then? Were you in the camp with the rest of the captives?"

"Yes, sir," Zak said, although that wasn't entirely true. He hadn't been *held* with the captives, but he *had been* in the same camp as them. He had decided long before arriving at the fort that the less they knew about his time at Little Crow's camp, the better. He had not been sent as a spy into the Dakota camp so he felt no obligation to tell more than he was asked. Further, he had not deserted the Army and he had not committed any treasonous acts, he reasoned, but anything—any type of consortium with the Dakota they knew of—would be liable to get him an appointment with the hangman's noose when it was all over.

"Indeed!" said Sibley again. He watched Zak closely, watching for anything that would indicate he was lying. He was obviously disappointed with the shortness of Zak's answers.

Suddenly he smiled and changed the subject. "I'm afraid I have forgotten my manners," he said. "Here I sit eating right in front of you and I haven't offered you anything. Are you hungry?"

191

"I could eat something, sir," Zak said, eyeing the food greedily.

"Of course. Of course. Lieutenant," he said to his hovering adjutant, "See to it that this young man is given the same meal I just had. Roast beef, potatoes and turnips." The adjutant clicked his heels together and left. "You have no idea how many cattle we had to confiscate from farms to feed the men," he said to Zak conspiratorially, winking.

"Yes, sir," Zak said.

Sibley read the note from Little Crow. "So he wants to use the captives as leverage," he mumbled mostly to himself. "He has murdered many people already without any sufficient cause. If he returns the prisoners first, then I will talk with him like a man. But only in that way. I will send such a reply tomorrow."

After a pause, while they waited for Zak's food, Sibley discussed the campaign so far. "Birch Coulee was a dreadful setback, to be sure," he said. "The newspapers in St. Paul have blamed me for that, but they do not know the realities of conducting an Indian war on the frontier. A commander is only as good as his subordinates. Captain Grant and Major Brown were in charge at Birch Coulee, and failed me by placing the camp where it was. They failed me, they failed the men, and they failed the wives and families of the dozens that perished."

Zak found himself silently agreeing with Sibley. Grant and Brown had caused the needless loss of many soldiers. But it all flows from the top down, from the General to his subordinates, he also thought.

"But we have pushed far into the wilderness, causing Little Crow to seek refuge farther and farther west," Sibley continued. "In just a few days the Third Minnesota will be joining us from down south and we will be 2,000 strong. Little Crow will not defeat such a force."

Again, Zak found himself agreeing with Sibley. The sad end of a proud nation was at hand, not by conquest, but by being overwhelmed by sheer numbers.

The adjutant arrived with Zak's meal and he ate politely but with gusto, answering the general's questions between mouthfuls. Yes sir, he had seen Little Crow himself. No sir, Little Crow did not confide in him any of his plans. Yes sir, Little Crow participated personally in the fighting. No sir, he did not personally see him kill anyone. No sir,

192

he hadn't seen all the captives. Yes sir, he'd heard they were still alive when he left. Yes sir, there was division among the Dakota, as attested by the secret note Campbell carried.

Apparently satisfied with Zak's answers, and apparently believing them to be true, Sibley left abruptly after his questioning with a curt order for him to report to him the next day for further duties. Little Crow *had* told Zak to return after delivering the message, but it looked like Sibley's order meant he would not be returning any time soon.

But no further duties came the next day, or the next day after that, or for the better part of two weeks. Sibley did not move the Army from Fort Ridgely, still playing his maddening waiting game. Zak heard he waited for more replacements and supplies. He still waited for the right opportunity, whatever that would be. He waited, waited, waited.

The air was cool, and it rained almost every day. The soldiers, cooped up in their tents outside the fort, fell into a routine of alternating frustration and boredom, and it took its toll. Fights and drunkenness increased, and the mood began to turn sour.

An epidemic of lice made its way through the ranks. The soldiers called them "graybacks." The wriggling little creatures disgusted Zak at first. He tried boiling his clothes to get rid of them, but most of them remained. After a couple of days of this, they got somewhat used to them. He and Buff counted the lice on each other—he had twenty on him; Buff had thirty-three on him. In the end they eliminated all of them only by picking them off each other and breaking them in two—like uncooked rice—between the nails of their thumbs and forefingers.

Zak managed to stay clear of Dougal Black, whose squad was well on the other side of the fort. He and Buff caught up on things and chewed the fat, as the corporal had said, but they, too grew restless. They played checkers and soon it grew into a sort of company tournament.

Still, Zak was restless. He had no desire to see further war between the Army and the Dakota, but he wanted *something* to happen, something that would break the ice and bring the situation to a close.

Yet a ray of sunshine penetrated the gloom, radiating warmth into Zak's heart. It came in the form of a letter with a return address of St. Paul and addressed to "Master Zakarias Hammer, U.S. Army, Minnesota Indian Campaign With General Sibley." Zak's head swam and his hands shook as he read:

Dearest Zak,

It has been weeks since I saw you last and I can't bear the silence any more. Now that I have stable living conditions I am taking the chance of writing you in hopes you will receive this and will be able to write me. I am living with my mother at my aunt's (her sister's) in St. Paul. The address here is on the front of the envelope.

I have heard only the most awful things from the frontier where you are and I pray nightly that they have avoided you. I play little games with myself, trying to guess what you have been doing. What have you seen? Are you frightened? When will I see you next?

I think about you all the time. Do you think about me?

All my love,

Hannah

What? Zak thought. Did he think about her? What a question! He hadn't been able to stop thinking of her since he'd met her! He read the letter again, and again, and again. She signed it *All my love*! A tremendous urge to see her filled him, tugging on his head and heart with a force heavier than gravity.

He sat down to write a letter. He wanted to tell her about everything—the slaughtered citizens; the battle of Birch Coulee; his capture; his time with the Dakota and his kin; Godspeed; and his meetings with Little Crow. He wanted to tell her that, yes, he was frightened, but it was better when he was able to think of her. But

194

when he set the pen to paper he found it was more difficult than he thought it would be—for some reason he found himself unable to write about what he'd seen. He came up with only a wishy-washy letter of two paragraphs stating he was happy Hannah was safe and that he would find her whenever he got to St. Paul. The letter conveyed the most essential information, and Hannah couldn't help but get the picture that Zak felt strongly about her, too, but it was not the romantic masterpiece he'd wanted. He sent it off, desperately wishing he could go with it.

Finally, at the end of the second week of September of 1862, something broke the ice and set the next chain of events in motion. Zak and the soldiers heard that after the Union defeat at the second battle of Bull Run, President Lincoln fired his ill-starred commander, Major General John Pope, and dispatched him to Minnesota to assume overall leadership of the war against the Dakota. The word was that Pope was breathing heavily down Sibley's back for closure, once and for all, of the conflict. Pope's career hinged on his success in Minnesota and he would not allow Henry Sibley to muck it up with his infernal delays. He told Sibley in no uncertain terms that he had better move against Little Crow, and soon.

Once joined by the Third Minnesota Regiment, they moved out. The Third Minnesota, true to what Sibley had said earlier, had been surrendered by their squeamish, incompetent officers in Tennessee. Paroled by the Confederates, they straggled home. Reassembled at Fort Snelling, Governor Ramsey sent them to Sibley. Sullen, disgraced, they were eager to fight Little Crow to gain some sort of redemption.

Again they rode by the ruins of the Lower Agency. Zak sighed resignedly. He decided that when this cruel war was over he would never come here again. Not ever.

Zak was sent forward with the other scouts and just past the Agency they came upon a strange sight—hundreds of three-foot tall poles stuck upright in the ground. When the head of the column of soldiers arrived shortly thereafter, Sibley and the officers sat in their saddles, gaping, confused at the spectacle.

Sibley counted the sticks. "Seven hundred thirty eight," he said. "What the devil do you suppose it is?"

"Maybe it's some religious thing," an officer volunteered.

"Maybe it's a burial ground," another said.

Not even close, Zak thought. He remembered the day he'd ridden out on the Hutchinson raid with the three hundred Dakota warriors. Half the total number, Circling Hawk had said. Zak knew that the seven hundred thirty eight poles in front of them represented the number of braves awaiting the Army.

Little Crow was taunting them.

On their fourth day out they camped near Wood Lake, more a marsh than a lake. Sibley sent Zak south to scout. The prairie seemed abandoned. As he neared camp upon his return, he heard a low rumbling.

Cannon!

Zak sped Sunny up and within an hour he was back with the Army. But it was already all over.

"What happened, sir?" he asked the nearest officer he could find, a young lieutenant.

"We were lyin' around," the lieutenant said, "and some of the boys heard there were some potato fields nearby, so they got their shovels and set out to find them. Sibley hasn't been much on keepin' those new boys from the Third in line, you know. Well, just outside of camp they surprised some redskins who were just lyin' in the grass! Turns out they were pickets, of sort, and when the shootin' started, why, if the whole redskin force didn't come down on us, whoopin' and makin' the most God-awful sounds I ever heard!"

"What!" Zak exclaimed. "So what happened next?"

"Well, there was a sharp fight," said the lieutenant. "Them Indians circled and circled us but we kept 'em at bay. They sure can ride them ponies, but they didn't have any type of coordinated attack, just kind of rode around pell-mell. A few of our boys went down, but it coulda been worse. When they brought up the cannon and started sprayin' canister out there, them savages packed it in and skedaddled. Look, I gotta go." He pointed out to the prairie just outside of camp. "Go see fer yerself."

196

Zak rode Sunny out to the battlefield. Chaos still reigned. Dead and wounded soldiers lay scattered about. The wounded moaned, asking for water, babbling, crying. Harried staff medics attended the wounded, Doc Mayo among them. Zak stopped and dismounted by one soldier, a private who looked even younger than him. The boy sat, dazed, rubbing his neck with a blood-covered hand. Zak was amazed at how bright red the blood was.

"You need some water?" Zak asked the boy.

The boy looked up at him with glassy, shock-dulled eyes. "Sure," he said weakly.

Zak knelt and held the canteen to the boy's mouth. He gulped eagerly, and the cool water seemed to revive him. He looked incredulously at his bloody hand.

"I—I been hit!" he exclaimed, as if it were the last thing he'd ever expected.

Zak felt the wound—it looked only like a deep scratch. The boy recoiled, but didn't cry out. Zak nodded to himself. There was a long bloody gash, but no puncture wound.

"What's your name?" Zak asked.

"Robert," he answered meekly.

"I'm Zak. Pleased to meet you." He felt like a seasoned veteran compared to this boy.

"You too."

"It's just a flesh wound," Zak told the boy. "The ball must've just grazed you. You're gonna be all right."

The boy breathed a sigh of relief, but then winced. "Mighty painful for just a flesh wound," he boy said.

"Reckon so," Zak said. "Here, do you want some more water?"

"Much obliged." The boy drank eagerly again.

Zak ripped off one of his shirttails. "Here," he said, handing it to the boy. "You just hold that back there. Put lots of pressure on it. The medics will get to you soon. You're gonna be just fine."

The boy seemed reassured by Zak's words, for he smiled. "Much obliged," he said again. He chuckled. "Never thought it could happen to me."

"Most guys don't," Zak said.

197

As Zak continued his ride around the scene, he spotted a group of soldiers gathered around something on the ground. As he got closer he saw the soldiers bending over a dead Dakota. They were stripping the Indian of his jewelry and trinkets, for souvenirs, no doubt. Then one soldiers produced a knife and cut one of the man's ears off.

Zak, revolted, opened his mouth as if to say something when General Sibley burst upon the scene on his stallion.

"You men!" he shouted angrily, stabbing his riding crop at them. "Get out of there! Leave that redskin alone! We are not the savages here!" He called out so that everyone around him could hear. "From now on it's courts martial for any men caught desecrating the dead!"

The men dispersed, grumbling to themselves. The man who cut off the ear threw it down, looking as if he was marking the spot to fetch it later.

Zak looked appraisingly at Sibley. Maybe he had misjudged him, he thought. He might not be the best commander, he thought, but he was still a gentleman, preserving the dignity of the fallen Dakota warriors. That counts for something.

But when the grumbling men were gone Zak heard Sibley say to his aide, "Get that stinking corpse out of here and bury it with the other savages in the common grave. Luckily they carry off most of their dead."

After Wood Lake the end came quickly for the Dakota. The scouts saw no sign of the once-formidable warrior force, and the word came that most had fled to the northwest, toward the Big Stone Lake and into Dakota territory. Although Little Crow, Shakopee, and Medicine Bottle escaped, the Dakota fled without many of their top warriors, including Mankato, killed at Wood Lake by a bouncing cannonball some said he refused to dodge.

Two days after the battle the Army marched into the camp of the Friendlies, flags flying, drums beating and fifes playing. The Friendlies, by advance agreement, turned over the hundreds of captives. "Camp Release," as Sibley had dubbed it, was at once a poignant and pathetic place. While the white women and children and the captive mixed-bloods wept with joy and relief at being liberated, the remaining Dakota, subdued and worried about their fate, coddled to Sibley in an effort to win his favor. White flags of truce flew everywhere: on top of the teepees, on poles stuck in the ground, tied to horses' manes. They waved the Stars and Stripes incessantly, and one Dakota wrapped a flag around his soldiers, pointing to himself and saying, "Me good Indian" over and over. The whole scene saddened Zak. It was a pitiful spectacle that stood in sharp contrast to the camp of proud and independent people in which he'd been only weeks before.

Sibley took all Dakota from Camp Release, women and children included, and placed them in a makeshift camp of internment nearby, merely a fenced-in area of an open field, a human corral. He sent mixed-blood couriers into the surrounding countryside to inform any holdouts that it was better to surrender and be treated humanely as a prisoner of war rather than to be hunted down and killed like rabid dogs. Later still, he sent word into the countryside that, despite the preceding conflict, the government annuity had finally arrived and would be dispersed to any Dakota who reported for a roll call at the ruins of the Lower Agency. It was merely a ruse. When more Dakota emerged from hiding and showed up to be counted and paid, they were quickly disarmed and placed into captivity with the rest. Almost fifteen hundred Dakota were rounded up through these methods and, incredibly, over three hundred of these were men identified as having participated in the conflict. They would now stand trial as "war criminals" and be hanged if convicted.

A couple of days after the annuity trick Buff approached Zak somberly. Silently he thrust a piece of paper at him. Zak looked questioningly, but Buff did not elaborate. Zak read the paper, and his stomach dropped.

He sat, holding his head in one hand and the paper in the other. He looked at it unbelievingly again. It was the list of the condemned Dakota. He looked up and away, desperately hoping that when he set eyes on the paper again, the name would be gone.

But when looked down he saw, through his tears, that the name was still there, and it read: *Cetan Okinyan.* Circling Hawk.

BOOK III:

Horse Dreamer

INDICTMENT

Charge and Specifications against one "Cetan Okinyan," also known as "Circling Hawk," of the Sioux Tribe of Indians.

Charge. MURDER.

Specification 1st. In this that the said defendant did, at or near Hutchinson, Minnesota, on or about the 4th day of September, 1862, join in a war party of Sioux tribe of Indians against citizens of the United States, and did with his own hand murder a white man and two white women, one being a child, all peaceable citizens of the United States.

Specification 2nd. In this that the said defendant did, at various times and places between the 17th of August, 1862, and the 28th of September, 1862, join and participate in the murders and massacre of soldiers of the United States Army committed by the Sioux Indians on the Minnesota frontier. By the order of:

Gen. H. H. Sibley, Com. Mil. Expedition.
Dated: October 5, 1862

Witnesses: Godspeed, a colored man connected with the Sioux tribe of Indians; Zakarias Hammer, associated with the United States Army.

17. Maniacs or Wild Beasts

THE LEAVES on the trees fought valiantly against the October chill to stay alive, straining in brilliant reds, oranges, and yellows before deadening to dull browns and blacks. Each morning a slight glaze frosted the tips of the long bluestem grass, now faded to a dull maize. The lakes cooled quickly, wisps of steam rising as misty ghosts from the water. Soon the nighttime temperatures would dip below the freezing point, and, although the day would provide brief respite with a lukewarm sun and tantalizing mildness, the lakes would freeze with only a few open patches of water in which migrating geese could rest before heading for Mexico. The winds turned vicious, massing with the savage Canadian packs of frigid air and racing wildly over the prairie, snapping hungrily at its occupants, maelstroms of dead leaves and stinging dirt punishing the weak and unprepared. It would only be weeks, days even, before snow buried the flat land, when the icy-sheened wasteland would just as well be the surface of a great frozen sea.

The Army and the captive Dakota shared the bitter wasteland near the ruins of the Lower Agency. The city of teepees belonging to the captives lay heavily guarded by soldiers on its perimeter by General Sibley. The war-crimes trials lay just over the horizon, and he had no intention of letting anyone escape.

Sibley maintained his field residence and command in one of the two houses that had escaped the Dakota torches. The other, a simple one-story log home, would be a makeshift courtroom.

Zak attempted several times to see General Sibley about Circling Hawk, but Sibley's aides granted no audience until Sergeant Buff Keegan intervened. Finally Sibley sent for him, the messenger informing Zak he had "about five minutes" to say what he had to say, for the General was a busy man with the trials and all.

"Your cousin is charged with two counts of murder," the general said, reading from some papers. "One specific, one general. First, he is charged with the murder of three white settlers in the vicinity of Hutchinson, Minnesota. Second, he is charged with aiding and abetting the murders of soldiers of the United States Army." The general looked up at Zak. "Extremely serious charges for which he will probably hang. I am sorry."

Stunned, Zak asked, "Are there witnesses to prove these charges?"

"Of course," the general said.

"Who?" asked Zak.

"Their identities are being withheld until they testify," the general answered. "To prevent any tampering or influence upon them. But I can assure you that I do not propose to try and execute any man, even a savage, without due process."

Zak thought. He didn't know whether Circling Hawk had killed any soldiers. It didn't seem like that should be an offense for which a person could be executed; after all, this was war. Soldiers got killed in war. But the first charge, the killing of the whites, was indeed serious. Zak's mind raced. He had been with Circling Hawk on the raid of Hutchinson, and hadn't seen him kill any settlers. There were those three people at the farm, but Godspeed had been the one that had killed them. He simply didn't see Circling Hawk kill anyone then, and couldn't see how there could be a witness to some killings that hadn't occurred. This he told to General Sibley.

Sibley shook his head. "I understand your concern for your cousin," he said. "But I assure you there will be proof at trial." ·

Sibley's adjutant strode in, interrupting them. "There is a Bishop Whipple to see you, sir," said the adjutant.

"Whipple? Here? Now?" The general seemed perplexed and a bit irritated. But he quickly recovered. "Oh, very well, send him in here in a minute." He looked at Zak. "You may stay while he visits. He is the Bishop of the Episcopal Church of Minnesota. I have mentioned him to you before. You will find him very interesting. Here is a man who truly loves the Indians. They call him `Straight Tongue,' for he supposedly has done much for their cause. You may wish to bend his ear about your cousin, for he is influential." But then he sniffed haughtily. "Not that his gilded oratory will influence me at all," he said.

Bishop Whipple entered, and Zak saw a tall man with a round face and shoulder-length graying hair, dressed almost completely in black: black suit, black overcoat, black hat, and black gloves, black boots. The only thing that wasn't black was his white button-down shirt, and that was offset by a black bow tie. He peered at them with hard, steel-blue eyes. Wise eyes, Zak thought. Eyes that saw and understood everything. Zak knew as soon as he saw the bishop that he was a man to be reckoned with.

"Bishop, how good it is to see you," Sibley said, extending his hand. The bishop strode purposefully across the floor and grasped the general's hand firmly, but with his left. His right was immobile and heavily bandaged. They shook hands, looking at each other. And, to Zak's amazement, Sibley dropped his eyes once, just the slightest bit, but it was still noticeable. The bishop intimidates him! Zak thought. Henry Hastings Sibley—pioneer, fur company magnate, former territorial governor and conqueror of the Sioux Indians, was intimidated by the bishop of a church!

"General Sibley, the pleasure is mine," said Whipple eloquently. "How are you? Our president Mr. Lincoln sends his regards and hopes you are enjoying your promotion."

"The president?" Sibley asked a little sheepishly. "You've seen the president recently?"

"I have," Bishop Whipple said, removing his hat in a dignified manner and sitting across the table from Sibley. He cast a glance at Zak and smiled.

"Of course," Sibley said, sitting. "Forgive me. How could I forget that your cousin is General Halleck at the War Department and that he is in close contact with the president?"

The bishop waved his hand. "It is quite all right," he said, smiling tolerantly. "I have found that my memory is disappearing as quickly as the years pass. Although you are much younger than I."

"Not much younger," Sibley said. Then he seemed to see the bishop's bandages for the first time. "If I may ask, Bishop, what is the matter with your hand? It is not serious I hope."

"I believe it was poisoned when I was helping with the wounded in St. Peter right after the outbreak," Whipple said. "I had a wound of my own—from shoeing a horse, of all things—and it was not quite healed when I helped bandage many bleeding people. I think it was a mixing of bad blood with mine, although from whom I do not know."

"I see," the general said. "And the physicians have not been able to cure it?"

"Ah, the physicians," the bishop said, "with their purgings and bleedings and obsessive love of amputations. One is probably better off appealing directly to God for healing and leaving the physicians out of the equation." He smiled. "In any event, the sickness comes and goes. I'm hoping it will improve in the near future."

The general nodded, signaling an end to the polite conversation. "Before we get to whatever business you have brought, let me introduce you one who is truly young," he said, referring to Zak. "This is Master Zak Hammer, who is under my direct charge. He has performed admirably as a messenger for me. He has also had the fortune—or misfortune, as some would see it—of seeing our terrible conflict from both sides."

"Is that so?" asked Whipple, turning towards Zak. "I should like to hear more about it in due time."

"Yes, sir," Zak said.

"Bishop, I am at your service," Sibley said. "What can I do for you today?"

"I am sure, General, that you knew the reason the moment you learned I was here," the bishop said wryly. "It is about this Indian business. I go to Washington three times a year to plead for my poor Indians. Sometimes with the Army, other times with the Congress, sometimes even with the president, as I did recently. I anticipate going there again this fall. I wish to see only the fair treatment of the Indians. I, along with the elders of my church and bishops from neighboring states, are gravely concerned about the trials and possible executions you have planned here on the frontier."

There it was. The bishop did not mince words. Right from the start the bishop let it be known that if he did not like what Sibley had planned, Abraham Lincoln himself would hear it!

The general drew a breath. "I seek only to punish the individuals who have committed murder and outrages upon white settlers."

"Perhaps you can tell me, then, why you have made the killing of white soldiers in battle a capital crime?" Whipple spoke crisply, demandingly. "Perhaps you can tell me why you intend to summarily try all adult males instead of making an investigation and trying those the evidence shows committed outrages against the settlers?"

The general produced a letter from his field desk. "Let me show something to you," he said. Whipple read the letter, and passed it to Zak, who read:

General Sibley:

The horrible massacres of women and children and the outrageous abuse of female prisoners, still alive, call for punishment beyond human power to inflict. There will be no peace in this region by virtue of treaties and Indian faith. It is my purpose utterly to exterminate the Sioux if I have the power to do so and even if it requires a campaign lasting the whole of next year. Destroy everything belonging to them, capture and execute the villains, and drive the rest out to the plains. They are to be treated as maniacs or wild beasts.

Maj. Gen. John Pope, U.S. Army

"So, you see, that is the pressure I am getting from above," Sibley said. "It was my intention at the beginning to conduct only a court of inquiry, designed to collect information for later use in prosecutions, but with no authority to pass judgment or sentences. But with a directive like this," he said, pointing to the letter from General Pope, "I must go farther. The plan has been adopted to subject all the grown men, with a few exceptions, to an investigation of the commission, trusting that the innocent will make their innocence appear. We will conduct trials and pass judgment, authorizing and carrying out the punishment of those convicted. General Pope has approved and ordered only this specific type of proceeding."

"I see," the bishop said. "Guilty until proven innocent, eh? I do not need to remind you, sir, that in the great courts of our nation it has always been the opposite: innocent until proven guilty. It is a hallowed principle and, combined with the placement of the burden of proof upon the prosecution, form the core of what is important in our system. To reverse that would be an abomination."

"This will not be a criminal trial before a jury of citizens," the general said. "It will be a military tribunal. The standards for a tribunal are not as high as in a criminal trial."

"Precisely!" Whipple boomed. "Innocent men may be convicted and sentenced to death! There is a broad distinction between the guilt of men who went through the country committing fiendish violence, massacring women and babes with the spirits of demons, and those who only participated in battles against soldiers and citizens!"

The general sighed. "This power of life and death is an awful thing to exercise," he said. "But, Bishop, this thing has taken on a life all its own. The wheels are in motion and can't be stopped. I have always valued your counsel, Bishop, but I fear your sympathies for the Indians cloud your judgment. If I do not visit quick and sharp retribution upon the Sioux, the people of this state will take the law into their own hands. Mob violence will rule, and none—including the women and children—will be saved." He threw his hands in the air. "Why, here in my own camp I am having trouble curbing the abuses of my own men. I have punished seven men already for abuses of the male captives, and I have also found the greatest difficulty in keeping them from the squaws. Some of them still manage to get among the gals."

He paused. "What I am going to do may not exactly be the type of 'due process' our forefathers imagined, but it is that amount of process, consistent with political realties, that is due the Sioux at this point in time." Sibley did not look the bishop in the eye when he delivered this short speech. Zak guessed that Sibley was not entirely sure about his authority to conduct the trials.

"Surely the prisoners will be granted counsel for their defense!" said Whipple.

"Not defense counsel *per se,*" Sibley said, hesitatingly. He was growing more uncomfortable as the bishop revealed, one by one, the flaws of the proposed system. "But one of my officers who will sit on the court is a lawyer in civilian life," Sibley continued, "as is the man who will record the proceedings. They are good Christians and I have directed them to intervene any time they see a violation of an individual's rights."

Whipple shook his head. He drew a breath and looked Sibley in the eye. "The law's final justification is in the good it does or fails to do to the society in a given place and time," he said sternly. "For years the Sioux have been treated as sub-human, less than human, by a dishonest government—a *Christian* government—and cheating Indian agents. A nation that sows robbery will reap a harvest of blood! That is what happened. You will merely perpetuate this harvest with your court of questionable legitimacy and purpose."

Sibley sat quietly. He had no further argument to give. Finally he turned his palms upward in a sign of closure. "What will happen will happen," he said. "Unless you are able to convince General Pope and Governor Ramsey that it should be different, many Sioux will be executed shortly."

After they were dismissed from the general's house, Whipple turned to Zak, putting on his hat and gloves. "The general must be fond of you if he let you sit through our conversation," he said.

"Perhaps, sir. He does not show any overt signs of affection, but he has treated me properly and well."

"How is it that you have come to see this dreadful war from both sides?" Whipple asked. He listened with great interest as Zak told him. Zak told him everything, including the details of the raid on Hutchinson. He felt that he could trust this man, and that he might do some good, help Circling Hawk, with the information he gave him.

"How difficult for you," Whipple said when Zak had finished. "I should think all of these events, happening so soon to one so young, would have left you weak and ill. But I see that you have grown strong, and that these experiences have benefited you in ways you do not yet recognize."

He offered his hand to Zak to shake. "The matters regarding your cousin and friend are most troubling," he said. "I will see to it that I use it as an example when I speak to those in authority about the wrongs being committed here. If there is something I can do to help your cousin I will do so."

"Thank you, sir," Zak said gratefully. Maybe there would be some action on behalf of Circling Hawk after all!

211

But before he left Sibley's camp Whipple must have again exerted his influence, for Zak received a subpoena to testify as a witness for Circling Hawk at his upcoming trial. The trials of other Dakota men were in full swing.

"Aw, shoot, buddy, all ya gotta do is tell the truth," Buff Keegan said when Zak told him about his nervousness surrounding his upcoming testimony. "Ya get up there and stick yer paw on the Good Book and swear ya won't lie." He punched Zak affectionately on the shoulder. "Ya got nothin' ta worry 'bout. They'll see yer tellin' it like it is. Why, when they hear ya they'll let that cousin a yours go faster'n ya kin shake a stick at 'em."

But Zak couldn't help worrying. He felt he had his cousin's life in his hands. The pressure was overwhelming. In the days before the trial he re-lived his days in Little Crow's camp over and over in his mind, seeing again the raid on Hutchinson, Godspeed's awful killing of the settler family. Zak began to think of questions the tribunal could ask, and he began to formulate answers for them. No, he did not hear his cousin brag of killing settlers. No, he did not hear his cousin brag of killing individual soldiers. No, he did not see him specifically kill anyone. No, he did not see his cousin force himself upon the captive white women. And on and on and on. The more he thought about it, the more he became convinced that the tribunal would believe him. They had to!

Zak envisioned what it would be like when his cousin was acquitted and released, and the joyful reunion they would have. Maybe Circling Hawk could come live with him, perhaps back in St. Peter at Mrs. Hinkel's boarding house.

He visited Circling Hawk the day before his trial, Sibley having approved it because of the kinship ties. Guards hauled Circling Hawk to him just inside the gate of the human corral. Soldiers stood guard vigilantly nearby, but they were afforded a modicum of privacy.

Zak choked up when he saw his cousin. Circling Hawk's clothing lay in tatters, the soldiers having stripped him of any vestment or article they thought could be religious or of a warrior nature so as to stir the passions of the other captive Dakota. This left him with a thin dirty shirt, leggings with holes in the knees, and bare feet, around which Circling Hawk had wrapped rags for warmth. Over his head and shoulders a thin gray woolen blanket lay draped, which he clutched against his chest with shivering hands. His face looked pinched, skin stretched, from a lack of adequate food. But he smiled when he saw Zak.

"My cousin and friend visits me," he said through chattering teeth.

Zak hardly knew where to start. He tried a couple of times to begin a conversation, but couldn't form the words to say what he was thinking. His cousin's wretched state clutched at his heart. He wondered if his cousin knew the precarious position he was in; he wondered if he understood what was going to happen; he wondered if he realized his life was on the line.

"These are not the circumstances we had hoped for," Circling Hawk said, seemingly reading Zak's mind. "We Dakota have heard Sibley wants to hang all of us."

The dam broke within Zak. "But I'm going to help you," he gushed. "You didn't do the things they say you did. There's going to be a trial where they're going to say you did some awful things but I was with you and I didn't see any of that and I'll testify to that, I swear I will, I'll make 'em see you're not guilty. They'll let you go. They'll have to!"

Circling Hawk smiled. "I see that I was right about you all along," he said. "Whirlwind, he doubted you at times because you lived like a white, but even he came to see that you are part of us, that you would never forsake your Dakota family. My heart has gladness in it because you are here."

"Where is Whirlwind?" Zak asked, looking around to make no soldiers were close enough to hear.

"He escaped with the others toward the Big Stone Lake," Circling Hawk said.

Zak breathed a sigh of relief. With any luck Whirlwind and the remaining Dakota would be keep moving and would be into Dakota Territory soon.

"How did you get caught?" Zak asked.

Circling Hawk smiled ruefully. "After the last battle the Dakota were scattered into many tiny camps. I was in a camp with Whirlwind and your grandfather Wounded Hand. Grandfather would not flee, saying he would not run like a scared rabbit in front of a fox. He did not believe like some others that the Dakota would be given their annuity after all that has happened, but he did not believe either that the long knives would imprison all Dakota for the actions of a few. I stayed with grandfather, telling Whirlwind to leave and that I would convince grandfather shortly to leave like the rest. I think I finally did, but it was too late. The long knives surrounded our camp and took all of us here."

"Where is Grandfather? And Grandmother? Are they all right?" Zak asked anxiously.

"They are in there, too," Circling Hawk said, gesturing into the internment camp. "They are not considered war criminals, but Grandfather prays every minute he is awake, convinced the Great Mystery will sweep down and free our people before any further harm comes to them." He sighed. "I pray, too, but I also know what is happening every day in the house of trials."

"Your trial's tomorrow," Zak said. "It will be like the Soldiers' Lodge, which decided my fate."

"I know," Circling Hawk said. "We have heard. Men have come back and told of it. They are taken before five long knives and are told they committed murder against the settlers and soldiers. White people tell the long knives of their sufferings and point to the men and say they did it, even if the men say they did not. In the end it does not matter because the men are told that because they murdered white soldiers they deserve to hang anyway."

"What?" Zak asked incredulously. "There has to be more proof than that! There has to be somebody who saw something before they can sentence a man to hang!"

Circling Hawk looked gravely at Zak. "There is one," he said. "Godspeed."

"Godspeed!"

"He was the first to be in a trial," Circling Hawk said. "It is said that he denied killing any whites but that he said he was forced to be in the fights and that he was once forced to strike a man with the flat of his hatchet."

"What! Why, I saw him kill three whites in one day! Including that girl he . . ." Zak remembered the horrible scene.

Circling Hawk nodded. "Yes, but after he was told he was guilty and should hang it is said that he told the long knives he knew of many more Dakota that had killed whites. He told them he would be very valuable to them, and they believed him. He has spoken against almost every man who has been there since, telling the long knives that he saw them do this or that, that he saw them kill this white man or that one, even if it is not really true."

"He's lying to save his own skin!" Zak exclaimed. "How can he do that? How can they believe him?"

"I do not know either," Circling Hawk said. "But it is happening. In our camp he is being called *Otakle*, or One Who Kills Many."

"Where is he? I'd like to wring his neck!"

"The long knives have removed him from this camp," Circling Hawk said. "I am sure the liar feared what those he falsely accused would do him in. I have heard he is being held in a tent in the camp of the long knives, where he is given special treatment."

"This can't be happening!" Zak said bitterly. "I'll straighten him out. When I testify I'll tell them what I saw Godspeed do that day. They'll have to start over and give every man he testified against a new trial!"

Circling Hawk looked at him with gratitude. "It is a good thing you are doing," he said. "You show much bravery in your actions."

"Well, let's just hope it works," Zak said. "Now let's get our stories straight so we both tell them the same thing."

Zak's heart sank when he saw the composition of the military tribunal that would decide his cousin's fate. At a table at the front of the room—there was only one room in the cabin—sat five Army officers in uniform. These men will not give Circling Hawk a fair trial, Zak thought. They fought against the Dakota and have sympathy for the soldiers and citizens that were killed. They no doubt sympathized with the public's calls for vengeance, which grew in strength daily. As he sat in the back of the room, waiting to testify, Zak saw an officer scowling at him—Captain Hiram Grant, who led his detachment to the disastrous defeat at Birch Coulee. Zak had heard that since that debacle Grant had been vociferously denying responsibility, claiming it was Major Brown who had ordered their ill-fated encampment by the creek.

Zak listened closely while the charges against Circling Hawk were read and translated through the interpreter. When the murders of one white man and two women were mentioned, Circling Hawk, seated in front of the tribunal with his hands and feet in irons, looked at Zak questioningly. But Zak shrugged his shoulders. He couldn't put any of it together. None of it made any sense.

"For the record," Captain Grant stated, speaking slowly so the court reporter could keep up, "this commission is comprised of Lieutenant Colonel William Marshall, Colonel William Crooks, Captain Hiram Bailey, Lieutenant Rollin Olin, and myself, Captain Hiram P. Grant." He still glared at Zak as he spoke.

"Does the defendant speak English?" he asked, now looking at Circling Hawk.

"De- fen- dant?" Circling Hawk repeated hesitatingly.

The interpreter spoke to Circling Hawk. He nodded.

"I am pleased to say English," he said.

Grant shook his head, apparently not satisfied with Circling Hawk's English usage. "The interpreter will translate every word," he sighed. "I want nothing in the record that indicates the defendant misunderstood anything." He cleared his throat. "To the charges just read into the record, how does the defendant plead?" he asked, motioning for him to stand. The interpreter translated for Circling Hawk. He looked about uncertainly.

"How does the defendant plead, guilty or not guilty?" Grant asked again impatiently. Circling Hawk looked at Zak. Zak shook his head.

Circling Hawk turned to face the tribunal. "I have done nothing against the law of my people," he said.

Grant sighed again. "That will suffice as a plea of not guilty," he said. "Very well. Sit down," he told Circling Hawk gruffly and then pointed to the back of the room. "Produce the first witness," he commanded.

The door opened and in walked Godspeed, flanked on each side by a private. Godspeed saw Zak and something indecipherable, a mixture of surprise and chagrin perhaps, flashed quickly across his face. But is disappeared just as quickly and was replaced by a blank look, a mask.

"The record will reflect the presence of one 'Godspeed,'" Grant said. "He has taken the oath previously and does not need to be sworn in again." He looked at the officer next to him. "If you please, Colonel Marshall, you may begin the questioning."

"Very well," Marshall said. "Godspeed, on or about September 5th of this year, were you part of a Sioux war party that attacked and burned the town of Hutchinson, Minnesota?"

"As the honorable Colonel knows, I was forced by the villainous Little Crow against my will to be part of such a party," Godspeed said, speaking very quietly.

"Yes, yes," Marshall said, nodding. "That has been established very well up to this point. Now," he said, shifting in his chair, "do you remember the details of that day sufficiently to be able to truthfully and accurately relate them to this court?"

"Yes, sir."

"Very good. Now, it is true that, having been forced into this war party, that you found yourself part of a small advance force that was to perform scouting duties for Little Crow?"

"Yes, sir."

"And is it true that the defendant . . . ," Marshall pointed at Circling Hawk, "was also part of the scout party?"

"Among others," Godspeed said, glancing slyly at Zak.

"Very good. Now, Godspeed, did you have an opportunity to observe the actions of the defendant at that time so as to be able to testify truthfully about them?"

"Yes, sir," Godspeed answered.

A moment of silence hung thickly in the air. Godspeed just sat there.

"Now would be the time to do so," Marshall said to him.

"Oh, yes. Yes, sir," Godspeed answered quietly, sheepishly.

He did that on purpose, Zak said to himself. He's putting on an act for the tribunal, acting all humble and confused so as to curry sympathy from them! And it apparently worked, for the officers beamed at Godspeed encouragingly as he began his narrative.

"I was with him," Godspeed began, pointing accusingly at Circling Hawk as Marshall did, "and we were sent out before the rest of the braves. We were to look for the Army and for anything else that might be trouble. If we saw anything we were to send one rider back to report to Little Crow while the rest rode on toward the settlements."

Sounds accurate so far, Zak thought grudgingly.

"We came upon a farm," Godspeed continued. "A husband and wife were tending a corn field and their daughter was doing something. Chopping wood, I think. We stopped and watched them. We were there for quite a while, watching, and I reminded the others that Little Crow had warned us not to kill any settlers because it would stir up trouble. The others, though, they wanted to attack and kill them, against Little Crow's word."

Zak's stomach turned. Godspeed's lying! he thought. He's the one that wanted to attack them!

Godspeed continued. The officers of the tribunal hung on his every word. "This one," he pointed again at Circling Hawk, "he rode down into the farm and shot the husband and wife. They were doing nothing except working in the field. I tried to stop him, but I was too late."

Zak's head spun. He couldn't believe what was happening. Godspeed was twisting the truth around! He was accusing Circling Hawk of the very murders he himself had committed! He looked at the members of the tribunal. They were glaring at Circling Hawk. Clearly they believed Godspeed spoke the truth.

"What happened next?" Marshall asked.

"The daughter ran away," Godspeed said, "and he chased after her. I ran my horse down onto the farm to stop him, but his horse was too fast. He was out of my sight right away, chasing after that poor girl. I did my best to track him but with no luck at first. But after a while I heard something in the woods. I rode that way and came upon them. I saw . . . ," He paused.

"Go on," Marshall said.

"I cannot. It is too terrible," Godspeed said, holding his hand over his eyes.

"Go on, son," Marshall said gently. "It is important for us to know the truth."

"I saw . . . ," Godspeed began again, quietly, dramatically, "I saw him take his hatchet and behead the girl."

The officers as one recoiled from Godspeed's words, their eyes large and round. Several audible gasps punctured the stunned silence. Godspeed stared at Circling Hawk triumphantly. Circling Hawk looked shocked, stunned. He slumped in his chair, chin down.

"You saw . . . ," Marshall began but then stopped. "Are you sure? You saw this man do that?"

"Yes, sir."

"Are you completely sure?"

"Yes, sir. I swear."

Several cries of anger rose from onlookers in the room. Captain Grant banged his gavel down and called for order. But Zak barely heard any of this. As Godspeed's lies piled up, Zak's anger had mounted until it was a swirling fury, roaring in his ears, white-hot behind his eyes. Finally he could contain himself no more.

"Liar!" he screamed, leaping to his feet. He stabbed a finger in the air toward Godspeed. "He's a liar! It didn't happen that way! I know! I was there! It was him that killed those people! Him!"

Grant banged his gavel sharply on the table, one, two, three times. "Order! Order, I say! You there," he shouted, pointing his gavel at Zak, "you are in contempt of this court! Bailiff! Have him removed!"

"But I am a witness!" Zak shouted. "I have been subpoenaed to testify!" He clutched the piece of paper in his hand, waving it over his head. "I am a witness!"

Grant seemed to consider this. Then he spoke. "Bailiff, bring that paper to me." The bailiff grabbed the subpoena from Zak's hand and brought it to Grant. After a few moments of scrutiny, Grant looked up at Zak. "Oh yes, Mr. Hammer," he said. "I remember you now." He motioned to Godspeed. "You can step down now," he said. Godspeed left the witness chair and walked out of the room without looking at Zak.

"Mr. Hammer, you indeed are a witness and you will testify when called upon," Grant said sternly. "But for now you will restrain yourself or I will indeed have you removed from the courtroom." He turned to Circling Hawk. "Does the defendant have anything he wishes to say in his own behalf?"

219

But Circling Hawk did not answer. He sat motionless in his seat, stunned, unable to speak.

Grant cleared his throat. "I said, does the defendant have anything he wishes to say in his own behalf?" Still Circling Hawk could not answer. "Very well," said Grant. "The record should reflect that the defendant has declined to testify in his own behalf. Call the next witness."

"Mr. Zakarias Hammer," the bailiff said.

"Sit down and raise your right hand," Grant said.

Zak raised his hand. The bailiff approached him and stood in front of him.

"Do you swear to tell the truth, the whole truth, so help you God?" he asked.

"I do," said Zak.

"State your name for the record," Grant said.

After Zak did so, Grant turned the questioning over to Colonel Marshall again. His preliminary questioning of Zak elicited the basic facts of his background and duties with the Army, including his ride from New Ulm to Shakopee, his participation in the battle of Birch Coulee, and his messenger duties for General Sibley. Marshall then turned to the subject at hand.

"Mr. Hammer, do you claim to have relevant testimony about the defendant?"

"Yes, sir," said Zak.

"And will your testimony be in support of the defendant?"

"Yes, sir."

"Very well. Please begin, if you would."

Zak cleared his throat. His mind raced ahead to what he would say. This was his time to save his cousin. He wanted to be sure of his every word and he wanted to be convincing. He would deliver a cogent, concise narrative of what he saw and remembered and he would finish by vouching for his cousin's character. When he was done they'd see they had accused the wrong man!

But he uttered only a few words before Captain Grant interrupted him.

"Excuse me, Mr. Hammer, but did I hear you say that you are related to the defendant?"

Zak, startled by the interruption, sputtered a flustered "Yes, sir."

"He is your cousin?"

"Yes, sir."

"Do you have a personal relationship with him? I mean, are you close?"

"Uh, yeah, I mean, yes, sir," Zak stammered. He didn't understand what any of this had to do with anything.

"I'll just bet that you're friends, aren't you?" Grant asked. He had taken on a kindly tone, condescending, mockingly conspiratorially. "You're friends, and you're kin, so it's natural to feel sympathy for him, isn't it?"

"I—I suppose so, sir."

"And you feel sympathy for him because he is in dire trouble now, right?"

"Yes, sir."

"And you want to help him in any way you can, right?"

Zak could see where this was leading, and he hated it. But he was trapped. He *had* to answer Grant's questions, lest they terminate his testimony right then and there.

"Yes, sir."

"You say you're going to give some testimony in favor of your cousin," Grant continued. "But you're worried for him. You want to do what you can to help." He looked slyly around at the other members of the tribunal before he focused back in on Zak. "Now, you're gonna tell us the truth, aren't you, son? I mean, you're not gonna tell us a bunch of good things about him, maybe shade things a bit in his favor, just because he's your cousin?"

Zak gritted his teeth, but he held his tongue, giving only the barest answer. "No, sir. I'm not gonna lie just to save him. Everything will be the truth."

Grant smiled. "I see," he said. He nodded. "Sure thing." He sat back in his chair and didn't say any more, but he had driven home his point. It would be impossible for the rest of the members of the tribunal to listen to anything Zak said without thinking he was lying to save his cousin's skin. They would view his testimony as tainted by bias, even though he hadn't even begun yet.

Zak was mad, and he briefly wondered why Grant had done that. What axe does he have to grind with me? he thought. But these thoughts were only fleeting, and he pushed them to the back of his mind. He must concentrate even harder now to convince them that what he saw was what had actually happened!

He began again, taking the members of the tribunal through his capture at Birch Coulee, his time in the Dakota camp, and the beginning of the raid on Hutchinson. When he got to the part about the killings at the farm he spoke slowly and clearly, telling them how it was Godspeed who had been the murderer, throwing in as many details as possible to bolster his credibility. He watched the faces of the tribunal members as he spoke but they were unreadable masks. He couldn't tell if they believed him or not. When finished his narrative he sat back in his chair and took a deep breath. He stole a glance at Circling Hawk, who had recovered enough from the shock of false accusation to give him a thin smile.

The members of the tribunal sat quietly in their chairs, appearing to digest what Zak had said. One officer—Lieutenant Olin—scribbled furiously on the pad of paper in front of him. After a few moments Captain Grant spoke again.

"Mr. Hammer, isn't it true that as part of the force sent by General Sibley, you were to act as scout to locate any trace of Sioux war parties that may be in the area?"

"Yes, sir." Now what does this have to do with anything? Zak thought. He had a sinking feeling in his stomach.

"And isn't it true that, as part of your duties, you were to act as a scout to locate any trace of Sioux war parties that may be in the area?"

"Yes, sir."

"And isn't it true also, that as part of your duties, you were to watch the horses and protect them in case of an attack?"

"Yes, sir. Me and Buff—I mean, Sergeant Keegan."

"Ah, yes, Keegan," Grant said, smiling at the other members of the tribunal conspiratorially. "Our colorful sergeant. A man of the spirits, and I don't mean ghosts." The other members of the tribunal chuckled, except for Lieutenant Olin, who regarded Zak seriously. Grant continued. "In any event, isn't it true that when you reported to me that night, that you indicated you had seen no sign of any Sioux war parties?"

Zak's mind reeled. They had clearly told Grant about the moccasin tracks and kinnikinnick that they'd seen!

"Uh, no sir," he said quietly. "With all due respect, we told you we'd seen war party sign."

"That is strange," Grant said haughtily. "That is not my recollection." He continued. "And isn't it also true that when the Dakota attacked—and in fact, killed all the horses you were supposed to be watching—that you weren't even down by the horse corral but were up in camp?"

Zak controlled his anger. "Yes, sir, but that's because I was up trying to get to see you to tell you that Sergeant Keegan had seen some unusual activity and that you should muster the men."

"You . . . ," Grant said, making like this was completely unbelievable, "*you* were trying to warn *me* about an attack? *You* were trying to tell *me* that I should muster the men? Well," he said, "I should have relinquished command, right? Why, better yet, I should have put you in command from the start!" Two members of the tribunal chuckled, but Lieutenant Olin did not. His face was serious, grim, and he watched Zak intently.

"Well . . . ," Zak stammered. He could not outwit a colonel. "Well . . ." He decided to say it. "You were still asleep, sir."

"Indeed!" Grant roared, slapping his knee as if he'd just been told a good joke. "I am in command of an important detail, at the direct orders of the general himself, and I am *asleep?*" Suddenly a stern looked crossed his face.

"I think we have had just about enough of this. Here we have a half-breed purporting to give truthful testimony that would exonerate the defendant, when in reality he is related to the defendant and would say anything to save him. When in reality he is a man—no, he is only a *boy*—who failed to obey orders in the field, whose gross dereliction of duty contributed to the deaths of dozens soldiers of the U.S. Army. When in reality he was with the enemy on a raid against the peaceable citizens of this state . . ." Lieutenant Olin started to object, but Grant raised his hand to cut him off. "Oh, I know, he *says* he was forced into it and took no part of it, but that is exactly what almost every defendant

223

has said in his own defense so far!" He pounded his fist on the table. "Enough! The boy is simply not credible! And I, for one, will not sit here and have *my* character and *my* abilities to lead questioned by such a boy! I make a motion that this young man's testimony be halted and, indeed, stricken from the record!"

"I second that," Colonel Marshall said.

"All those in favor, signify by saying `aye,'" Grant said.

Four of the members did just that. But not Lieutenant Olin.

"I say 'nay'," he said.

"Lieutenant Olin says `nay,'" Grant said incredulously. He glowered at him. "And why is that?"

Olin looked at his notes. "What we have is the word of one man against another—this Godspeed, against Mr. Hammer," he said. "Now, I understand why the Colonel has called the testimony of Mr. Hammer into question. I can see that there is at least the appearance of bias and impropriety, although I am not convinced that these exist. But it goes both ways." He held up his notepad. "I have been keeping track, too, of what Mr. Godspeed has been saying. By my count, he has testified in almost two dozen trials so far. In each one he has taken careful pains to deflect any blame from himself, saying he was forced into something, or he didn't really do something else, or he doesn't remember everything. But he has certainly been able to recall the bad deeds of others! By my count, he claims to have personally witnessed the murders of over fifty settlers! How can that be? How could one man have been in so many different places, at so many different times, to have seen this? I submit to you it's impossible!" He took a deep breath. "Godspeed's testimony has been self-serving, and is as questionable—no—is *more* questionable than that of this young man before us. I submit that this young man may be telling the truth. His answers should not be stricken; we should take them into account when judging the defendant's guilt, and they be a part of the permanent record."

"Your objection is noted," Grant said crossly. "But the motion carries by a vote of four to one. The testimony of Mr. Zakarias Hammer is hereby terminated and what he has said before is stricken entirely from the record."

"We haven't even heard any testimony about his alleged murder of soldiers," Lieutenant Olin said.

A pained look came over Grant's face. But he immediately recovered. "I make a motion that the second specification, that of murder of soldiers of the U.S. Army, be dropped." He clearly just wanted the hearing to be over.

"I second the motion," Marshall said.

"All those in favor, signify by saying `aye'," Grant said. All five officers did just that.

"I believe we have enough evidence to deliberate on the first specification, then," Grant said. He rapped his gavel on the table. "The members of the tribunal will each write `guilty' or `not guilty' on a piece of paper and pass them to the bailiff."

They did this quickly, and the bailiff gathered the papers. The vote was four to one for conviction.

Grant spoke with authority. "It is the judgment of this court that the defendant, one *Cetan Okinyan*, of the Sioux tribe of Indians, is convicted of the first specification of the charge of murder. Thus convicted, it is the further judgment and order of this court that the defendant be hanged by his neck until dead at a time and place to be determined by the commander of the U.S. Army in the state of Minnesota, Major General John Pope." He rapped his gavel sharply on the table. The members of the tribunal stood.

"We are in recess."

18. *Such Sad Eyes*

"LOUSY CRETINS," Buff Keegan growled when Zak told him of the verdict and of his rough treatment at the hands of the tribunal. "Lousy cretins! Didn't even give a guy a fair shake." He placed a hand sympathetically on Zak's shoulder. "Ya did what ya could. I'm right proud a ya."

But Zak miserably felt he'd let Circling Hawk down, although his cousin had vigorously denied such a thing when they'd spoken after the trial. Zak still felt he'd been intimidated and tricked. Captain Grant had snared him like a blind rabbit in a trap, and he remained angry with himself.

"Nonsense! Nonsense!" Buff roared when Zak told him how he felt. "They had their minds made up 'afore ya even opened yer mouth. It ain't none a yer fault!"

While Buff's words were comforting, Zak felt little of it. He kept thinking of the trial, going over it again and again, beating himself up over it, thinking of all sorts of things he should have said but didn't. But slowly, over the course of a couple of days, a steely resolve replaced his sadness and anger. He wasn't finished fighting for Circling Hawk yet. He'd try to see Sibley again, to explain how the tribunal was wrong. He'd write a letter to Bishop Whipple and tell him what happened. Maybe he could intervene somehow. He'd write a letter to Governor Ramsey—heck, he'd write President Lincoln himself, if he could just figure out how to do it and where to send the letter.

He never got that chance. Less than a week after the last of the trials, in which the military tribunal convicted—and sentenced to death—over three hundred Dakota men, Sibley ordered him to St. Paul. While the convicted were to be taken to Mankato to await execution, the remaining captives were to be shipped like cattle to an internment camp at Fort Snelling to await further disposition. Rumors of their fate included everything from imprisonment to lifetime banishment from the state.

Zak's orders required him to accompany the soldiers taking the Dakota to the fort, acting as a guard against escapes and carrying dispatches to General Pope. Zak attempted to get re-assigned to the company that was headed for Mankato so he could accompany Circling Hawk, but his request fell on deaf ears. His disappointment eased somewhat, though, when he remembered that Hannah was in St. Paul. Somehow he'd finagle a leave when he got there so he could find her.

A bitter November gale, brutally strong and razor-sharp, slashed at them as they left for Fort Snelling. Driving rain pelted them mercilessly, chilling Zak to the center of his bones. The column sprawled for four miles—fifteen hundred Dakota people, including women and children and the men who had not been convicted, closely guarded by five hundred wary, hateful soldiers and civilian guards. Zak rode near the front of the column and suffered under the suspicious glare of Lieutenant Colonel Marshall, now in command of the column.

They progressed painfully slowly, burdened by the cumbersome Red River oxcarts that hauled the captives like cattle, and by the sheer difficulty of managing such a lengthy procession. For four eternal days the forlorn column traversed the icy, wind-ravaged prairie between the Lower Agency and Henderson. But as they approached Henderson Zak smiled, recalling his exploits there with Hannah and old Mr. Grady, the man who had traveled the world. He wondered if Grady was all right. He wondered if the town was still abandoned.

He quickly received a deadly answer. As they approached from the south a dozen citizen pickets met them on horseback. When the pickets saw the Dakota captives they wheeled their horses around and dashed back into town. By the time the column reached the outskirts, it seemed as if every person in town waited their arrival.

Before Colonel Marshall positioned his men to protect the vulnerable captives, the frenzied citizens lit into them. Screaming, cursing, and howling, they beat them with whatever weapons they had—boards, clubs, fists, and feet. Cries of pain rose from the helpless Dakota as they squirmed in their bindings, trying to protect themselves and their children. Zak urged Sunny forward into the throng, knocking over a man and a woman who pummeled an old man.

"Get back! Get back!" Zak tried to scream over the noise. The man leapt to his feet and grabbed for Zak, trying to pull him out of his saddle. Zak pulled his right foot out of the stirrup and kicked the man squarely in the jaw. He went down again as if shot, and then Zak and Sunny surged forward.

"Company forward!" Colonel Marshall shouted. "Company forward! Fix bayonets!" Several dozen infantrymen rushed forward, struggling to fix their bayonets to their muskets as they ran. They formed a loose skirmish line and faced the mob.

"Advance!" cried Colonel Marshall. The soldiers surged toward the throng, bayonets leading them. Facing a possible bayonet charge, most members of the throng quickly lost their appetite for trouble. The crowd began to disperse, the soldiers advancing on them steadily.

Zak couldn't believe what had happened. These were supposed to be the "civilized" people of the frontier, as the whites always held themselves out to be; yet here they were committing this barbarism against helpless prisoners!

If this was any indication of the mood of the general citizenry of Minnesota, Zak thought, nothing but the darkest days awaited the Dakota.

Zak marveled at the changes around Fort Snelling. During his childhood, the fort stood only as a lonely army outpost surrounded by scattered cabins, teepees, and ramshackle settlements. Now it acted as the center of a bustling river port in an up-and-coming state. On any side of the fort, dozens of new homes and stables gleamed, whitewashed and tidy. At the docks below the fort half a dozen steamboats floated in their moorings, and scores of soldiers and civilians scurried about like worker ants, simultaneously loading and unloading crates of every imaginable type of cargo—crates of weapons, kegs of beer, casks of hardtack and pork. When they arrived at the gates of the fort, hundreds of people materialized, rushing onto the parade ground to gape at the Dakota prisoners.

Zak asked for directions to General Pope's office and he walked there to deliver the dispatches from Sibley. Some of the men had already warned him about the general. Pope led the Union Army to a disastrous defeat just weeks before at the Second Battle of Bull Run. Lincoln relieved him of that command promptly and sent him west to "attend to the Indians." Word had it that Pope, a self-righteous type, didn't like being banished to the frontier and would do whatever it took to get back east to "civilization."

That does not bode well for the Dakota, Zak thought.

Pope's office was a madhouse, with officers and aides rushing about pell-mell trying to figure out what to do with the Dakota captives. Zak surveyed the chaotic scene and wondered how he would find Pope and then how he would get his attention. He did not have to wait long to find out.

"You there!" a booming voice called out behind him. Zak turned and met the glare of a massive man with a round face and hair on his chin. He amply filled out an elaborate uniform, with both a sword and pistol hanging and bouncing jauntily at his side. Two stars adorned each shoulder.

"You there!" he shouted again, pointing at Zak. "Who are you and what are you doing here?"

"Excuse me, sir," Zak said. "I have some dispatches for General Pope."

"I'm Pope!" the man growled belligerently. "Dispatches? From who?"

"From General Sibley, sir," Zak said.

"Sibley? Well! It's about time!" He snorted contemptuously. "It's bad enough that I have to deal with this penny-ante little war without my subordinates taking their time in updating me on their situations." He snapped his fingers twice. "Don't just stand there, damn it! Bring them to me!"

Zak handed the satchel to Pope, who flung open the cover. "Ah. I've been waiting for these." He grabbed a sheaf of papers and handed them to a harried aide. "The transcripts from the Sioux trials. See to it that copies are written immediately. The originals will go to Lincoln."

He sniffed, clearly still angry with the president over his transfer. "He's asked to see every one, the meddling oaf," he muttered. "I'll bet he's going to second-guess the verdicts, as if we don't know what we're doing out here in the sticks."

Pope continued ranting, but Zak barely heard him. Stunned, he realized he'd been carrying the transcripts of the trials, including Circling Hawk's! Had he known that, he could have done something!

The very papers condemning his cousin and friend had been in his hand! Maybe he could have conveniently "lost" them. What could they have done with him? They couldn't court martial him—he wasn't a soldier, was he? But now it was too late! He'd handed them over to Pope himself!

Zak didn't have long to contemplate the irony, for Pope bellowed at him again. "Did you hear me? I asked who you are! Where's your uniform?"

Zak explained his situation to Pope, who sniffed again and drew himself up. "Well, you *were* in the charge of Sibley," he said. "You're under my charge now. You will be my personal aide. Fetch me things, do errands, and the like. If I'm going to be stuck out here in this godforsaken wilderness I might as well make myself as comfortable as possible."

Personal aide my eye, Zak thought when he left the general. He means *servant*. Glumly he walked toward the general's quarters—he'd been ordered to shine his boots—and contemplated his situation. The future looked bleak indeed. The only silver lining in the gathering black clouds was that Pope had given him a leave in St. Paul, starting the next day. He'd been ordered to deliver some of the general's personal things for shipment to his family back east, and after that Zak could, as Pope put it, "sow some wild oats" for two days before getting back to business.

Zak's interests were far from sowing any oats. His only desire was to comb St. Paul until he found Hannah.

Zak's amazement at the growth of Fort Snelling gave way to utter incredulity at the explosion of life and activity in St. Paul. The once-tiny river town now qualified as a bona fide metropolis. Dozens of steamboats chugged in and out of dozens of docks and the river was choked with every other type of watercraft in existence—canoes, longboats, ferries, and barges. As Zak rode into the city he gaped, open-mouthed, at the brick buildings of the downtown area. He'd never seen buildings so sturdy or so tall—some of them had five or six stories! The city's streets teemed with throngs of people moving about on foot, horseback, or in every make and model of carriage available. A saloon inhabited every street, each one filled with boozing revelers who serenaded passersby with the same maudlin tunes, accompanied by tinny-sounding pianos. Every few minutes a pistol shot rang out from some corner of the city, each proclaiming something new to the world—celebration of a birth, the fatal finality of a duel, a cold-blooded murder, or just someone having a good time.

Zak waylaid several townfolk before he finally got the right street address to Hannah's aunt. Nervousness rose in him as he rode in that direction—the thought of seeing Hannah again; the promise of that moment. He'd rehearsed the moment in his mind a thousand times—what to say, how to act, how to show respect to her mother and aunt to get on their good sides. He stopped twice at barber shops to check his appearance in the mirror—acceptable, he thought, but certainly not handsome. He suddenly felt very insecure. While he believed he was in love with Hannah, he harbored a terrible fear of fouling it up. He was terrified that her feelings toward him might have changed.

"Clarice!" a heavy-set, middle-aged woman shrieked after answering Zak's knock at the door. "He's here! He's here!"

"Landsakes!" called another female voice from inside the house. "Martha, what are you shouting about? Who's here?"

"The young man who saved your daughter!" cried the woman named Martha, whom Zak guessed to be Hannah's aunt. The woman swept Zak up in a hug, then held him at arm's length. "Well, look at you. Just like Hannah said! Handsome as all get out."

"Why, Mr. Hammer, it's our pleasure to meet you," said the other woman as she approached the door. "My daughter and I can't thank you enough and we . . ."

She stopped short. Hannah must not have detailed Zak's dual heritage. Clearly her mother was not ready for her daughter's savior to be an Indian. Or at least Indian-looking. A cloud passed over her face.

She recovered quickly, though, and made a pretense of being polite. She offered her hand, stiffly, for Zak to shake, and cleared her throat uneasily.

"I can't thank you enough for saving my dear child," she said formally and moved back into the parlor of the house. Her eyes found a spot on the floor and remained fixed there.

After entering the parlor dominated in a corner by a grand piano, Zak looked around anxiously for Hannah. Martha advised him that Hannah would return shortly from errands. She sat Zak down in a cushy love seat and begged him to tell them of his adventures since he and Hannah had been separated. Zak recounted the events as best he could, sparing them the grim details, but he was distracted. His mouth worked the words but his mind pondered Hannah's return. But if he wasn't giving Martha full attention she didn't seem to notice for she sat, enraptured, listening to his account.

Finally, as he wound down his tale with a description of the events at Camp Release, the front door opened and Hannah strode in. When Zak turned to her she caught her breath sharply and her hand flew to her mouth. She dropped the bag of fruit she was carried. Their eyes locked for a second and color crept into her face, in her lovely high cheekbones, and into her ears. Zak could feel his own ears suddenly aflame.

"Why, Hannah, you've dropped your bag!" Martha cried, and the spell was broken. Hannah recovered and bent to pick up the items she'd dropped. Zak rushed forward gentlemanly to help her. They stuffed the fruit back in the bag, stealing glances at each other. When they each reached for the same apple she gave Zak's hand a wonderful, cool, tight squeeze.

Martha begged Zak to finish his tale and he did, trying his best to shorten it up as much as possible. Hannah sat quietly, her eyes wide as she looked at him, her cheeks still rosy and flushed. When he was through speaking Martha peppered him with questions and Hannah even chimed in with two or three polite queries. Zak answered all questions politely and thoroughly, but inside he chafed. He wanted to be alone with Hannah, to talk just to her, to look into her eyes.

Deliverance came from an unexpected source. A sharp rapping propelled Martha to the door.

"Why, Bishop Whipple!" she cried. "What a pleasure it is to see you! Come in! Come in!"

In walked the bishop with his sophisticated air. He tipped his hat at all three women and turned to do the same to Zak. His eyes lit up with recognition and a little surprise, but he managed to tip his hat anyway.

233

"Well, young Mr. Hammer," he said, his deep voice resonating in the parlor. "It is an honor to see you again. How is it that you come to be in the presence of these lovely ladies—my sisters and my niece?"

Zak didn't have to answer the bishop's question, for Martha did it for him in excited fashion. While she did, Zak's mind raced. Did Whipple say his *sisters* and his *niece*? Hannah was his niece? He almost chuckled out loud. Another in a string of amazing coincidences. He briefly pondered this until Whipple spoke directly to him.

"Master Hammer, whatever became of your cousin? The one your age that was to be put on trial?"

Zak sadly related the outcome of the trial and their separation thereafter, careful to point out the unfairness of the proceedings and the unjust verdict.

"Scandalous!" roared Whipple. "Scandalous and shameful! I pleaded with General Sibley, even with Pope and the governor, to instill fairness and equity into the trials. But my requests fell on ears already filled with the retributive howls of the populace, of the newspapers." He sniffed at the indignity of it all. "Well, we'll just see about that. I'm going to Washington, D.C., to plead with the Army, with the politicians, with anyone who will listen about the injustices that have been wrought and . . ." He stopped himself in mid-sentence and turned his gaze once again to Zak. "Young man, how would you like to accompany me on my journey east?"

Zak was taken aback. Go to Washington, D.C.? Him? He'd never even been out of the state.

"Well, now's your chance!" Bishop Whipple said, nodding, a twinkle in his eye. "It'll put a face to the story when I meet the powers that be. They'll be able to look at you, listen to you as you describe the sham trials. You may even be of some help to your cousin."

Suddenly Zak saw what the bishop was saying. Maybe he *could* help. If he just convinced the right person, a senator or whoever, he could save Circling Hawk or at least get him a new trial. A fair trial, in front of an impartial tribunal. Excitement and hope surged through him. But a couple of nagging thoughts hit him.

"But what about General Pope? What about my horse?" he asked.

234

"Pope? What has he to do with this?" Whipple asked.

When Zak told him of Pope's desires to have a personal servant, Bishop Whipple chuckled and shook his head.

"The pompous fool," he said. "Don't worry about that! Pope knows that my cousin is none other than Henry Halleck, Lincoln's General-in-Chief of the Army. Pope used to serve under Halleck out west. He'll be anxious to curry any favor with Halleck in hopes of getting back to Washington. He'll grant me any request or favor I ask, thinking I'll put in a good word with Halleck."

He laughed. "No, Pope won't give us any trouble. You leave him to me. And as far as your horse, he can be put up in the stable at my home church here in St. Paul."

He turned to Hannah and her mother. "Dear sister," he said. "Why don't you let your lovely daughter accompany me on the trip? I would like nothing better than to show her the sights of that city."

Hannah's eyes lit up. "Really?" she exclaimed. "Really? Oh, mother, can I? I would so love to go!"

"I'm not so sure," Clarice said. "It's a long ways to go for a young woman."

"Mother, I'm almost *seventeen,*" Hannah said. "I can take care of myself. Besides, I won't be alone. I'll be in the company of these two gentlemen."

It took a little more convincing, but Clarice finally capitulated. In two days the three of them would travel to the nation's capital.

Hannah finally asked to be excused and in all the excitement of the bishop's visit she slipped out without waiting for an answer. As she walked out past Zak she looked hard into his eyes. Zak pretended not to notice her absence and engaged in polite chit-chat for little while, but then he too begged leave, saying he needed to attend to his horse.

Hannah stood in the yard behind the house. When he reached her she grabbed his shirtsleeve and they ran, giggling, behind a couple of weeping willows. Concealed from the view of the house, Hannah turned to Zak, placed her hand on his cheek, and kissed him once, gently, on his lips. He stood there, transfixed, eyes closed, for what seemed a full minute. Nothing in his life could match what he'd just felt—so soft, so pleasurably cool. When he dared open his eyes again he summoned all of his nerve and returned her kiss.

"I can't believe you're here, you're *actually here,*" Hannah whispered breathlessly. "I've thought about little else but this moment since I left you." She stroked his hair. "I've worried so. For a time I was absolutely sure I'd never see you again, the news was so terrible."

"I've thought about you, too," Zak said. "All the time. Through all the bad times, I'd wonder what you were doing, what you were thinking. I'd wonder if you were thinking of me."

"Was it bad out there? Really bad?" Hannah asked. She looked concernedly at him. Then she placed her finger on his lips. "You don't need to answer that. I can see it in your eyes. You seem different."

"Different?"

"Yes. I've never seen such sad eyes." She peered into his eyes as one might into darkened cave. "Maybe I'll call you 'Sad Eyes' from now on." But she beamed. "There's something else, too," she said. "I can't quite describe it. You seem stronger, I guess. Less shy." She smiled. "I like it."

"I am different, I guess," Zak said. "I can feel it. It's strange—I always wondered how I'd react in tough situations and if I would hold up. I guess I did. I know one thing. I don't want to be a soldier any more. For either side."

"Oh, Zak, you don't have to be!" Hannah cried. "At least for the next few weeks! Just think—us, together, in our nation's capital! What a fine time we'll have! Can you think of anything more grand?"

He couldn't. And, as they embraced tightly, he told her so.

19. The Phantom Ship

THE SEVEN-DAY journey east enthralled Zak. Accustomed only to travel on foot or horseback, he marveled at the fascinating machines which carried them and at the wondrous places they passed through. First the steamboats carried them south from port to port on the monstrous Mississippi, the paddlewheels of the giant ships whipping a creamy froth behind them as they passed between the ominous bluffs flanking the river. Then they caught a train in Illinois right across the river from St. Louis and chugged east at thirty miles an hour—*thirty miles an hour!* Zak couldn't help thinking about the many hours he spent with Flandrau's advance party traveling the same distance between St. Peter and New Ulm.

Zak and Hannah, sitting comfortably side-by-side in the passenger car, could hardly keep up with the countryside as it flew by—the seemingly endless flatlands of Illinois and Indiana, the rolling river country of Ohio, and the beautiful Allegheny Mountains of southern Pennsylvania. On the last day they passed through the Appalachians at dawn and worked southeasterly toward Baltimore and Washington. They tracked the Potomac River and passed near Sharpsburg, site of the recent dreadful conflict at Antietam Creek. Along the way they gleefully pointed out things that interested them—marvelous-looking spotted cows that looked so *fat* and *healthy* compared to the scrawny, morose ones that inhabited the farms on the prairie; tidy little villages with their two- and three-story homes and beautiful spired churches that shamed the log-hut and clapboard settlements of Minnesota; the striking contrasts between the sooty, dark coal fields of Ohio and Pennsylvania and the sunny, gleaming, churning azure waters of Chesapeake Bay in the distance.

The capital city seemed a bit of a disappointment after their spectacular odyssey. Bishop Whipple told them how a Frenchman named L'Enfant had been hired by the founding fathers to design a city that would leave room for expansion and aggrandizement as the wealth of the nation increased. Zak observed this as they rolled into the city—wide thoroughfares and open spaces gave the city an open, promising feel. However, apparently the nation wasn't as wealthy yet as had been imagined, for many of the avenues seemed to lead nowhere. The only thing constant about the streets was the near-impassable mud through which citizens and soldiers trudged. Scrubby trees and the run-down shanties of former slaves, liberated in the capital city by an act of Congress only the year before, blighted the landscape. An air of incompleteness hovered above the city. And when they got off the train at the depot, Zak discovered that there was something else in the air, a lingering stench, and the fetid smell of polluted, stagnant, brackish water. He guessed that the sewage and waste runoff from the city wasn't always reaching the Potomac as planned.

Still, the city boasted many interesting sights. Just a few hundred yards from the Potomac sat the White House, dominating Pennsylvania Avenue with its white sandstone columns, terraces, and porticos. Bishop Whipple said this was the "new" White House, and Zak remembered Mr. Grady relating the story of the burning of the building by the British during the War of 1812. A few blocks southeast of the White House was the Mall, a four-hundred-foot wide thoroughfare that was flanked by the still-incomplete Washington Monument—which they said was going to be the world's tallest marble structure when done—and by the Capitol, with its still-incomplete cast-iron dome. Bishop Whipple said President Lincoln had been recently criticized for continuing construction of the dome despite the travails and expenses of the War Between the States, but Lincoln insisted that it was "a sign we intend the Union shall go on." Just to the southwest of the mall, right on the Potomac, was an open area they said might be excavated and turned into a Tidal Basin, near which would be future monuments and memorials to those who fall in war.

"This unfortunate war between the states will be the promulgation of many of such memorials," Whipple said.

The city swarmed with soldiers, tens of thousands of men in the "rear guard" defending the capital city while the Army of the Potomac under General Ambrose Burnside plodded maddeningly toward Richmond. Zak recalled a newspaper article recounting how Lincoln had finally relieved General McClellan of command for failing to pursue Lee after the bloodbath at Antietam and because he had a perpetual case of the "slows," refusing to move his army until he was over-prepared and then only haltingly so. Zak chuckled when he remembered Buff's comparison of General Sibley to McClellen on the very same point. Lincoln should have removed Sibley from command for the very same reasons. His plodding, blunderous movements through southern Minnesota prolonged that conflict unnecessarily and only added to the misery of all involved.

After a couple of days of sightseeing they got down to business. Zak and Hannah accompanied Bishop Whipple when he called on his cousin, General Henry Halleck, President Lincoln's Chief General of the entire Union Army. A round, solid man with receding gray hair and protruding eyes, Halleck was nicknamed "Old Brains" in the Army because of his astute leadership. But Zak read in the papers only the day before that some, including Lincoln, were growing dissatisfied with his handling of the Army. The bloody War Between the States, which some had predicted would last only a month, still raged with no end in sight. But he remained Lincoln's general in command, and Zak relished having the opportunity to tell him of the travesty of the Indian trials back in Minnesota.

He got an even bigger opportunity.

"You can tell that to the President himself!" General Halleck boomed when the bishop introduced them.

"The Pre- President?" Zak stammered.

"Yes, son," the general said. "It just so happens that I have an appointment with him in the forenoon." He winked at Whipple. "I was hoping my country cousin would be here in time for the meeting so he could meet the Great Father himself." He spread his arms out, smiling.

"Now you all can."

Zak felt beside himself on the carriage ride to the White House. He was going to meet the President! Little ol' Zak from Minnesota meeting none other than Abraham Lincoln! What would he say? He hadn't planned on this development. Suddenly he felt very giddy. He began to chuckle to himself. What if he called him Honest Abe? Would the president laugh with him, or would he be thrown out on his ear?

Zak chuckled to himself, and Bishop Whipple cast him a quizzical glance. Hannah beamed at him but did not ask about the source of his merriment.

When they entered the White House a huge man who introduced himself as "Ward Lamon, His Honor's bodyguard," searched them thoroughly. Zak barely noticed, though, for he was too in awe of his surroundings: imported French drapes and Swiss lace curtains; elegantly carved furniture; vases and other glassware that glittered in the flickering candlelight; luxurious carpeting covering all the floors. He and Hannah stared, wide-eyed, at a cabinet filled with fine china emblazoned with the presidential emblem.

A dapper man in a blue suit and red tie came down a staircase toward them, exuding an air of quiet confidence and importance about him.

"Hello, General," he said before he reached the bottom step.

"Good day, Mr. Hay," General Halleck said. They shook hands. Then Halleck turned to Zak and the rest of them. "This is Mr. Hay, the president's secretary," he said. They greeted him, and he nodded graciously in return. "These are our guests from Minnesota," Halleck continued. "Bishop Whipple, Ms. Hanna Smith, and Master Zak Hammer."

Mr. Hay shook hands with Whipple. "I've heard much about you, sir," he said. "I have enormous respect for what you have attempted out there with the Indians."

"Thank you for those kind words, Mr. Hay," Whipple said. "I'm afraid, though, that my efforts may be too little, and too late."

"I sincerely regret to hear that," Hay said.

A high-pitched voice with just a touch of a Southern accent called out from somewhere upstairs. "Mr. Hay, have our guests arrived?"

"Yes, Mr. President," Mr. Hay answered.

"Very well. Please show them up here."

"Yes, sir." Hay turned back to them. "Right this way," he said, and they followed him to the second floor.

They entered a large, bright room. Zak scanned it quickly—there was a marble fireplace, two sofas, and a desk with papers strewn about it. In the center of the room stood a large, polished, wooden table capable of seating twenty people for meetings. Military maps detailing

Union campaigns covered the walls, as well as a painting of Andrew Jackson. An air of authority and urgency filled the room.

On the far wall a large window looked out over Washington. At the window stood a very tall man dressed in a black suit, his back to them, hands clasped behind him. He stood that way, gazing out the window, for what seemed a full minute before Hay gently cleared his throat.

President Lincoln turned away from the window and strode toward them.

"Hello, Henry," he said, smiling, to the general. "It is a pleasure to see you." They shook hands. If the president had lost confidence in his general-in-chief, he did not show it in front of others. "How is your family?"

"Fine, Mr. President," Halleck answered. "Thank you for asking."

"I always ask after the families of my acquaintances," Lincoln said. "We've had so little cheer around here recently between this dreadful war and the death of our darling Willie, that I hope only to hear of good tidings elsewhere."

On the carriage ride over, Bishop Whipple told them about the illness and death of the president's eleven-year-old son. It had cast a pall over the White House and over the Lincolns' marriage. Mrs. Lincoln apparently suffered some sort of breakdown and hadn't been the same ever since.

"I trust that these are our guests from the frontier?" Lincoln asked.

General Halleck made the introductions. The President smiled at Zak and Hannah when they were introduced. The president and the bishop talked about the journey from Minnesota after they were introduced.

Zak studied the appearance of this great man. In newspapers at his father's store he had seen drawings of the President right after his election in 1860. They showed a tall, gaunt, clean-shaven man with black hair and bushy black eyebrows who, with arms folded defiantly and with bow tie arrogantly askance, epitomized confidence and authority.

The man before Zak now was different. The events of the past two years had changed him. He was still tall, but not intimidatingly so because he walked slightly hunched over, as if someone had just punched him in the stomach. His hair receded a bit and was graying on the sides. As if to compensate the President had grown a beard, but it was somewhat scruffy and patchy and couldn't conceal the great hollowness of his cheeks. He looked at them from behind sunken eye sockets with dark circles under them. The pair of dark eyes looked upon them kindly, but with no real life or sparkle. It was if the candles behind them had been snuffed out.

Zak thought it was the saddest face he'd ever seen.

The President motioned for them to sit around the large wooden table. General Halleck and Bishop Whipple sat across the table from the President, while Zak, to his surprise, found himself next to the great man. Hannah sat on the other side of him. The President leaned back in his chair, crossed his legs under the table, and held open arms to the bishop.

"Bishop, I understand you're here to talk about the Indian troubles in your state," he said.

"Yes, sir," said Whipple. "About the Dakota war and its aftermath."

The President nodded. "I was involved in an Indian war once," he said, "back when I was in Illinois. Ol' Chief Blackhawk and his men took up arms against the citizenry and the Army was called out. I was elected captain of our local militia. I couldn't have been more than twenty-two, twenty-three years old at the time. We didn't know what we were doing. *I* certainly didn't." He chuckled, shaking his head. "All we did was march and camp, march and camp. We never saw any Indians to make war on. The only war we made was on the local farmers' livestock and chickens and onion patches. Seeing as how we were so ill-equipped for food, we had to get it from somewhere."

The President looked over their heads with a far-off look in his eyes and a wistful expression, as if recalling a better time. He's trying to recapture his youth, Zak thought. I don't blame him.

"The mosquitoes were so bad," the President continued, "we had to cover ourselves from head to foot in the thick of summer, even when you slept. Especially when you slept. In the morning you woke soaked in your own sweat and you were a lot more ornery than when you went to bed."

He smiled. "Mosquitoes and onion patches. That was *my* Indian war."

In a moment the President shook off his wistful state and returned to the conversation. "But I suppose this war out in Minnesota is a little more serious than that," he said.

"Yes, sir," Whipple said.

The President suddenly grew grave. "Tell me about it."

Whipple recounted the war. Lincoln studied a map of Minnesota a mapmaker had sketched for Whipple before they left St. Paul, and upon which Zak had made notes about his journeys. They talked about the proposed executions.

"General Sibley and Governor Ramsey have been pressing me by telegraph for an immediate execution of each and every one of the condemned Indians," Lincoln said. "They have been saying that if I don't order it, the people of Minnesota will take the law into their own hands. Vigilantism will be rampant. What do you think of those statements, Bishop?"

"I don't think that is necessarily true," said the bishop. "There may be some trouble, yes, but it won't be widespread. They are exaggerating."

"That's what I thought," Lincoln said.

"Ordering the executions may curry favor with the voters for the next election," Lincoln's aide, Hay, said.

Lincoln shook his head. "I'll not hang men for votes. There are too many. There has to be some other way."

He shook his head again. "Cruel ironies abound. Our nation is involved in a great civil war over the fate of one race—the Negroes. At the same time, in a distant frontier state like Minnesota another people—the Indians—fight their own civil war to be free. One people I support; the other I must suppress." He ran his hand through his hair. "As I prepare the final drafts of an Emancipation Proclamation that will free one race, I must order the executions of those in another that will never be free again."

243

Lincoln fell silent again, brooding. The weight of such decision-making seemed to make his lines of worry even deeper on his face. Zak got the feeling that Lincoln was prone to many of these bouts of melancholy as he considered the fates of many peoples daily.

"I was a lawyer in prior days," Lincoln said. "I have read the Sioux trial transcripts, and I must say most are paper-thin. So-and-so admitted to being at a battle, and so that person is sentenced to death. That's not good enough. Just participating in a war is not good enough."

"What about those who did things that are not part of the normal scope of war?" General Halleck said. "I know I'm not familiar with the situation out there and I have no say in what happens, but that might be the bright line."

Lincoln leaned forward in his chair. "Go on, Henry."

"Well, when I used to command in the field, men would do all sorts of things to get themselves into trouble. Gambling. Drinking. Sneaking away from camp to meet women. Some were even accused of rape. These men committed acts not associated with the customary rules of warfare. Maybe you could come up with the same sort of standard here. Bishop Whipple has suggested that the cases of those men convicted for merely participating in armed conflict with the whites must be distinguished from those who committed acts outside the scope of customary warfare—murders of civilians, rapes. Maybe you could distinguish those who participated in *battles* from those who participated in *massacres.*"

Lincoln nodded vigorously. "I think you may have hit on something there, Henry," he said. "Bishop, tell me what you personally know about the trials."

While they talked, Zak began thought about what he'd say to the President. He'd have to say things just right in order to get his points across. He had to make the President see just how serious the situation with Circling Hawk was. But when would he say it? What would be his cue?

Suddenly the President turned to him and spoke. Zak was startled back to reality.

"What?" he said. "I mean, excuse me, sir?"

Lincoln smiled. "Welcome back," he said. "I hope it was nice wherever you were."

The others chuckled. Zak felt his face and ears reddening. He cringed inside. He was making a fool of himself in front of the President.

"Is that true how they convicted your cousin—" Lincoln consulted his notes, "—Circling Hawk?"

"Um, yes," Zak answered. He hadn't heard what had been said, but this looked like his opportunity to discuss it.

Lincoln stood. "Son, I think you and I should take a little walk," he said to Zak. Lincoln looked across the table at the general and the bishop. "I'm sure you gentlemen will excuse us for a few minutes. You know of my fondness for boys this age." They nodded. "Ma'am," Lincoln said to Hannah, executing a small bow.

Stunned, Zak followed Lincoln out into the hallway. They walked downstairs and out into the back yard.

"My boy, Robert, is nineteen now and wants very badly to be involved in the war," Lincoln said as they walked slowly about the yard. The air was chilly, but not cold. The snow crunched beneath their shoes. Zak saw the frozen vapors of Lincoln's breath when he spoke. "Mary and I have done our best so far to shield him from it, but I know it's an eventuality that he will respond to the calling and suit up."

Lincoln turned to Zak. "How old are you, son?" he asked.

"Almost seventeen, sir," Zak answered.

"Seventeen," Lincoln repeated. "So young to be involved in something so terrible."

They stopped near a bench. Lincoln motioned for them to sit.

"Tell me about your cousin's situation," he said.

Zak took a deep breath and did just that, speaking the words he'd carefully rehearsed inside his head. When he was through, Lincoln sat motionless, staring off into the distance.

"And you want me to spare your cousin if I can," he finally said.

"Yes, sir," said Zak. "More than anything."

Lincoln sat silently for another moment before speaking again.

"Before this cruel civil war I did not believe in fate, that some unseen giant hand was directing our lives," he said. "But now, after two years of terrible bloodshed, I have come to think differently. I think there is a Divinity that shapes our lives. In my case, I have come to believe that I am the instrument of Providence who has been placed on this earth, in the center of this war, for God's own designs."

Zak fidgeted on the bench beside Lincoln. He had no idea why Lincoln was telling him all of these personal things. But he did not interrupt.

"I have become accustomed to that thought," Lincoln continued. "But not comfortable with it. I think it is affecting me. Every night, when I am fortunate enough to actually fall asleep, I have the same dream—I am on some sort of a phantom ship moving silently through a thick fog toward a distant shore. But I never seem to reach that shore."

Lincoln sat, absorbed in that thought, for a few seconds.

"Do you have any dreams?" he finally asked Zak.

Zak told him about his recurring visions of flying away as a free bird. Lincoln nodded.

"Well, if your dreams come true," he said, "it looks like you'll be able to get away from it all. I'm afraid that when I finally reach that distant shore in my dreams, it will be the day I die. I fear it will be before the war is over and I will not see its end."

Together they rose from the bench and walked back toward the entrance to the White House. Lincoln placed his hand on Zak's shoulder kindly as they walked.

"My son Willie was like you," Lincoln said quietly. "He was smart and always wanted to do the right thing. You are doing the right thing by trying to save your cousin. It may be that God has placed you on this Earth for that very reason."

Lincoln squeezed his shoulder. "I will spare him if I can."

Later that afternoon Zak and Hannah received permission from Whipple to leave their hotel and walk down to the Potomac River. They brought some milk and sandwiches and sat on the shore of the river that was the dividing line between the Union and the Confederacy. On the hilltop in Arlington, just over on the Virginia side, they saw the former estate of Robert E. Lee, the revered Confederate general. The yard and buildings, now occupied by the

Union Army as a command post, swarmed with officers and orderlies as they scurried around like ants. Zak and Hannah could not see beyond Lee's estate, but they knew that just a couple of miles past it were the Confederate armies protecting Richmond, the Southern capital.

Just to the east was the area they were going to dredge for the Tidal Pool. Although the area was a nondescript swamp now, Zak could imagine what it would be like in a few years, with monuments and memorials. He could imagine taking a son here and looking into the reflecting pool and seeing their faces, placing them in context with the statues of great men that would decorate the grounds. Great men like Abraham Lincoln.

"It's beautiful," Hannah said of the scenery.

"Yes, it is," Zak said, still in his wistful state. "And so are you."

Criminey! Did he just say that? Zak felt his face and ears reddening. What did he have to say that for? Too embarrassed to look up at Hannah on the blanket across from him, he kept his eyes on the Potomac.

Hannah placed her hand under his chin and lifted it. She looked at him with shining eyes.

"I think you're beautiful, too," she said, and she smiled. "After all, you saved me."

Zak thought of his rescue of Hannah while the Dakota burned her mother's farm. The events of the past months flashed before his eyes—his induction into the militia at St. Peter after the first Dakota attack; his midnight ride over the prairie to alert the Army; the dreadful battle at Birch Coulee; his capture by the Dakota and his reuniting with kin; accompanying Little Crow as he raided the settlements; the capture of his cousin and the sham war crimes trials. He thought of how, during all of these frightening dark times, his thoughts of Hannah, the sound of her voice in his head, had sustained him. How the thought of her helped him change, helped him become someone trying to do the right thing. Her entrance into his life had truly been a gift.

"No, Hannah," he finally said, quietly. "You saved *me*."

20. The Bright Line

ZAK BARELY took note of the journey back to Minnesota. He still basked in the glow of meeting Abraham Lincoln. Hope for saving Circling Hawk surged in him. And, most overwhelmingly, he knew he was in love with Hannah. He felt, for the first time since his mother's death, good about life and the future.

But reality whacked him upon his return to Fort Snelling. General Pope remembered all too well that he wanted Zak as an errand boy. Pope ran him ragged, shuttling messages around town, doing personal errands for him, cleaning his quarters, shining his boots. Zak chafed at the duties that kept him from Hannah.

No word about Lincoln's decisions regarding the executions came, even though it was already mid-December. Zak received orders to leave for Mankato, where the condemned Dakota were being held in a stockade ironically named "Camp Lincoln." Frantic to see Hannah again, Zak wheedled a ten-hour leave in St. Paul, but a blizzard howled in from the northwest, with deadly white-out conditions, and nobody left the fort for almost two days. When the storm finally broke everyone who had been detained at the fort left for Mankato at the same time, and Zak with them. He did not even get to say good-bye to Hannah.

Zak wanted to visit Circling Hawk as soon as he got to Mankato. But just moments after he arrived at Camp Lincoln, an officer rode up to them.

"You men! Come with me!"

"We just got in from Snelling," said one of the men.

"Get back on your horses!" cried the officer.

"But it's nearly midnight! And we're tired and hungry!" protested the man.

"Never mind that!" barked the officer. "Get on your horses and follow me. There's trouble heading this way!"

Confused but obedient, Zak and the rest of the men saddled their weary horses again and followed the officer. Another unit of mounted soldiers under the command of one Colonel Stephen Miller joined them. Soon they saw the source of the trouble.

A mob of men filled the road leading to Camp Lincoln. In the moonlight Zak saw that some were armed with rifles, others with axes and pitchforks. He counted at least eight dozen men. Zak didn't recognize most of them, but he did recognize a few soldiers who must have been in town on passes.

Zak started in his saddle when he saw one of the mob's leaders—Dougal Black. When Dougal saw him, he grinned contemptuously.

The two sides faced each other in a temporary stalemate. Finally Colonel Miller broke the silence.

"What are you men doing out here?" he called out.

No answer.

"I said, what are you men doing out here?"

"None a yer business," sneered an unidentified man from the back of the mob. Some chuckling arose from the group.

"We have heard that a mob of men drunk with whiskey was on its way to storm the stockade and kill the prisoners," Miller called out. "You wouldn't happen to be that mob, would you?"

Stony silence again.

"So what if we are?" Dougal Black finally challenged. "Maybe we ain't. Maybe we're just men out enjoying a walk in the country."

More chuckling. But, from the back of the mob, a restlessness seemed to rise. The mob moved forward, just a little.

Colonel Miller did not waste time. There was just too much potential for violence.

"Draw sabers!" he commanded. At once three dozen sabers glinted in the pale light. "Forward!"

Zak and the soldiers rode into the midst of the mob. Cursing men stumbled everywhere, running away from the soldiers, tripping, falling, bowled over by horses. The soldiers did not strike with their sabers, but the threat of receiving a two-hander with the flat of a steel blade was enough. In seconds the would-be vigilantes were scattered, the wind taken out of their sails. Miller identified the ringleaders and ordered them held. They stood glumly, hands in the air. All except Dougal Black, who stood defiantly with his arms crossed in front of him

Colonel Miller addressed the captives. "I've a good mind to run you men in on charges," he growled, "if I thought you really were a threat. But you're not. What would you have done when you got to the stockade? Overpower an army brigade and kill three hundred Indians? I don't think so. It is the absurdity of the situation that saves you. You all turn around and walk back where you came from. It will be forgotten this time. But only this time. If any of you were my soldiers it would be different. I'd throw you in the brig so quickly you wouldn't have known what happened."

"But some of them are soldiers!" called out an officer on horseback. "I recognize him—" he said, pointing to a man cowering toward the back of the captives, "—and him," pointing to another.

"Arrest those men!" Colonel Miller commanded. "Take them back immediately under charges. Does anyone else recognize any other men here?"

Zak and Dougal Black stared at each other. Zak hardly wished more trouble with Dougal. But something in Black's eyes changed his mind. Black stood there, grinning at him, practically saying, *I dare you.* I dare you to turn me in. But you won't, because you are afraid to. You are afraid of me.

You are a coward.

"I recognize him!" Zak cried, pointing accusingly at Dougal. "He is in the Sixth Regiment!"

"Arrest him!" Miller commanded. Soldiers led him away, wrists tied behind him. But before he was gone, Dougal turned and glared at Zak. He said nothing; he didn't have to. Zak shuddered. He'd just seen the coldest look of hatred anyone had ever given him.

Zak forgot all about Dougal Black when he reunited with Buff Keegan. The gigantic sergeant squeezed him until he thought his ribs would cave in. Later Buff sat, enthralled, as Zak recounted his trip to Washington. He wanted to know everything about the city—how it looked, how it smelled, how it *felt*. What interested him most was Zak's description of the ladies of the capital city—how they looked, how they dressed. Apparently satisfied with Zak's descriptions, he drew in a deep breath and nodded his head, declaring his firm intention to visit there some time during his life.

Judgment for the condemned Dakota arrived the next day. Zak and Buff read the accounts of Lincoln's decision first in the St. Paul newspaper, copies of which were delivered daily to Camp Lincoln. Together they read that Lincoln commuted the sentences of 263 men! Out of 303 Dakota who'd been convicted and sentenced to death by the military tribunal, only forty would be now be executed!

The soldiers, especially the officers, reacted in a surprisingly subdued manner. While some cursed President Lincoln softly, their reactions were nowhere near as shrill as those of the newspaper editors. They brought fire and brimstone down upon Lincoln's head, declaring him to be nothing more than a traitor, a turncoat. Zak shook his head ruefully at the gall of these editors, who just recently proclaimed Lincoln as a hero for his Emancipation Proclamation. The editors seemed blind to this terrific irony.

When Zak saw the newspaper listing those remaining condemned to die, he grabbed the paper away from Buff and scanned the list, convinced his cousin would not be on it. But, as he scrolled down the list, his heart dropped down into the hollow of his chest when he read, at the bottom of the page, the name of his cousin. Tears filled his eyes as he stared, unbelieving, at the paper. He felt short of breath, as if someone had just filled his lungs with water. He had been so sure Lincoln would save him! He had virtually promised it!

Zak's head suddenly ached, a pounding directly behind his eyes. How would he explain this to Circling Hawk? According to the paper, the condemned men were to be hanged in one mass execution on December 26. He gulped. That was only four days away!

In a fit of rage he shredded the newspaper. When the pieces floated to the ground, he stomped on them in overkill. He suddenly felt like doing something violent, like beating someone up. Anger and sadness washed over him like a steaming rain.

He clenched his teeth to control himself. His sanity hung on a string, just a hair's breadth from being snipped right off.

A stone-shed-turned-prison served as death row for the condemned men once they were separated from the others. Zak watched as guards led the men, each one chained to those in front and behind, in a solemn procession into the prison. Circling Hawk met his troubled stare as he passed, and returned his own one of confusion and fright.

Zak passed by the hastily-constructed gallows—a huge, wooden, square-shaped platform sitting smack-dab in the middle of the Mankato town square. Forty rope nooses swayed in the bitter winter wind. Evidently there was a mechanism that would enable the executioner to drop a gigantic trap door, plummeting all to their deaths at the same instant. Colonel Miller was up on the platform, testing the strength of one of the nooses with a sandbag tied to it. *Whap!* went the trapdoor as the bag dropped. Zak shuddered.

Later that day a courier delivered a letter him from General Sibley. Sibley had conferred with Pope and Judge Flandrau; together they decided that Zak's service to the Army had been meritorious. As of New Year's Day 1863, his service would be over. Furthermore, he would face no charges in connection with the assault of Olson at the mercantile in St. Peter. Judge Flandrau was true to his word.

In just over a week Zak would be a free man. It should have been great news, but in his misery over his cousin's plight he took no comfort from it. If anything, it made him even more acutely aware of the short time his cousin had left. He needed to see his cousin and explain that he had done all he could. With the help of Buff Keegan, who had been assigned as one of the guards of the prison of the condemned men, Zak managed to finagle a job as a server bringing food to the captives. That way he could speak to his cousin whenever he had a break.

When he entered the stone prison for the first time, the sights and smells of the dark, dank building assaulted him. The condemned sat with their legs crossed, ankles chained to the floor. One wood-burning stove sat in the middle of the room, its firelight casting eerie dancing shadows on the walls. Greasy smoke from the stove polluted the air, mixing with the fragrant smells of tobacco as some of the men smoked pipes. Uniformed guards paced back and forth constantly, as if the captives might actually be able to miraculously shed their chains and run out.

After delivering a meal of boiled pork to the captives, Zak stopped to talk with Circling Hawk. His eyes locked with those of his condemned cousin as they sat across from each other. Zak didn't know what to say. Even if he did, he didn't know if he could talk, the lump in his throat felt so big.

Circling Hawk finally broke the tension. "I take it from my current position that your efforts have not won success," he said, and smiled. Zak half-heartedly smiled back

"How can you make fun at a time like this?" Zak asked.

Circling Hawk shrugged. "All is not lost yet. I have been praying to *Wakan Tanka*, calling for help from the ghosts of my ancestors. They will deliver me from this trouble."

Zak marveled at his cousin's courage. Wrongly accused, unjustly convicted, and sentenced to die, he was still as brave as anyone he'd ever seen.

"I tried," Zak finally said after a lengthy silence. "I saw the Great Father, Lincoln, and asked him to save you. We sat face-to-face and I thought I got through to him. I am sorry that I did not."

His cousin nodded, thanking him. They sat in silence for a while longer while Circling Hawk finished his meal. The uncomfortable silence grew. Zak miserably felt he had not communicated his regret well enough. His mind filled so many things he wanted to say, but he felt stuck and the impassive face across from him asked for no sympathy. Finally he tried.

"Look, cousin," he said. He was in agony. How do you communicate your life's greatest guilt to the subject of it? "Look," he said again, but he choked up.

Circling Hawk placed his hand on Zak's shoulder. "You do not need so say anything more," he said. "I know you did as best as you knew how. Remember back to our time together in the village." He raised his hand to show the scar from the knife wound. "You are my cousin but you are my brother as well. In this time of trouble and grief I have given many thanks to *Wakan Tanka* for the friendship we have had. In this life and the next, we will always be friends."

Zak raised his scarred hand and placed it in Circling Hawk's. Once again they were blood brothers. Once again they were unified as one.

Behind them someone banged open the prison door. They turned to see Buff Keegan burst in. With a piece of paper in each hand, he scanned the room.

"Tate Hminyan!" he called out. "Round Wind! Which one of you is Round Wind?"

Across the room a captive raised his hand tentatively. Buff strode purposefully toward him.

"Your sentence has been commuted!" he bellowed as he stood in front of the confused man. He waved the piece of paper he held in his right hand. "This is a letter from President Abraham Lincoln saying your conviction is thrown out and you will not be executed!" Keegan motioned to a private to unfasten the man's chains.

"Stand up!" Buff commanded. "You will now taken back to the stockade for further proceedings under the law."

Round Wind rose slowly, stiff from sitting so long. He still looked confused, but he followed a couple of soldiers as they escorted him from the room. All eyes followed him.

Suddenly Buff called out again. "Zak Hammer! Hammer, are you in here?"

Zak raised his hand. Buff stomped towards him. He held out another piece of paper in his left hand.

"A letter for you, too, son," he said, eyes gleaming. "From the White House! It's marked `Personal and Confidential,' so it's not been opened."

Keegan smiled at him. "I bet it's what we been hopin' for," he whispered.

Across from the Washington, D.C. postmark, the return address of `Executive Mansion' leapt out at him. Neat handwriting addressed the letter to "Master Zakarias Hammer, c/o U.S. Army, Fort Snelling, Minnesota." The army's marks on the envelope indicated it had been received at Fort Snelling some two weeks previously. That meant it had been mailed from Washington almost three weeks ago, about the time the President had finalized the list of those to be executed. Through some bureaucratic foul-up at the Fort, Zak had not been given the letter until now.

He held his breath a moment before opening it. Maybe this was the good news he'd been waiting for! Maybe Circling Hawk was to be saved just like Round Wind!

Zak opened it with trembling hands. It was hand-written in the same thick, neat script as on the envelope. He could almost hear the President's high-pitched, slightly Southern drawl as he read:

Executive Mansion,
Washington, Dec. 6, 1862.

Master Zakarias Hammer
St. Paul, Minnesota.

Dear Master Hammer:

I hope this letter finds you in good health. I have heard that a Minnesota winter is a force to be reckoned with, and that we here in Washington "have it easy" that way, although I am afraid that the dampness we have had here recently has put me "under the weather," so to speak.

I have often thought of our visit together at the Mansion. After speaking with Bishop Whipple, and after speaking particularly with you, I felt the rascality of the Indian business "down to my boots." The subject has invaded my thoughts, both waking and sleeping, for much of the time since you left the city. I have agonized at length over your request for clemency for your cousin.

After another careful review of the trial transcripts, I am afraid that I cannot accommodate your request. The "bright line" General Halleck suggested was indeed the standard I used when making my judgments for clemency. Because your cousin was convicted, upon uncontroverted testimony, not of merely being present at a battle, but rather of killing unarmed settlers—including a young girl—I could not remove him from the category of the condemned. Please do not take this as a signal that I did not believe what you said. I did. But I was called upon to make a decision, and I finally decided that, for

*the sake of consistency, I could not differentiate the facts of
your cousin's case from those that were similar. It was as
much a political decision as anything, although I am sure that
is little comfort to you or to your cousin. I am so sorry.*

*With each letter like this I write, I can feel the phantom
ship moving closer through the fog toward that distant shore.
My fate, I am afraid, is already sealed.*

*There is nothing I can do with this knowledge. But it is
different in your case. Whether you know it or not, whether
you want it or not, your fortunes are inextricably intertwined
with those of your cousin. How you choose to act upon that
knowledge will be your fate. May God bless you as you rise to
meet it.*

Very sincerely,

A. Lincoln.

That night, Zak purified himself in a sweat bath in his tent.
Remembering his uncle Whirlwind's actions, he made his tent as
airtight as he could by placing blankets—he had no buffalo
robes—over the poles and banking snow against any gaps at the
bottom. He removed all blankets from the floor of the tent and dug a
small hole in the snow, into which he placed stones he'd been heating
in a fire for hours. After he'd stripped down to his union suit and sat
on a blanket, he poured water on the heated stones.

The steam drifted throughout the tent-turned-sweat lodge,
warming him to the point of perspiration. Zak breathed deeply, eyes
closed, and contemplated the overall situation. He cleared his head of
all distractions and only dwelled upon those thoughts concerning
Circling Hawk. As he did, voices resonated in his mind, bouncing
around off the corners of his skull like angry bees in a glass jar. He
heard the voices of the military tribunal as they issued their conviction.
He heard Circling Hawk praying to his ancestors for deliverance. He
heard President Lincoln ordering the execution of his cousin but
practically challenging Zak to do something about it. He saw

257

faces—his father, his mother, Dougal Black, Hannah, Buff Keegan. It all rushed together into one great swirling mass, a cyclone that whirled behind his eyes and roared in his ears. It seemed to go on and on and on, and he seemed to go down, down, down into the depths of his own mind.

A sudden iciness washed over him. Startled, he sat up and rubbed his eyes. He must have fallen asleep. The stones had cooled and the steam evaporated. But he did not feel the cold. He did not really feel anything at all. He sat, numb, as if a chemical reaction had deadened his body.

Then, suddenly, a tingling crept through him, an all-over awakening that made him look, anew, at his arms, his hands. He wiggled his fingers, seeming to discover them again in the manner of an amazed baby. He rubbed his face, searching, feeling, as if expecting physical signs of a transformation, a change in features. When the tingling reached his mind, his senses heightened and the spaces occupied by ghosts and voices were purged as if by a sucking whirlpool. He felt one great moment of emptiness, an instant of soul-cleansing, and then white-hot flashes of clarity seared his mind. Eyes shut tight against the pain, he sat completely motionless.

When he opened his eyes again, the pain gone, he realized he was still here, still in his tent, still in the Army. But it was not really *him*, not really *Zak Hammer*, that was here. Something else—*someone else*—occupied the shell of his body, filled his mind. Someone he knew he'd been all along.

Sungahamades'a.

He was Horse Dreamer.

He knew what he had to do.

21. *Whether It Be Treason*

"ARE YOU crazy?" Buff roared when Zak told him his plan. "That's the most harebrained scheme I've ever heard of!"

"It's not harebrained," Zak said confidently. "I think it'll work."

Buff stomped around the little room in the back of the stone prison. Although they were alone, he checked the door again—and again—to see that it was locked. He huffed and puffed and pulled on his beard and ran his hands through his hair in exasperation. Twice he stopped and glared at Zak, on the verge of saying something, but then he huffed and continued pacing around the room. Finally he wheeled around and faced Zak again.

"So let's assume you get him outta the prison!" he bellowed. Then, with a fearful glance at the door, he reduced his voice to a hoarse whisper. "Then what? How are you gonna get away? There's a thousand extra soldiers here just ta keep order for the hangin'!"

Zak sighed. "All right," he said, "let's go over it again." He took a deep breath. "I fake a letter of reprieve. It'll be nothing more than a forgery—I've already got a piece of paper from Lincoln with his handwriting. I just write up a note similar to the one that saved Round Wind—you know, something saying that, based on new evidence, Circling Hawk is not to be executed. Signed, old Abe himself."

"All right," Buff said. "I'm followin' so far. Then what?"

"Well, tomorrow night, you just bring it into the prison. I'll be there, for I'm due to work again. You wave the paper around, announcing he's been saved—just like you did with Round Wind—and show the paper to the guards. It'll be Christmas Eve, and only the most junior of privates will be on guard. The officers will all be off getting drunk. No one will question it. They've seen this happen once already."

Buff stood silently for a moment, and then he grudgingly nodded his head. "I'm still followin'," he said. "But, again, what about when I get you two out? You just can't waltz off into the sunset without anyone noticin'!"

"That's where you come in," Zak said. "You can escort us toward the stockade. Cover for us if anyone stops us. But then we won't go to the stockade after all. We'll go to the stable and get on Sunny. If there *is* a problem, you can create a diversion."

"A diversion! What kind of diversion?"

"You can figure that out. You're loud. You can pretend you're drunk. Start a fight. Anything to buy us a couple of minutes to slip out of camp unnoticed."

Buff thought for a few moments, then shook his head vigorously. "I don't know," he said. "I just don't know. What if we get caught?"

"Look, you're not going to get caught. You know it as well as I. I'm not asking you to help with the actual escape from camp. Just a diversion if needed."

"Do you know what they do for treason?" Buff whispered incredulously. "They'd string you up by your neck along with all the Indians!"

"That's a chance I'll have to take," Zak said, "whether it be treason or not. It's gotten beyond that issue for me. During this whole bloody time I haven't known which side I was on. Am I white or am I Indian? Well, I'm both. I *want* to be both.

"But there's more. I've made some bad decisions along the way, decisions that have gotten me into trouble. Gotten me to where I am now." He clenched his fists. "Well, that stops right now. My cousin—my blood brother—Circling Hawk was wrongly accused and convicted. He's sentenced to death. But I can't—*won't*—let that happen. He's family, from the side that's always treated me well.

"I've seen so many bad things in the last few months. My mother dying, my father abandoning me. War, death, destruction. I've wept over so many of these things, but I'm getting to the point where I can't cry any more. Like I'm not human anymore. And that scares me.

"This plan to save my cousin, it's the right decision! I'm doing the right thing, finally! Don't you see? Like Lincoln said, maybe I was put on this Earth just for this reason! It makes me feel human again! It gives me hope!"

They silently regarded each other. Zak could see the stress of the decision-making contorting Buff's face. His eyes bulged in and out and he licked his lips over and over. Twice he ran his hand over his sweaty face.

"So, how about it?" Zak asked after he'd given Buff a chance to digest everything. "Will you help me?"

Buff looked at the floor. He looked at his hands, turning them over and over as he thought. He was silent for a long time.

Finally, he shook his head and looked up. "I'm sorry, son," he said hoarsely. "After my woman and kid died, I had nothing. Joinin' the Army saved me from bein' a homeless beggar! It's the only thing I've known since then, and I've come too far to throw it all away now if we get caught."

Tears filled his eyes. He shook his head again.

"I can't, youngster. *I just can't.*"

And he left the room.

Christmas Eve. Darkness crept in quietly as the usual hubbub of officers barking orders and the incessant clatter of horses and wagons was stilled by observance of the occasion. Barracks and tents glowed invitingly as the men congregated to share the Christmas spirit and to keep the loneliness at bay. The sounds of carols and hymns drifted in the air:

Silent night, holy night,
All is calm, all is bright
Round yon Virgin Mother and Child.
Holy Infant, so tender and mild,
Sleep in heavenly peace,
Sleep in heavenly peace.

Zak's suspicions proved correct—only a few junior officers and the youngest privates were on duty throughout the camp. Zak was spared further duty by the head cook, who, with the help of a flask of whiskey, had a sudden streak of generosity. Christmas cheer pervaded the entire camp. Even the prisoners in the soldiers brig had been furloughed, released for the evening. Zak absentmindedly wondered if that included Dougal Black, but the thought quickly left his preoccupied head as he contemplated his plans.

After the bugler signaled the day's end, Zak stole through the darkness to the stable through a light snowfall. The temperature must have hovered just above freezing—warm for this time of year—for a low rumble of thunder rolled in the distance. But Zak barely noticed this peculiarity of Minnesota weather. The saddle slung over his shoulder made him terribly conscious of unwanted attention. Luckily nobody questioned him and he made it to the stable unmolested. Inside, he doused the lantern and made his way through the failing light to Sunny's stall. When he spoke softly to him, the horse greeted him with the familiar soft nicker and a bob of the head.

Zak patted him as he saddled him. "We're going away tonight," he whispered. "We've gotten through some tough times together, but this will be the toughest." Sunny bobbed his head again as if he understood. "You're gonna have double the load, with two people on your back. But you're strong. You've done it before." Sunny looked at him with dark eyes, blinking with his long lashes.

Zak hugged his horse and almost wept with fear. But he'd steeled himself for his mission, and gradually his fear gave way to a quiet confidence, something that never used to happen. Sunny and he could do this, with or without the help of Sergeant Buff Keegan. They could do it together.

Zak took a deep breath, summoning all the resolve he had. This was it. Now or never. "I'll be back soon," he whispered to Sunny, and left the stable, saying a silent prayer.

Scarcely anyone raised a head when he entered the prison. The outside guard, a boy no older than Zak, recognized him and opened the door without any questions. Inside, the scene was the same as it had been—the condemned men chained to the floor, the soft flickering glow of a fire, dozing guards against the wall. Zak saw one guard in the far corner look around surreptitiously, then take a swig from a tin flask he'd secreted in.

Another young guard rose to meet Zak when he entered. "What do you want?" he asked sleepily.

Zak pulled the letter from his pocket. "It's another reprieve from the president," he said quietly.

The young guard yawned and took the letter. "Another one?" he asked. "Ain't gonna be no one left to hang if this keeps up," he said. He read the letter, which was written in thick, neat script. It had taken Zak two hours, and three drafts, to forge President Lincoln's writing to his satisfaction. He'd even addressed the envelope identically to the one he'd received, though of course this one had no postmark from Washington. Zak held his breath as the guard read the letter again. He did not even check the envelope.

But still he frowned. "I don't know," he said dubiously. "I'll have to show it to my sergeant, I guess."

Zak's heart leapt into his throat. This was one thing he hadn't thought of! He thought quickly. "Aw, you don't have to do that," he said in his best tone of camaraderie. He leaned in close to the guard's face conspiratorially and pointed to the sergeant, asleep on a stool against the wall. "Look at him. You want to wake him up? He'll just meddle and muck things up. When he's done with that he'll find something else for us to do. He'll want us to get him some food or something. Let him be."

The young guard looked at the sergeant and turned back to Zak. He shook his head. "I know you're right," he said regretfully, "but I still better check. I don't want my head on the chopping block in case there's a foul-up."

The guard started toward the sergeant. Frantic, Zak thought wildly. His plans were about to be foiled! He would be caught! He had to stop him!

He started to reach for the guard when a voice stopped him.

"Private, I don't think it's necessary to bother the sergeant."

Zak and the guard wheeled around. Facing them was Lieutenant Olin, one of the members of the tribunal that had judged the Dakota prisoners. Zak had seen him in the compound earlier. A surge of hope electrified him. Olin had been the only one who'd believed him when he'd testified for Circling Hawk!

"That's not necessary," Olin said again to the guard. "Here, let me see that letter." He shot a knowing glance at Zak as he reached for it.

Olin took a long time reading the letter, frowning thoughtfully, nodding his head seriously. Finally he folded the letter and looked at them.

"Everything seems to be in order," he said. "Another reprieve straight from Lincoln himself." He pointed at Circling Hawk. "Private, get the keys and unchain this prisoner."

"But that letter . . . ," the guard protested, "my sergeant . . ."

"Private, that is a direct order," Olin said quietly. "I'm not gonna say it again." He folded the letter and placed it in his breast pocket. "You don't need to worry about this letter. I'll see to it that it's filed with the proper authorities." He gave Zak another meaningful look.

"Yes, sir," the guard said sheepishly, face reddening. He crouched in front of Circling Hawk, fumbling to find the right key. In his nervousness he dropped the keychain and cursed softly. Zak looked around fearfully—the sound of the jangling keys seemed amplified in the dead silence. But none of the guards stirred. A few of the captives next to them stared at them questioningly, but they kept quiet.

Circling Hawk rubbed his ankles where the chains had been and then stood. He was quiet but his eyes were alert and still locked on Zak's. If he wondered what was happening, he didn't show it.

"Now I'm sure that you will take this prisoner right over to the stockade with the other one who had his sentence commuted," Olin said to Zak. The thinnest of smiles graced his lips. "There aren't going to be any left to hang if this keeps up."

Circling Hawk seemed to sense that silence and stealth were necessary, for he followed Zak out of the prison without making a sound, padding quietly across the floor behind them.

Zak breathed a sigh of relief outside the prison. They were out! Now all they had to do was quickly cover the few hundred yards through the open camp to the stable without being noticed. This just might work after all!

He motioned for his cousin to follow him. The snow fell faster and thicker. Big, wet, fluffy flakes landed on Zak's eyelashes and he cleaned his eyes every few steps. The darkness was punctuated by only a few dimly lit lanterns hung on posts. Zak silently rebuked himself.

I should've doused those, too, he thought. But he quickly shook himself out of it and resolutely walked on.

He saw the stable ahead, only a hundred yards away. He quickened his pace, Circling Hawk right beside him.

Suddenly their path was blocked. A man materialized from nowhere, right in front of them. He held a lantern, framing his face in the yellow glow.

Dougal Black.

The hair on the back of Zak's neck stood on end.

"Well, well, well," Black sneered. "What do we have here? The snitch who sent me to the brig!" He looked from Zak to Circling Hawk. "And his Injun kin." He cocked his head sideways and peered at them. "Where y'all goin'? Plannin' on leavin'?"

"Stay out of this, Dougal," Zak said through clenched teeth. "This ain't none of your affair."

"Oh, it's my affair, all right," Black said. "Bet you didn't think I'd be outta the brig so quick, did you? Bet you didn't count on ol' Dougal Black spoilin' your getaway plans, did you? Nothin' like a Christmas furlough to make a man feel free again." He grinned wickedly. "I always knew you'd turn Injun in the end," he said. "And I always knew I'd get my revenge against you. Well, this is where it happens. This is where I win. I'm a-gonna yell real loud, get the attention of everyone, and turn ya in. I'm gonna be a hero."

For a moment nobody spoke. Nobody moved.

Then Black opened his mouth as if to yell. Zak leapt forward and in one motion clamped his hand over Black's mouth and wrestled him down into the snow. The lantern crashed, glass shattering, and the flame snuffed out.

Zak put Black in a chokehold and squeezed. Black tried to scream but all that came out was a gurgling wheeze.

Circling Hawk bolted for the stable, but Black got an arm free and tripped him. He fell onto the pile, breaking the chokehold.

Black rolled out from under Zak, took two heaving breaths, and yelled at the top of his lungs.

"Help! Somebody help me! They're escapin'!"

Zak and Circling Hawk struggled to their feet. All around them men tumbled from their tents, rubbing their eyes, shaking off drunkenness or sleep. They gaped at the three snow-covered boys in front of them.

Nobody moved for what seemed like an eternity. Then, as if on cue, Zak and Circling Hawk ran.

"Stop them!" Black screamed from the ground. "They're Injuns! They're gettin' away!"

They ran. But the snow had deepened, and Zak fell. He felt Circling Hawk lifting him up and then he sighted the stable, just ahead of them. Out of the corner of his eye he saw dark shapes moving toward him, soldiers moving to block their path.

It would be close.

An explosion shattered the air. Then another, and another. A gargantuan fireball billowed into the night sky behind them, brilliantly blue-red against the blackness. In two seconds shock waves reached them. Zak and Circling Hawk fell as the earth shook. Men fell around them left and right.

Before anyone recovered their senses, a pair of strong hands lifted Zak and Circling Hawk to their feet. They came face-to-face with Buff Keegan.

"Did you see it blow?" Buff bellowed. "The gunpowder cache behind the stockade!" He roared with laughter. "That was the most fun I've had in a long time! Here, take these!" He shoved leather reins into their hands. "Now get outta here!"

Zak found himself being shoved up into a saddle. When he righted himself he found he was astride Sunny. Circling Hawk was on Buff's horse right next to them.

"I said get outta here!" Buff roared, and he slapped the horses. Sunny lurched forward. Zak barely held on as they plowed ahead through the drifts. He craned his head to look back.

A fiery light bathed the surreal scene. Buff stood rigidly in the falling snow, mouth open in a roar, fist raised in the air. Another blast rocked the air and Dougal Black, trying to get up, was flattened again. Soldiers ran about every which way, utterly confused by the explosions. They acted as though the compound was under attack. They knocked each other over, trampled each other in their panic.

Zak and Circling Hawk held tight as the horses took them away. In just minutes they were far enough away so that the falling snow blocked the glow from the burning gunpowder cache. They could no longer hear the sounds of the rampant chaos. They slowed the horses down and Zak led them onto the frozen Minnesota River. Leading north, it stretched ahead of them like a road in the darkness.

22. *This Final Journey*

NEITHER OF them spoke as they wound their way on the snow-covered ice. Huge flakes continued to fall, piling quickly and slowing their progress. The darkness was deadly. Several times Sunny led them around patches of open water, bitter death they barely missed.

Zak peered behind them frequently, fearing they were being followed. He imagined being overtaken by a pursuing squad and shooting it out with them. He pictured being captured and paraded back into camp as a traitor to be executed. He could see himself up on the gallows waiting to dangle at the end of the hangman's rope.

But he saw no followers. After a couple of hours the snow let up, and soon after the clouds parted and the moon emerged. The temperature dropped in the clear air, and they shivered while they rode. The landscape, buried beneath the deep snowfall, gleamed a crystalline white in the pale light. They left the relative openness of the river and wound their way along the bank, where they could be less easily spotted in the moonlight. Zak took a long last look behind him. He could see well up the river—nobody. He began to relax and looked at his pocket watch—just after midnight, Christmas Day.

At last they neared their destination. Zak held his breath as they approached, fearing they'd ride right by it. But finally he spotted the tangle of trees and brush that hid Dougal Black's shack. Up on the bank, hundreds of yards above them, Zak saw the twinkling lights of St. Peter. The stiff crunching of the horses' hooves was the only sound in the chilled air.

They had made it! According to Zak's plan, they would stop overnight and get some sleep. Before dawn, when the horses were rested, they would sneak out of town and head for the northwest. While everyone down here concentrated first on Christmas Day and then on the hanging in Mankato, they would be well on their way toward Dakota Territory to join the rest of the Dakota who had fled after their defeat at Wood Lake. With any luck they would be reunited with Whirlwind and the rest of the family within a month.

Zak dismounted and patted Sunny on the flank. "Good boy," he said. Circling Hawk dismounted as well and they tied the horses to a fallen tree. They fought through the brush wall and stood in front of the little shack.

Zak looked at it thoughtfully. How many hours had he spent here with Dougal Black? Doing nothing. Hiding from everything. He never thought he'd see it again. But now here he was, using it as a hiding place again. But this time he was doing something good, something right. He considered the irony. If only Dougal knew what he was doing!

"We'll be safe here," he finally said.

Circling Hawk smiled and spoke for the first time since they'd fled Camp Lincoln. "When we are many days away from here I will believe we are safe," he said.

Inside, Zak fired up the stove, using wood that was still piled in the corner. I probably cut this wood myself, he thought. When it warmed up they sat on the floor and removed their wet outer clothing, draping the sodden articles over chairs near the stove to dry. Zak got out the hunk of boiled beef he'd stuffed in his saddlebag earlier. He pulled his knife out of his waistband and cut off a slice for himself. He handed his knife to Circling Hawk, who did the same. It was good, but it was not much. They would need to steal some food from town on their way out.

They dozed, each lying to one side of the stove. But sleep came fitfully, and Zak started awake with every sound—the crackling of the fire, the groaning of the ice in the river. Twice he dreamt a squad of uniformed soldiers broke down the door of the shack, guns blazing. Each time he jerked awake, disoriented until he came back to the present, back to the little shack with his cousin asleep across from him.

Zak awoke again just as the fire went out. The shack had cooled. He looked at his watch again—4:30 a.m. It would be dawn in a couple of hours. He sat up, rubbed his eyes, and looked over at Circling Hawk. His cousin was already awake and fully dressed, quiet and alert.

They nodded at each other. Time to go.

"I'll go down and check on the horses," Zak said as he put the last of his outer garments on. "You make sure the fire is out." Circling Hawk nodded.

Zak left the shack and pushed through the brush wall to the horses. Sunny greeted him with a low snuffle. Zak patted his shoulder. "You did real well earlier," he said. "Real well. We've been through so much together." He caressed the horse's neck and scratched behind his ears. "We'll get you some food in just a little bit. Then we've just got this final journey to make and then there won't be any more. I promise." And he meant it.

Suddenly a crunching blow to his head staggered him. White spots exploded behind his eyes. As he doubled over, a kick to his side shot through him as if he'd been stabbed with a hot poker. He tumbled to his hands and knees and then fell prone, face-down, as if a giant hand had flattened him.

He felt himself being rolled over. Through tears of pain he stared straight up into the barrel of a gun.

"You didn't really think you'd get away with it, did you?" Dougal Black sneered. He shoved the barrel roughly into Zak's open mouth, splitting open his lower lip.

"I knew where you'd go," Dougal crowed breathlessly. "You idiot! It was easy! Once it quit snowing and the moon came out I followed the tracks. But I didn't need 'em anyway! I just knew!"

Black stood, pulled the pistol out of Zak's mouth, pointing it at his head.

"Get up!" he commanded. When Zak didn't move—he couldn't yet—Black kicked him again. Zak rolled over again, clutching his side. Gasping, he couldn't seem to catch his breath. Finally it came, but in great racking wheezes that Zak struggled to control.

Zak lay in the snow a moment more, recovering. Finally he rose to his knees in preparation to stand. Covertly he reached into his waistband for his knife.

It was gone! His heart plummeted—he'd given it to Circling Hawk in the shack. He was defenseless!

Zak stood shakily. He faced Dougal in the pale moonlight.

"What are you going to do?" Zak sputtered through bloody lips.

Black laughed. "What do you think? I'm going to shoot you, and then I'm going to shoot that flea-bit horse of yours, and then I'm going to shoot that Injun relative of yours." He grinned wickedly. "Then I'm gonna drape your corpses over my saddle and haul you in. Yep, it'll be promotion time for Dougal Black."

"You can't shoot all of us," Zak protested. "Not like this. It'd be murder!"

Black laughed again. His pistol dropped just a bit as his body shook.

"Then murder it is," he said.

They faced each other silently. Zak racked his brain trying to find a way out of this. Maybe he could trick him. Maybe if he called back over his shoulder to . . .

"Don't even think of tryin' anything," Dougal sneered, seeming to read his mind. "It won't work. Nothin's gonna work. This time you've had it!"

Dougal's smile vanished and something dark, something inhuman flashed over his face.

"Now you're a dead man."

He cocked the hammer on his pistol.

Zak prepared for the impact of the bullet.

It never came. Out of the corner of his eye he saw a flash of movement. Circling Hawk tackled Dougal with full force from the side. Dougal dropped like a stone, pistol waving wildly. A deafening roar and a blinding flash ripped the night. A horse squealed and there was a *thump!* in the brush beside them.

Circling Hawk and Black rolled furiously in the snow. Black screamed incoherently. Somehow Circling Hawk got on top of him. Another roar shattered the night and Zak saw a flame stab directly into Dougal Black's chest.

He lay still.

Circling Hawk stood over Black. Shaking, Zak walked to his side. Together they looked down on the dead boy. Dougal's terrified expression was frozen on his face, his eyes wide, his mouth open in a silent scream. Zak suddenly felt sorry for him.

A gurgling wheeze rose from behind them.

"Sunny!" Zak screamed, and wheeled toward the horses.

Buff's horse had snapped the reins in terror and had bolted toward the river.

But, right where he'd been tied, Sunny lay on his side, eyes closed. Black blood ran thickly from his belly into the snow.

"No!" screamed Zak, sinking down beside his friend. "No! This wasn't supposed to happen!" Hot tears streamed down his face. "Sunny! Please!"

He stroked the horse's neck. The head tilted, and those long, beautiful lashes opened. One dark eye looked up at him.

"Sunny!"

The horse gave a low snuffle in response. He began to tremble and his ears flattened, but the one eye remained locked on Zak.

"Sunny, no! Don't leave me! We're gonna make it!"

The horse snuffled again, as if to say he understood Zak's anguish. That he knew his pain. But the snuffle also indicated an understanding—that Sunny knew it was over—that he'd done his part but he wouldn't make it after all. That it was time to go.

And that it was all right.

Because they would always be friends.

When the eye closed again the breathing came in short, raspy bursts. Zak felt a hand on his shoulder. He turned to see Circling Hawk standing over him, holding Black's pistol out to him.

Zak shook his head, but deep in his heart he knew it was the right thing. Weeping openly, he finally took the pistol and stood. It was the least he could do for his suffering friend.

It was not necessary. The end came mercifully quick.

After a few more breaths, and a final, soft nicker, Sunny died.

An observer on the river bluff—or a bird in flight overhead—would have found the scene below neither surprising nor particularly tragic. There had been many such scenes throughout the bloody country. But the sounds coming from below would have startled the callused observer, and maybe even the bird.

Wrenching, heaving sounds tore from the boy kneeling in the snow near the dead horse. They were strange sounds; yet they were familiar. They were the sounds of howling wolves as they projected their loneliness into the air. They were the sounds of solitary loons as they cried for missing mates. They were the sounds of the mourning

273

doves as they sang of the tragedies that had been so common throughout the land.

To the observer—and maybe even the bird—the sounds would have served to show there were those who still cared about what happened; there were those in whom kindness and empathy still remained; and that there were those who, despite all the hatred and killing, remained good and true in heart and spirit.

Epilogue

Dear Hannah,

If you receive this note it will mean that Buff Keegan has found you. I hope that when you read it you are well and the sun is shining. I can't tell you where I am now. It could be anywhere. I could even be with my family on the plains west of the Big Stone Lake.

Some people may say some bad things about me. That what I did was illegal, maybe treason. That I am a traitor. But I didn't do what I did for anybody or any country. I did it only because it was right. It wasn't a hard choice. I know you will understand.

The really hard choice was leaving you behind. I'm sure I never told you just how I feel about you, but I think you are a beautiful person and that the world is a brighter place with you in it. I'll never forget our trip out east. I meant it when I said that you have saved me.

I don't know when we will meet again. I hope it will be sooner than later. But I want to tell you that I will think of you every day. That I will pray for you and your family.

And that I still love you.

Zak

Historical Note

This is a work of fiction. I know of no plot or any last-minute attempt to rescue the Dakota captives slated for death. The main characters—Zak Hammer, Buff Keegan, Circling Hawk, Whirlwind, Hannah and Dougal Black—came only from my imagination. Some of the peripheral characters were real people and some, while fictional, are amalgamations of many real people who lived.

The events involved, though, were all too real. Between August and December 1862, the fledgling state of Minnesota was a cauldron in which one of the bloodiest conflicts between U.S. citizens and Native Americans raged. Hundreds, perhaps a thousand, people were killed on both sides. Tens of thousands of settlers fled, some of whom later returned, some that did not. Retribution on the Dakota was swift and severe. On December 26, 1862, the 38 condemned Dakota were hanged in Mankato in one of the largest mass executions in American history. The remainder of those captured endured a harsh, disease-ridden winter in captivity at Fort Snelling before being permanently banished to an inhospitable reservation in South Dakota. The army pursued the escapees into Dakota territory in 1863 and several battles ensued. Little Crow stole back into Minnesota that year and was killed by farmers while he was picking berries near Hutchinson. Shakopee and Medicine Bottle escaped into Canada, but were kidnapped in 1864 and taken back to Minnesota where they were condemned to death without proper trials. When they stepped into their nooses, a locomotive train—one of the first in Minnesota—whistled in the distance. Shakopee reportedly said, "As the white man comes in, the Indian goes out."

To a large part, this novel accurately portrays the events and people involved in the 1862 war. The timeline is substantially accurate, as are the descriptions of the forces and battles. Little Crow, Shakopee, General Henry Sibley, Captain Hiram Grant, Major General John Pope, Bishop Henry Whipple and, of course, Abraham Lincoln all played vital roles in the horrible drama that unfolded. To a large part, this novel accurately reflects their actions, altered only when they come in contact with Zak Hammer. My interpretations of their characters and the reasons for their actions are of my opinion, based on my studies of historical accounts, biographies, personal letters and writings, and memoirs.

    D.W.H.

Printed in the United States
3468